THE NASEBY HORSES

THE NASEBY HORSES

Dominic Brownlow

2019
Louise Walters Books

The Naseby Horses
by Dominic Brownlow

A catalogue card for this book is available from the British Library.

Produced and published in 2019
by Louise Walters Books

ISBN 978 1 999 630560
eISBN 978 1 999 630546

Typeset in PTSerif 11pt by Blot Publishing

Printed and bound by Clays Ltd, Elcograf S.p.A

louisewaltersbooks.co.uk

info@louisewaltersbooks.co.uk

Louise Walters Books
PO Box 755
Banbury
OX16 6PJ

For Jessica and Sam

DAY THREE

DAY THREE

ONE

It's another day and a night before they let me leave the hospital. Uncle Pete picks me up in his black Rover, driving slowly over the chain of mini roundabouts that gets us out of Spalding on to the straight lonely roads of the Fens. There's still been no word from Charlotte.

'Hobby,' he says, ducking his head to look at a small bird of prey hovering by the side of the road. The hobby drops to the ground, bouncing back into view with a field mouse locked in its talons, before disappearing low across the fields. I press my head against the warm glass, my mind weighed down with the hazy fug of medication, and watch the earth stream by in an endless blur of yellow and green and gold.

Above stretch millions of square miles of unsullied blue sky.

Years ago, in my grandfather's living room, I read that the mean radius of the earth is three thousand, nine hundred and fifty-nine miles. I remember thinking how disappointingly small this was and how anxious I became at the idea of billions of minuscule people and animals and cities being stuck to this minute green and blue ball out in the middle of space. A few months later I threw a marble out to sea on Brancaster beach, proclaiming to my family that the marble in the sea was as proportionally irrelevant in terms of mass to the unknown mass of the ocean as the earth was to space. They had laughed and continued walking ahead, the wind tugging at their clothes as though trying to pull them into the water.

The sea was choppy that day. I remember this vividly, but I remember everything vividly. That's the problem. It had swayed and dipped like crude oil, its surface veined with seaweed where thin dirty crests appeared and disappeared unevenly in the swell as though they weren't quite sure which way they should be heading. I remember, too, grains of sand skimming across the hard plane of the beach, a sharp January wind that carried with it the decaying scents of the sea and the marshes to the east. On the hazy spine of Scolt Head avocets gather in their hundreds. To my left, like the iron finger of some long-fallen robot, I can just make out the top of the wreck poking through the water.

Back in the car, I stare directly at the sun. It's high and bright, and I'm thinking someone, God perhaps, is trying to burn a hole through the universe with a magnifying glass when the scent of sulphur drifts eerily through me. I've half been expecting it. After a seizure of that size, there are often little aftershocks: partial seizures no one can see but me.

'You OK?' Uncle Pete asks.

I hold out my fingers and study them in the strange fluorescent light. It feels like I'm in space. Everything is both big and small at the same time. Everything is beautiful yet frightening. There is something quite beguiling about the aura, before it takes me, that is, something about the intensity of the light, its still prismatic sharpness before it shatters into millions of glittering particles. When I'm in the aura I get to see below the surface of everything. I get to see the wires that hold the universe together. Within it, I listen to the even hum of the Rover and I can't help thinking about that marble, only I'm not thinking about it floating freely in the clear abyss of the ocean. I'm thinking about it covered in silt on the sea bed.

Uncle Pete clears his throat, like he's testing a microphone. The resonant boom distorts in my head. He looks at me for a few seconds, dark eyebrows pinching over a flat nose, but whatever it was he was going to say, he doesn't say it. Instead, he looks back to the road flowing smoothly beneath us. He screws up his forehead as he thinks, concentrating on his driving even though there are no other cars about. It's just an empty straight line pointing forward, its neat edges trying to join up somewhere in the distance. I could even drive on a road like this.

I like Uncle Pete. He doesn't talk to me like I'm an exchange student. He doesn't shadow me as everyone else seems to do. He and Aunty Anne own a white-bricked cottage on the North Norfolk coast where Charlotte and I spent part of our holidays when Mum and Dad were both working. There's a long sandy nature reserve there. For most of the year you can spot curlews, godwits and lapwings, and in the winter, when the sky feels as cold as the sea, there are geese, twite and redstarts.

'She didn't want to come here in the first place,' I say in a monotone voice that doesn't really sound like my own.

'No,' he says. 'But that's no reason for her to put your mum and dad through all this, is it?' He's trying to sound angry, but I know he isn't, and as though to compensate, he runs his right hand awkwardly through his hair.

'Do they still think that's what happened?' I say. 'Do they think she's run away?'

5

Ahead, a tractor and trailer pull out of a farm track. Uncle Pete tilts his head to the right as he indicates, overtakes, then gently straightens the Rover, the sun catching on the windscreen in thin ripples of white light. 'We just can't understand it,' he says and he sucks in air and turns away and stares out of his driver's window.

I, too, look away, pinching the bridge of my nose against a swell of nausea, and try to organise my thoughts, but it's almost impossible. My mind is like an aviary. It has been since I came round that night, the smells of linoleum and disinfectant expanding relentlessly in the warm synthetic air. Mum is sitting forward on a wooden chair designed for sitting back on, that hurried look of hers accentuated in the artificial light.

'We can't find Charlotte,' she says. 'We can't find her anywhere.'

When I was younger, my dad gave me one of his old cameras. He had a small but unusual collection, which he stored in an antique ottoman chest along with numerous flashes and different types of lenses, most of which I don't think ever worked. The camera was a Yashica. It had a worn brown leather case with a sleek metal handle shaped like a comma that would wind each frame forward with an unhurried and satisfying clicking sound. For a short while I photographed everything: people, birds, the sea, the sky, the sun, its glare almost blinding me every time and scorching indiscriminate coronas of light across the images.

The films were developed in a tiny shop beside the little cafe our nanny used to take us to after school, opposite Tooting Bec Tube station. I remember clearly the smells of bacon and cheese, wet hats and coats in the winter. Umbrellas would be crammed by the door, dripping onto the tiles like game fowl. We'd eat cake. Charlotte would look boredly out onto the street as, restive with excitement, I would pull free from their colourful envelope my new set of prints, releasing into the stuffy air the vinegary waft of developing fluid. The pictures were always disappointing. It was as though from each one something was missing, yet every now and again, by some technical fault caused either by myself or the camera or the machine at the shop, there would appear two images on the same photograph, one neither more prominent than the other, as if in some way both moments of time had aligned before me, the edges of these strange ghostly images always burnt a little in the corners.

There was one I framed. I remember. It was of Charlotte standing before an enormous Brancaster sky out of which had appeared a huge flock of crows, their wings curved like scythes and almost blocking out the light. This is what my memories look like: images and sounds and smells as clear and as vivid as that moment on the beach randomly superimposed onto the present. It's been like this since I was seven years old, since my first seizure.

There's a navy-blue car coming towards us. It's so low to the ground it looks like a boat. Black smoke pours out behind it, trailing in thin spiralling ribbons into the sky. The sun glares in its windscreen. Uncle Pete winds up his window as a whiskery grey-haired man forms out of the sharp white light. He looks directly at me and smiles. His teeth are rotten. His eyes are as blue as crystals and make me think of the bright blue light in the centre of the ophthalmoscope Dr Chatterton used to peer into the back of my eyes. He has that innately contented look about him only people in the Fens seem to have, as though nothing can reach him out here, as though he is still miles from the mainland in every way possible. Something fires in his engine, sending two grouse up into the afternoon heat like deflating balloons. They collide with each other before settling back on the grass verge, shuddering and staring intently into the light as though not sure where they have just come from.

Uncle Pete glares in the rear-view mirror. When he feels he's covered enough distance, he opens the window again and releases an exaggerated breath. 'Your dad tells me she came to your room to see you that night, before they found you,' he says, eyes set back on the road.

'I don't really remember,' I say.

'No,' he says after a moment. 'I don't suppose you do.'

We don't speak after that. Through the glassy air I watch the countryside unfurl, its tirelessly neat edge only occasionally knotted by a farm building or distant house corralled within a barricade of poplar trees. Wind turbines glimmer on the skyline. We pass three red-bricked houses moored at the side of the road. There are no others on our journey. They're packed tightly together as though whoever built them was in some way concerned about space. A caravan, bruised with rust and dirt, balances on breeze blocks in one of the front gardens. Next door, sunflowers stare at the sun. The windows are boarded up on the third.

Like splatters of blood, poppies dot-to-dot the grassy verge as I go over in my head all I can remember from that night, trying to filter old memories from those of the last few days. Somewhere in the darkness I hear the blistering crackle of rain. I go to the window nearest my bed, where the sky is bearing down like an enormous sheet of beaten metal. Lightning flickers behind it. I blink, startled, as a bee thumps softly against the windscreen, leaving the faintest smudge of grey and red on the glass.

8

Uncle Pete swerves around a dead rabbit. 'She'll be OK,' he says quietly, I think more to himself than to me.

Glennfield appears as a pale green smear on the horizon. As we draw closer, the shapes of the church bell tower and the tall grey chimneys of the Manor House slip gently into focus. Crows and rooks, minute specks of black against the clear blue of the sky, circle above. Our new home, our new start, the Old Abbey, had centuries ago been built on what is now the southern furthest edge of the village. For over ten years it had been boarded up and left to ruin. Lined up along the road by the village sign are two police cars and two large white vans.

The Rover slows and stops as a full-set officer in a short-sleeved white shirt beneath a bulletproof vest leans into Uncle Pete's window. He has a thin moustache and a face that on other occasions, I guess, would be cheery. He looks around the car. 'You from the village, sir?' he says. There's an even note of distrust to his voice.

'My sister-in-law lives in the Old Abbey there,' Uncle Pete informs him. 'What's going on?'

'Procedure, sir,' he says calmly, 'that's all,' and he looks across at me. 'You must be Simon.'

I don't answer this. In the rape field to the west of the village I've noticed a long line of men and women dressed in dark blue overalls wading waist high through the scraggly green crop that just a fortnight ago had been yellow and luminous. A hundred metres or so up the farm track villagers are gathered, keeping a respectful but observant distance.

Uncle Pete speaks but I can't hear his words anymore. I can't hear anything. The aura's turning. It's darkening its edges. I need to focus, concentrate on my breathing just as I've been taught: in through the nose, out through the nose. At the same time my brain begins to recite whole

9

passages of text from memory, trying to anchor itself to the present. The words appear as a landscape of tiny black dots in my head. They're from *Bewick's Swan*, the book Dad bought me from the Wildfowl Trust at the far end of the village.

Whatever this is, it feels real. It is no longer in the safe immunity of my mind. It's out there in that field, where everything is clear and solid and comprehensible, where men and women are poking at the land with sticks, looking for my sister. My mouth droops. It tastes bitter and metallic. I widen my eyes and tilt my head as distances become undefined, as though in forced perspective, uncertain of exactly where they belong in this unfamiliar terrain. I don't want her to be missing anymore. I don't want her to be out there, cold and lonely and frightened. I want her to be safe, and as I think this, time separating itself imperceptibly from the now, I see through the radiant glare of Uncle Pete's windscreen little bugs of rain crawling down the glass from the night Charlotte disappeared.

I'm at my bedroom window. Squares of netted light float in the darkness, scarred by the rain and seemingly unattached to the village itself. In the distance, thunder breaks from where, out over the fields, the clouds are dark and foreboding, twisting and turning like waves, making shapes in the sky.

There's another police car parked outside our front path. Uncle Pete pulls up before it, where we sit for a while not talking until eventually the aura settles and I am fairly confident I won't black out. A small group of people are standing outside Mrs Neal's house. They look as frightened and uncertain as we do, staring at us through the soft bleary air. I want to be seven years old again, I tell myself, in a cafe looking at photographs, back in the time before the fits started, before my memories began to layer themselves on top of each other like reels of film, before the blackouts and the not knowing.

'Ready?' Uncle Pete says. A single bead of sweat drips down the side of his face.

'I'm scared.'

'We're all scared,' he says, and he takes a breath through his nose. 'But it's going to be alright. You're going to get through this. You're a good person. Remember that.'

But as I step out of the car into the bright day and head up the stone path to the front door, I wonder how true that is. I am a good person in that I love nature and birds and life and I don't want to harm people even if they are cruel to me, but I also know I am uncommunicative and solitary. And I'm a liar. These are not attributes that make a good person.

It's been three months since the move. The scaffolding is down and the house stands tall and pallid against the empty sky. I half expect to see a face up in my window as I did on our first day, but there is no one there.

TWO

Mum is standing in the kitchen at the other end of the hallway with Aunty Anne and a policewoman. Her face is partly hidden in her hands. Her hair is unbrushed. I shiver, but it's not from the coldness of the house. It's from the way she's looking at me, eyes seared with fear, and for a moment I feel as though the air between us is parting, the molecules backing away in the dusty light. She didn't come and visit at all yesterday.

Uncle Pete crab-walks past me with my bag. 'You'll be OK,' he whispers before disappearing up the stairs in the hallway. I don't follow immediately. Something holds me back in the shadows of the stone arch in the porch. It's the only visible remains of the abbey itself on the inside, other than some of the windows and the cellar. It still has that discerning musty aroma ancient buildings possess, even though it's now only a fragment of what it once was. I'm in the present, I tell myself. That's what it is. I'm in that tiny sentient space between the past and the future. I'm safe here. So congested is my past with memories and half memories and dreams, I can't seem to filter them properly, not with any certainty, and there is nothing in the future because it hasn't happened yet.

I breathe through my nose, studying my fingers in the strange syrupy light. They're tingling still, thick and numb. A reverent smile eases its way into the corner of my mouth.

'Is everything alright?' Mum asks.

'Is Dad here?'

Her lips move but she doesn't say anything else. She just watches, nails tapping incessantly against her teeth.

Tiny streaks of phosphorescent light glimmer on the perimeter of my vision and I notice for the first time, dripping into the hallway from the living room, various muffled voices I don't recognise. They sound hushed and distant. Above the fireplace is an arch-top mantelpiece clock, which Mum was given after Grandpa died. He kept it over his fireplace too, in his living room in Cambridge, where, smothered in a warm russet light, old books lined every wall. It's set within a walnut case balanced on four brass balls. Its thin metal pulse counts time as eventually I take a breath and step forward.

There are two men in the living room with Dad. They stop talking when they see me. I haven't been inside this room since the day we arrived, but I know the painting is there, hanging over the mantelpiece. Part of me wants to go in now, though, just to see it, to prove to myself that everything my brain thinks happened the night Charlotte disappeared didn't happen, that it was all conjured up within the existential walls of the aura. But I don't go in. I put a hand to my mouth, remembering the stench from the first time I stood here. Something was holding me back then, too.

Spring sunlight surges through the wedged-open front door, carving a long waxy path down the full length of the hallway. While Charlotte heads towards the dining room behind me, I stand here in the thick decaying air, not wanting to move.

13

Removal men clatter above as eventually I take a breath, step forward and reach for the glass handle, but my fingers stop just a few centimetres short of touching it. It's as though there is some sort of force field around it, or around me, I'm not sure, but however much I want to go inside, I can't seem to push my fingers through that last little pocket of air. My breaths ebb and flow. Something bangs on the landing. A door creaks. When I look up, I hear Dr Chatterton's voice in my head, his calm sagacious tone. 'Fight the fear, fight the triggers,' he tells me, but still my fingers won't move. They're trembling pathetically, hovering over the complex glass prism of the handle beneath them, when Charlotte screams from inside the dining room.

When I get to her, she's laughing, both hands pressed against her chest. There are the skeletons of maybe two dozen birds splayed across the floor among feathers and broken bones and smeared streaks of bird muck. They glimmer in thin strips of sunlight slanting through a small stained-glass window high on the wall facing the village. Behind her, sheets and blankets, crusty with dust and filth, cover a large table and a dozen chairs.

One of the removal men rushes in behind me. He's not much older than us, with short black hair and a t-shirt that can barely contain him. 'What happened?' he says. His accent is Eastern European.

Charlotte laughs, properly this time. 'It's fine,' she says, flicking her hair. 'They frightened me, that's all.'

'Must have come down the chimney,' he says.

I look around. There are what I assume to be paintings stacked against the wall, also covered in sheets. Shutters block the windows. Each of them is latched on the inside. I leave them to it and head straight across the hallway to the living room door. I turn the handle and push it open, where

14

I'm greeted with the stench of a dead rat lying face up on the timber floorboards. Its insides are bubbling with maggots.

'You sure you want to live here, son?' one of the removal men says behind me.

I can still hear him laughing as I step around the rat into the room. The space is enormous. Great cathedral arches of cobwebs laden with dust span its length, flies scrawling through long beams of sunlight squeezed through shutters that cover two large stone windows. It's cold, a feverish sort of cold that makes me shudder, as though it's coming from inside me. It catches my breaths, turning them into crystals that dissipate in the fetid air.

Double doors, panelled in diamonds of glass and boarded up on the outside, lead on to the main lawn. Beneath the smell of damp and decay, I think I can smell ash. There is no furniture other than a rocking chair facing a deep gothic fireplace. Above it hangs a large oil painting in a gilded frame. It's of a Fenland sky. Ink-black clouds pour out of the night like smoke, twisting into the shape of a horse's head.

There's a hand on my shoulder. Dad's looking at me. His eyes are glazed and empty.

'You alright?' he says.

I'm not, but I don't tell him that. I don't tell him anything. I look at the painting, aware that, once again, time has moved on without me. My arms are tingly. My mouth is dry. Threads of electricity, their tails lithe and bright, curl themselves guilefully back into the darkness as the painting bears down like a cliff face. It's exactly the same image I saw the night Charlotte went missing: the same shades, the same dimensions, the same wiry veins of lightning striking the earth beneath it. I can even make out the shape of the copse on the horizon. It's the view from my window.

15

Aware of my wrist convulsively beating a rhythm into my side, I study the painting, picturing every stroke being meticulously moulded, listening to the coarse whisper of the artist's brush until part of me can almost smell the peat lifting from beneath the gauzy aroma of dried oil. Despite the obvious deftness of hand, it's not in any way pleasant to look at. It's as though it was purposely designed to incite revulsion, to pull me inside its two-dimensional walls, only it's not two-dimensional anymore. It's real. I can see my face against it, blue and ghostlike and staring back at me through the darkness of that night.

I can hear the rain pounding on the roof tiles. I can smell the sulphuric breath of the storm, lightning flailing both out across empty fields and inside my head. Like a downed power cable, it fizzles and hisses across the rubbery surface of my brain, and when the door opens behind me, I realise I've bitten down so hard on my lip I've drawn blood. I wipe it away with the back of my finger. Charlotte is staring at me from the door. A sudden glare fossilises the delicate ivory-white features of her skin, her dark glistening hair and the scar that drips like ice from the corner of her eye to her mouth. Overhead, thunder breaks. As the sound falls away, I think I hear the church bell peal a long single chime.

Behind me, the mantelpiece clock does the same.

'He alright?' one of the men says.

Dad ignores him. He takes hold of my elbow.

'It's OK,' he says quietly, so only I can hear, and he turns me around, placing us inside our own little pocket of space, from where he looks probingly into my eyes as though searching for something dropped in a pond. 'Are you having a seizure?'

16

'No,' I tell him and I look away because I don't like people looking into my eyes, not even Dad, especially when the world beyond my memories is fast disappearing and my thoughts are left unguarded. A large mirror is attached to the wall behind him. Hand-painted wild flowers adorn its frame. Hummingbirds, aqua blue with delicate silver wings set back like springs, are feeding on the nectar, and for the briefest of moments one of them flashes across my line of sight, passing from here into a place beyond the glass, the light so white and radiant I can hardly see the men at the back of the room and for a moment I am not even convinced they are there. This isn't unusual. Sometimes my brain tricks me into thinking there is someone standing beside me when there isn't. It's not uncommon for people like me, according to Dr Chatterton, to think they've seen someone in the room with them when all they've seen is a subliminal reflection of themselves.

'It's going to be OK,' Dad whispers, tightening his grip on my arms.

'I'm scared.'

'I know,' he says. 'We all are.'

The elder of the two men clears his throat as he steps on to the hearth beside me. 'My name is Sly,' he says. There's a ritualistic note to his voice. It's smooth and measured, emitting from the back of his throat, the accent vaguely local, its edges having long ago been refined somewhere south of here. Cambridge, perhaps. His coarse grey suit smells of cigarette smoke and cats. 'And this is Detective Sergeant Daniels,' he adds. 'Your father tells me you've not been well. I'm sorry to hear that. It's an interesting painting, is it not?'

'I guess,' I say, half shrugging and stepping off the hearth. 'I don't think I like it much.'

'No,' he says, leaning studiously into the canvas as though remnants of my thoughts are visible there. 'Can you remember when you last spoke to your sister?' he says. His voice is at once steady and suggestive.

I shake my head. 'No,' I tell him.

Without turning, his body hunched, his narrow gaze fixed on the intricate details of the painting, he says softly, 'And has she spoken to you recently about anything that may have upset her, that may have caused her to run off?'

'No,' I say.

'And would she have told you if there had been?' His small eyes lift from the canvas. 'Are you close like that?'

'If you think she's run off,' I say, 'why are you searching the fields?'

Sly, moving slowly, seemingly without the need for haste despite the terrible air of desperation exuding from Dad's nervous little movements beside me, the abortive sentences stammering from his lips, pulls himself away from the grip of the painting and I become acutely aware of the presence of the other man in the room, Daniels. He's tall and ectomorphic, bright blue eyes set back in a gaunt face shadowed by a cap of snow-white hair which seems almost invisible in the halo of bright sunlight behind him.

I look to Dad for support, but his mind is clearly elsewhere, somewhere out in the fields, where men and women are making their way through the dirty green entanglement of rape stems looking for his daughter, and I feel alone standing in this large bright room with two complete strangers. I'm not really sure why I didn't tell the inspector about her coming to see me. Maybe I need to get things straight in my head first, put things in the right order before I say something I don't want to say, sieve out the false memories from the real ones. I don't know.

'So can you remember?' he says again.

'Remember what?' I reply, my wrist tapping methodically against my thigh, letting me know, for now at least, my body and mind are still attached to each other, that they're on the same side, that what one says the other will do.

He offers a placatory smile. 'When you last spoke to your sister,' he says. 'When did you last speak to your sister, Simon?'

THREE

Everything changes with the tone of his voice. It's almost as though he's been saving it for this moment. Its meas-ured evenness punctures a hole in the room. Everything deflates.

'I feel sick,' I say.

Thin pencil-black eyes stare back at me, the crystal light picking out long vertical lines in his face, and I notice for the first time the smell of flowers in the room. It's coming from the roses hanging languidly in a vase on the glass coffee table and clashes with the latent scent of sulphur. Some of the petals are lying on their backs, on their own reflections, like peels of dead skin. Annie Proctor brought them over last week.

A bird flashes across the sky, its flight sliced neatly in half by the wall between the windows. It was either a rook or a crow. I couldn't tell. It was too quick for me to see. A corvid anyway. They're about the only birds that seem to settle here, appearing randomly in the village on the corners of walls or the tops of houses, black and jigsaw-shaped, like missing pieces of the day.

'Would you like me to do this another time?' Sly asks.

I shake my head. 'That morning,' I tell him. 'We walked into the village together. I went to the Wildfowl Trust.

Charlotte caught a bus into Peterborough.' I'm talking now as though reading from a prepared speech.

The village is eerily quiet, the low morning sun offering a glittery warmth as we walk past the line of cherry and almond trees that parade its only road. The sun out here in the mornings is like an enormous spotlight shining through tracing paper. It turns everything bright and opaque, even the petals above us and those scattered loosely on the ground. Someone is practising a violin. When I look towards where I think it's coming from, I see the face of a young girl, seven or eight years old, appear in a top-floor window. She hides behind the curtain as though she doesn't want me to see her. The violin continues. It's slightly out of tune and being played without too much care, and for the briefest of moments I feel as though I've heard it before, in this exact same moment of time, like a déjà vu.

On the verge by the wooden bus stop a jackdaw is picking at the freshly cut grass like a mechanical toy. It stops as we approach, looking up at us disconcertingly before getting back to looking for bugs.

Mary Murphy is already here, sitting on the wooden bench. Long straight hair mirrors her black dress. Piercings of gothic design – peace signs and pentacles, inverted crosses and a goat's head – bead the curve of her ear. There are also strange demonic-looking symbols painted on the caps of her Dr Marten boots in white paint: a circled pentagram and a star I recognise as the Sigil of Baphomet. In her lap, I notice, is a small brown paper bag. A long spar of shadow from the lamp post splits her full and waxen face in two as she looks up from a dog-eared copy of *Macbeth* covered in blue biro: moustache, glasses, names of obscure bands. She smiles at Charlotte. She doesn't speak to me. She doesn't seem to notice I'm here.

'The Wildfowl Trust,' Sly says. 'Arthur Skinner's place?'

I blink, finding myself once again in the prickling heat of the living room. 'Yes,' I tell him. I pull at my collar. 'I found a Bewick's Swan by the railway lines when we first came here. Mr Skinner's looking after her. I go whenever I can to help with the feeds. We're hoping to get her strong enough for winter migration.'

'And you didn't see her after that?' he says.

I don't reply. I didn't see her after that, I tell myself, closing my eyes and trying to think. I came back from the Trust just before lunch and read in my room all afternoon.

'And has Charlotte ever been to the Trust, do you know?'

'No.'

'You're sure about that?'

'Yes.'

'What about the old people's home?'

'I don't think so. Why?'

He half smiles. 'What about you, Simon? Have you ever been to the old people's home?'

I shake my head and look away. Partly hidden by the glow of light, Daniels takes out a small black notebook from his jacket and makes notes.

'And you say you can't think of anything that's happened recently that would have upset her. At school, in the village.' Sly glances at Dad. 'At home maybe?'

'No,' I say. 'We didn't really talk. Not like that anyway.'

He smiles again. 'It's OK, Simon,' he says. 'This isn't an interrogation. We just need to obtain as definitive a timeline as we possibly can for that evening, to try and understand what was going on in her head. Your mum and dad suggested she may have been to see you. Is that correct?'

A car drives slowly past the house, the groan of its engine low and stuttery. I look to the window and scratch the back of my neck just below the right ear, where a small rash has started to develop. It's one of the side effects of the medication.

'I'm not sure,' I say.

'You're not sure or she didn't come and see you. Which is it, Simon? This is important.'

'I can't remember,' I tell him.

His smile tapers. He turns back to the painting, where fewer than a hundred metres beyond the canvas, trawling through the exact same landscape, his men are searching for Charlotte.

Dad pulls me towards him. He is tall and slim and his long arm knots around me like a coil of rope. He smells of coffee and stale sweat, like he did in London last summer. He's unshaven, too, and his skin has become sickly yellow. 'We'll do this another time, Inspector,' he says, at last finding his voice. 'If you don't mind. Simon needs rest. These things sometimes get mixed up in his head.'

'Of course,' Sly says, stepping back to give us space.

Something whimsical glimmers in the corners of Daniels's eyes. His silver ring catches the light. I look away, down to the ground, the vignetted edges of my vision blocking everything but my trainers and the tawny sheen of the floorboards. Clumsily, I wipe my sleeve across my face and mutter a paragraph from *Bewick's Swan*. 'Ever since the study started, adult and yearling swans recorded at Slimbridge have each been given a name, making it easier to remember the birds thereafter.'

Dad swallows noisily by my ear.

'What's going on, Dad?'

He looks directly at me, tears forming in his eyes. One of the windows rattles as a train passes on the tracks behind the house. It shakes the light in the room as though it's resting on water. 'They found something,' he says, quickly swallowing the words back into his chest and looking away up to the ceiling, drawing a long concentrated breath into his lungs as though he is about to free-dive to the bottom of the ocean.

I follow his stare. A large Georgian ceiling rose peers down like a giant eye. Above it is my room, where the windows look out across the fields as the painting looks out across the fields. For a moment nothing else happens. Sound stops and I'm overcome for some unexplainable reason with a sensation I can only think of as guilt. It's unfounded, but still it claws at my insides as the strain of those awful words plays in the stillness. *They found something.* I don't know exactly what the something they found is, but I know it's a bad thing and I probably only have a second or two of my previous life remaining. His next words will change everything. The past and the future will no longer recall each other in the same light. They will be forever tied. My mouth dries. Time stops. It's a reprieve. Fear does this to me. It's the same as when I'm in the aura. It can somehow bring the world outside of my world to a complete halt, while my world continues to race at thousands of miles an hour inside its own little bubble of confusion, like a snow globe. Possibly they are the same glassy walls. I don't know. I haven't worked that out yet.

Dad whispers something into the top of my head but the words don't get through my skull, not as words anyway. They're just meaningless reverberations. Steadily I start to breathe through my nose, focusing on the now, and speak aloud more sentences from *Bewick's Swan*. 'In the field, Bewick's Swans are more likely to be confused with Whooper Swans than with any other swans because they are superficially similar in appearance and their ranges overlap.'

'It was found at the copse,' Daniels says. There's something almost gloating about the way he says this. 'We're still trying to ascertain whether it has any connection to Charlotte or not but, if so, would you have any idea why she would have gone there that night?'

'She wouldn't have done,' I say. 'No one ever goes there,' and I pad an urgent rhythm into my side, but Daniels doesn't let up. He simply waits, watching me in the glow of bright white light streaming in through the windows. He makes sure he catches my eye then looks to the door.

When I turn, Mum is standing there, arms wrapped around her chest as though she's been placed inside an invisible straight jacket. She looks like she's been poisoned. Her skin is pale. Her eyes are red and puffy.

'Mum,' I say, 'what's going on?' But her face doesn't change. She just stares at me, a bitter emptiness in her eyes I have never seen before.

'I've made a sandwich,' she says in a monotone. 'You should probably eat something.'

I shake my head, unable to convert thoughts into words. Somewhere in my mind, I see Charlotte standing on a beach hut, the brightest sky imaginable set behind her. The world is swimming around me like glass. I don't know where it ends and I begin. And I don't understand what is going on here. Nothing is making sense.

Dad guides me past her and takes me up the stairs. They are bare, the edges freshly painted white, ready for a carpet. As we walk, they groan dispassionately, releasing a damp fusty scent of age with each creak, and I think about the empty space beneath them: a dark inverted door-less space with a ceiling that zigzags into nothing, a forgotten void so black there are no shadows. It will always be there,

25

I think, even though I can't see it, nor will ever touch it, the same as the unmapped passageways and corridors in my brain will always be there. Not seeing them doesn't mean they don't exist, the same as seeing something doesn't always make it real.

Below, the mantelpiece clock taps out its metronomic dance. It's better suited to this house, I think. The cold stone walls in the hallway give it the sepulchral voice it deserves. I look up at Dad, but he isn't here anymore. I'm standing at the top of the landing the night Charlotte disappeared, looking down.

Darkness laps at the bottom steps. Behind me there's an empty corridor dimly lit with wall lamps, four on each side, the light making grainy crescent shapes on the wall like little fires through which I can just make out the shape of the attic door on the ceiling. The laundry room door at the end is closed.

Mum and Dad are downstairs in the kitchen. I can hear them moving around each other, the way they do. I need to concentrate, I tell myself. I need to get help, and when the floor shifts beneath me, I have to hold on to the wall to stop myself falling into the darkness below. I sniff, looking for a scent, but the smell of sulphur has gone. The aura has passed and yet I feel extraordinarily strange, as though in two places at once, alive and dead at the same time, inside my own dream. Rain is hammering down on the domed roof light over my head. In the distance, thunder breaks. As it fades, I hear the corridor behind me creak. At first, I just stand here, too afraid to turn around, part of my brain telling me it's just the wind and the house and my imagination, but the feeling doesn't go away. It only gets stronger. All I can hear are my breaths. All I can feel is someone standing behind me, watching me. They're so real I can smell them, but it's not the sulphur I smell in the aura. It's a brighter smell, lavender.

I feel sick, I'm so scared. This isn't a trick anymore. This isn't an abandoned memory, some random feeling finding its way to the surface of my brain. There is someone standing behind me. Mum and Dad are downstairs. So is Charlotte. I can hear them. They're arguing. No one else is in the house. I turn, as though to catch them off guard, a punch ready in my fist.

The corridor is empty. Something's wrong though. It seems twice as long as it actually is. The walls are leaning obliquely to the right. One of the lights flickers and hisses, and I think for a moment there may be a moth caught in the lamp, but it stops as soon as I think this. I squint as my eyes try to adjust to the darkness and it takes a while for me to figure out what it is that's different. It's the laundry room door. It's open. I can see the shelves and the white towels in the subdued light.

Lightning flashes overhead, splintering metallic grey through the domed roof light, and for the tiniest fraction of a second I see him standing by the laundry door. The boy I had seen at my window the first day we arrived. Then he's gone.

When I look back down the stairs, the kitchen door is open. There's shouting coming from inside. There wasn't supposed to be shouting anymore.

FOUR

There are clean sheets on my bed. My clothes are folded on the wooden chair in the corner of the room, my sketchbook, laptop and pot of pencils neatly positioned on my desk just as I left them. The walls and ceiling are gleaming white, as is the bookshelf with my bird books and the boarded-up fireplace set between the windows. On my bedside table is a lamp, a digital alarm clock and my book, *Bewick's Swan*.

'You should get some sleep,' Dad says with deliberate calmness.

'Where do you think she is?'

His expression wavers. 'I don't know,' he says, 'London? She wasn't happy here. We knew that,' and he sits me down on the edge of the bed, takes two Diazepam from my bedside table drawer, places them in my hand and goes to get a glass of water from the bathroom.

I sit and wait with them balancing in my palm, wondering if this is the start of the end of our family. Everything has to start somewhere, even the end of something. I study the pale blue pills, a sharp tremor running up my arm, and briefly imagine being taken to a place far away from here, to Alice's Wonderland perhaps, but the illusion is shattered as I remember all Alice had to do to get home again was accept the ludicrousness of her situation. I can't do that. It would only bring me back to the same spot. The room smells of dust and furniture polish. It reminds me of Aunty Anne and Uncle Pete's house. Our house only smells of polish on a Friday afternoon after Mrs Yearsly has been. Sunlight slants through two Georgian windows, sketching distorted frames of burnt yellow onto a white rug and wide wooden boards. On the day we moved in, Mum had ushered me inside, saying she thought this should be my room. She thought I'd like the view. My bed and furniture and boxes were already here.

'You can see both the world and the village from here,' she says, as though the two are not connected. Carved into one of the floorboards are some letters. We look at them a while, a little uncertainly, until Mum gets to her knees and brushes away some of the dust. 'A R,' she says, looking up with a strained fervour, as if she wants me to clarify this with her, for us to discover it together, mother and son, that unbreakable bond.

I step back, frightened, although of what I'm not sure. I'm not trying to spoil the moment. I know what this move means to her. That's not it. It's just sometimes I get a feeling I am not supposed to be in a place, as though I've accidentally stumbled on something I wasn't meant to see, a dream or memory that doesn't belong to me.

'No,' Mum says, rubbing the letters excitedly. 'It's an H. Look. H R '50. It must have been carved by someone who used to have this room. What do you think?' She looks up with a grin. 'You should put your initials somewhere.'

'No,' I tell her flatly. 'I don't think so.'

'Well,' she says, getting up and brushing the front of her jeans with the backs of her hands. 'We'll put a rug over it then. How about that?'

'Yes,' I say. 'It's my room now.'

29

Dad hands me the glass, hovering over me as I take the pills.

'And the painting?' I say. 'Why was Sly interested in the painting?'

'I don't know. Listen, Simon, I'm sorry but I have to go. The inspector, he's going to want to ask me more questions.' He turns to the door but I don't let him leave.

'It's the view from my window,' I tell him.

He pauses mid-step, releasing a long composing breath, and I imagine him, as I've seen before, briefly closing his eyes, telling himself to be patient with me, as everyone seems to have to be.

'What's going on, Dad?' I say. 'That night, before the fit, I saw the same horse's head in the painting downstairs out there over the fields.' I point to the window with a straight arm.

'It was a dream,' he says. 'We'll talk about it later, OK? Now I need to speak with the inspector.'

'What did they find at the copse?'

He composes himself a moment, looking back to the door as though someone is waiting for him outside, the light collecting in the folds between his eyes. 'A white rose,' he says reluctantly, 'on the stone circle there.'

The words fail to settle among my thoughts. 'What does that have to do with Charlotte?'

'Probably nothing, just that someone was there the night she disappeared.'

'I don't understand.'

He shakes his head and goes to the door. 'Nor do I,' he says.

'Is that why they're searching the fields?'

He nods without turning his head.

'Who found it?' I say.

30

He grips the door handle, but still he doesn't leave. He lets out a breath through his teeth, agitation sharpening the course of its release. 'One of the Burton boys,' he says, half looking over his shoulder. He looks as sceptical as he does frightened, standing there by the door in the harsh glare of the day. The reflection of a fly on the window pane moves across his nose without him realising as he stares up to the ceiling, as though the words he's about to say have been printed across it. He inhales deeply and blinks away the start of tears. 'This is that thing, Simon,' he says. 'Do you understand? This is that thing that only happens to other people, but it's not happening to other people. It's happening to us.'

'Why were they even looking there?' I say.

He frowns. 'I don't know,' he says. 'Get some rest. I'll let you know if any news comes in.'

I allow my gaze to drift towards a painting of a pair of Montagu's harriers hanging on the wall beside the door. Uncle Pete bought it for me. It was Christmas, ten years ago. I remember. He owned a Triumph Spitfire at the time, bright yellow with a convertible roof. Through the blue haze of morning he drove me to Lakenheath Fen, the engine groaning ardently beneath our feet, the acetic smell of petrol leaking through the floor and the worn leather seats, the steady vibration of its shell shaking me like a chill.

It was there I saw my first and only Montagu's harrier. It was a male. They are rarely found in the winter, usually migrating to Africa, especially when among the larger more aggressive marsh harriers who dominate the nesting areas there.

Cumbersome low-flying American jets had been thundering overhead that day, but I hardly noticed. I was too engrossed in listening to every word Uncle Pete was saying, my eyes pressed against the glass viewfinder of a brand-new set of 8 x 32 DPSI binoculars. The fetid stench of reeds and wildfowl clung to the air. The taste of salt played on my lips. Huge snow-white clouds loomed in a December sky which seemed to have been wrapped like cellophane around the universe. I remember thinking, even then, how vast everything was, that we merely subsisted on this tiny rock floating through a fathomless ocean of matter and antimatter we know almost nothing about. I understood not just how expendable but how irrelevant we are, that there are things around us we will never comprehend, that we're not supposed to comprehend, a knowledge we are not yet to be trusted with.

A train races south on the tracks behind the house. It's the fast train to London. It sucks a hole through the air like a drill. I wait for the sound to fade entirely, the distant calling of Charlotte's name faintly breaking as an ebb tide into the stillness, before going to my desk drawer and taking out a sugar-free cola cube from a brown paper bag. I suck on it. Quickly it combats the bitterness of Diazepam.

The search party is gathered in the far corner of the rape field, its cluttered tea-stain shadow spilling lightly across a mat of green. Behind it, rising out of the flat earth like a sea monster, is the copse. It's bulbous and solid, an incongruously dark shape watching from just above the surface of this calm and subdued land, its untold vastness hidden in the earth below. Birds circle overhead. There are two policemen, I notice, standing at its edge in the sunlight, out of its shadow.

Most of the villagers who had been to look are heading back along the path. I count fourteen of them. They're walking with no real pace, no conviction. Occasionally they stop to look behind, uncertain, perhaps, of whether or not they should be going home yet, or if they should have gone down there at all. A man in a faded Barbour jacket points towards the house. His frothy golden hair gleams in the hot sun. Behind them neat regiments of colour, green, silver and beige, stretch back to an unbroken horizon that shimmers in the distant heat, making it hard to distinguish where the earth stops and the sky begins. There's something oddly synthetic about this vast two-dimensional landscape. There is the sky and there is the land. There is nothing else but us, lost within it.

When we first arrived, I stood at this window looking out across the fields in the low evening light. Villagers were gathered outside Mrs Neal's house, watching the removal men carrying in the last of our furniture. In the middle of the road some kids were playing a game with sticks and a deflated orange football. I remember clearly as the sound of thunder broke somewhere off in the distance that none of them looked up. They simply continued playing their game or watching the house or drinking tea, as though oblivious to the presence of nature. Huge clouds, bruised with rain, had congealed over the horizon, their edges bright like fire where they touched the lowering sun. The earth was so clean and fluid I could have just as easily been looking out to sea, staring at the grey weight of a storm as it edged its way to shore, which is when the sky flashed for the tiniest fraction of a second, as though it hadn't really happened at all, as though there had simply been a technical glitch in time, and in that moment the air in the room had thickened with the most intense smell of sulphur. Then it was gone.

The monks who resided here from the tenth century would have shared almost the same view, other than woodland being replaced with farmland, and it occurred to me why they would have contemplated the world and its secrets with such ascetic resolve, why they would have lived their lives with the sole purpose of questioning the very meaning of it.

Somewhere, way off in the distance, sunlight glares off a moving car.

I notice Mr Scott limping a few paces behind the rest of the group. His black Labrador, Jet, is at his side. Sometimes I walk Jet. He's old and slow and barks at blackbirds. Mr Scott lives next door to Mrs Neal. He is mute. Mrs Neal told me, after I had helped her with her shopping one afternoon soon after we moved in, that the splinter of a battleship had pierced his throat during the Falkland's War. Emma Proctor told me this wasn't true. She said he had been born that way. I don't know which is the truth, but I remember thinking I liked the idea of being able to pass through this life without having to talk to anyone, like the monks who once lived here. Mum and Dad said it was just a phase I was going through, although I am sure I meant it at the time.

The angle and perspective of the copse are exactly the same as in the painting. Whoever created it, I think, must have once stood here, exactly where I am now. Did I see what they painted or did they paint what I saw?

There's a fly trying to get out. It's a bluebottle and it fizzes every time it hits the pane, and I wonder how long it will continue to keep hurting itself like this, relentlessly knocking into the glass, before it occurs to me that it doesn't even know what glass is. It will just keep flying into this invisible wall until it dies. It's not its fault. It's not stupid. It simply doesn't understand that not everything is as it seems, that this imperceptible barrier stopping it from doing something as innate to a fly as flying is actually solid material made from the same atoms and particles that it is.

The front door closes beneath me. I watch Daniels and Sly get into their cars. The fly continues to hit the glass. Sly heads south out of the village. Daniels goes the other way, turning into the stone gateway of the Manor House, where crows and rooks perch on the tops of the tall chimneys. All but one leap into the air as the car rolls across the gravel before settling lazily back down on their plinths like falling ash.

FIVE

As I turn back into the room, a sense of displacement
seethes through me as a current. Within it, her image
transposed without effort onto the present, I see Charlotte
standing by the door. Her hair is wet, her face taut with
fear, ashen white and faux, a flicker of metallic light
blazing across her right cheek and the scar that seeps from
her eye to the corner of her mouth. Thunder breaks
overhead. Rain scratches the window. 'Simon,' she says,
'you have to listen to me. There's something I have to tell
you. It's important,' and then she's gone, floating shape-
lessly over the edge of my memories, ghostly and
evanescent.

Dazed, I walk towards the middle of the room, stand in
the centre of the white rug and try to bring back the
memory, but it's impossible. For a while it flitters on the
surface of my mind, like a piece of wreckage, but every time
I reach for it, it sinks back into the depths, discarding as it
does the essence of Charlotte: her skin, her hair, the
skulking aromas of cider and cannabis. I see myself on the
bed in the green glow of the digital clock. I hear the rain at
the window. I feel each scrape of thunder against my skin,
and glazed indistinctly over the memory, I see the horse's
head daubed like paint in the savage sky. I let the lightning

inside. I let it rush through me, soldering violently the past and the present and the future.

Downstairs the telephone rings, jolting the house back to life. It's answered instantly. Silence pitches once again. Within it, a train skates north on the tracks behind the house. I look to the window nearest the desk, the top pane trembling slightly, shaking a poster-size mark on the wall. On the bookshelf is a framed photograph of a kingfisher. I had taken it at Pensthorpe Nature Reserve in Norfolk just moments before the fit that hospitalised me for a week last summer. It's why, I guess, the move to the middle of nowhere, as Charlotte delighted in calling it, happened so quickly, to get me out of the city into the calm unexacting flow of the countryside. And Mum too, I suspect. The photograph is completely blurred. On the back, Aunty Anne has written *Our greatest glory is not in never falling, but in rising every time we fall*. I think it was meant to inspire me.

It was Uncle Pete who introduced me to ornithology. When I turned seven he gave me a set of 8 x 32 DPSI binoculars. He had been fascinated with birds all his life, and from a young age I remember the two of us would take walks along the beach or spend hours peering through binoculars out of his conservatory window, nothing but the sea and the vacuous grey sky before us. Charlotte read or played chess with Aunty Anne. Sometimes I would sketch the birds, either from memory or copying them from a book, as Uncle Pete explained to me how each one behaved and how to identify them. There are hundreds of different varieties of seabird that gather on the marshes there and often the identifiable feature of a particular type can be very small: a slight colouring on the wing, or the shape of the beak. He had books too, old encyclopaedias Grandpa had given him, in wooden covers with golden lettering, plus more modern volumes in laminate dust jackets. I read all I could, logging every detail, and soon I had slipped quite eagerly into their complex avian world, leaving a little bit of my own behind.

I found feathers on the marshes and beaches and in ivy-covered hedgerows. Where other children collected shells and stones, I collected these feathers, cataloguing them in a hardback notebook Uncle Pete had given me, and in the quiet nights I would stand in the conservatory, encased in black glass, scrolling through pages and pages of drawings and photographs of birds until I could identify each and every species.

I open the window and watch the fly disappear into the bright day, rubbing my finger over the brass latch as the search party makes its way through to the next field. The phone rings once again and I find myself straightening the books on the desk and smoothing out the creases on my bed until it looks as though it has never been slept in. I pick up *Bewick's Swan* and read a new paragraph to try and calm myself. I can't risk another fit. Not now. I can't go back to hospital and so I read that in 1963 Sir Peter Scott at the Wildfowl Trust at Slimbridge began a study of the bill patterns of certain Bewick's Swans. He had noticed that each bird possessed a unique design. He drew the bills by hand. The following winter, thirteen of the eighteen birds he had identified returned to Slimbridge.

I close the book. I already know this.

Beneath the white rug, I picture Dad on the telephone in the kitchen, Mum standing irresolutely by the sink, clutching her arms together, trembling as though caught in the icy chill of winter. I can't hear what Dad's saying. I can only hear Aunty Anne crying at the bottom of the stairs, and all the while, like the distant tapping of a bell buoy, the immutable sound of the mantelpiece clock.

The shadows on the landing are long and hazy, spilling diagonally from the roof light and encaging little orbs of colour that have fallen through its faded band of decorative roses. They shimmer on the floor by my feet. The laundry room door is closed. I stare at it for a while, allowing my memories of that night a moment to settle, then go to Charlotte's door. My reflection looms in the glass handle, serious and frightened and distorted. Beneath me, voices coming from the kitchen are once again halted by the phone. I stop and wait, as I imagine those in the kitchen are also doing, until Dad quietly thanks whoever it is at the other end and replaces the receiver.

The curtains are drawn. Neat lines of sunlight wrap around their square frames. Already it feels like a tomb. Charlotte's scent: cheap joss sticks, hairspray and stale cigarettes, hangs faintly in the air beneath an ambivalent scent of perfume. Carefully I pass through it, pull the curtains apart and open both windows. Sunlight floods past me, shredding the room's dreary skin into millions of particles of dust. There's a photographer positioned on the bench by the village sign. He's leaning forward as though praying. Dirty grey hair covers his head. He is dressed entirely in black, eyes fixed on the house as though half expecting it to vanish at any moment. When he sees me at the window, he lifts his camera to his face.

I step back, startled but invigorated with a fresh supply of oxygen in my lungs, and start to look around. I have no idea what I'm looking for, but whatever it is, something tells me I need to find it soon, before the police take everything away, before these empty white walls really do become a shrine.

Charlotte's room is bigger than mine even though she's younger than me. There are two single beds, a desk, chest of drawers and a large fitted wardrobe. There are none of the garnishments I imagine most other teenage girls' rooms would possess. There's no bric-a-brac. There's no pink. There are no horses or posters of boy bands. Instead, there's a shelf full of books, a plasma ball supporting them at one end, and a pile of unopened boxes in the far corner of the room. Various garments spill out of her chest of drawers. The wardrobe door is open. I can see her black boots and an old leather jacket collapsed like a corpse on top of them. Other jackets and shirts, long knitted jumpers hang limply above. Everything looks so normal and unaffected, I think, and, as I'm standing here, it's hard to get my head around the fact that she is actually missing, that she has not physically been here, in this room, for two days and two nights.

Her bed is unmade. Clothes are scattered across the floor as though washed up in a flood. The lid of a roll-on deodorant lies beneath a small table cluttered with lipsticks and make-up pencils, a small ceramic bowl filled with bracelets and rings and hair-bands. Beside it is a bangle, which I've never seen before. Attached to it by a thin black chain is a ring encrusted cheaply with a red flower design. It is not something Charlotte would ever wear. I pick up the lid, place it back on the deodorant and go to her desk. It's Grandpa's old desk, mahogany with a scuffed leather writing pad and drawers on both sides. There are notepads and A-level English Literature text books stacked around the edges: *Birdsong, Dr Faustus, Macbeth, The Wife of Bath*. Other subjects lie adrift on the floor. Her laptop isn't here. I guess it has already been taken away.

With the sun warming one side of my face, I let my finger run over the waxy new cover of a copy of *Lolita* and sit in her chair, hoping, perhaps, for some kind of metaphysical inspiration. When it doesn't appear, I make myself comfortable and pick up one of her notebooks, noticing a sketch of mine stuck to the wall by her exam timetable. I lean forward, carefully tracing my finger over the pencil lines. I've not seen it here before. I didn't even know she had taken it. I don't know why she would have done. It's of a Bewick's Swan lying inert in brambles. In the right-hand corner, in blue biro, she has written in her small disparate handwriting *Silence in Heaven about the space of half an hour.*

It's our first week here and we are taking a rest from pulling up carpets and breaking up old pieces of furniture when Charlotte, surreptitiously tapping the top pocket of her shirt, the way she does, suggests we go and explore by the railway lines.

A broken gate set in a tall row of poplar trees takes us through a ley of meadow grass. It sways and ripples like the ocean. Insects scratch at its surface, the tart scents of pollen and thistle catching in my throat as I follow her, thankful for a distant wind that has carried with it the smell of the sea. The stump of an oak tree pushes its way out of the earth like a giant fist. Cabbage white butterflies balance on the nettles that surround it, wings arched and ready. There's hardly any sound: the faintest buzzing from bees and wasps, crows in the tops of the trees, finches on the other side of the tracks. There is not a single sound of human life or machine. It's as though we are the last two people left on earth.

Charlotte lights up as I make my way through a dense brier of nettles and brambles, careful not to brush against the soft white domes of giant hogweed standing straight and rigid like guards at the side of the makeshift path. The marshy odour of Charlotte's joint follows me. Crows circle endlessly above, breaking up the sharp lines of light as eventually I find an old railway sleeper beneath my feet that must have once been laid as a track. It's shaded beneath wild elderflower and yew trees, which I have to hold onto for balance until I reach a tall mesh fence. Beyond it, eight glimmering steel lines stretch uninterrupted towards the horizon.

'So,' Charlotte calls from the edge of the meadow, 'is this everything you ever wanted then? Birds, the open land, train lines but no station.'

'It wasn't my idea,' I say, my fingers slipping through the wire. I'm not sure if she hears me or not.

I see a gap in the fence, five metres or so away. There is another sleeper leading to it but it looks too overgrown for me to reach. Even so, I take one step, then another, supporting myself on a wooden post, damp and black with rot, and swollen with ivy. Nettles grope at my ankles, thorns scrape my arms until, at last, my foot rests on the soft timber, which is when I see the swan.

'It's a desert,' Charlotte calls out behind me. Her voice is laced with contempt. 'That's what it is. A desert.'

My warm face presses against the cool metal as I try to weave my way further through the brier. 'It wasn't my idea,' I repeat even though I know she can't hear me. Pollen sticks to the side of my face. The air chills as the sun disappears behind a sluggish grey cloud. I hook a bramble onto the fence, duck my head beneath it and inch my way closer to the dead bird. 'If you don't like it, you can leave. No one will care. I won't care.'

'Maybe I'll go back to London,' she says, seemingly unaware of my comment. 'We're seventeen. We can do that, you know.'

'Do what you like,' I say beneath my breath. The swan is about two metres away now, entangled in thick coils of bramble.

42

'It's alright for you,' she says. 'You're all at home out here, aren't you, with your feathered friends?'

When I look back, her fingers offer me an indulgent little wave. She drags on the joint, releasing its thick grey essence into the slanting light. Her stare is tight and inimical. She looks like Mum, I think, pretty in that gaunt angular way which magazines seem to like, high-ridged cheekbones and hollowed out eyes. Only her hair is different and that's been dyed. It's almost impossible to think we were created in the same womb.

'What are you actually doing?'

'There's a swan.'

'A what?'

I ignore her. I am desperately trying to stop myself from falling back into the undergrowth, and besides, I know she heard me, so taking a sharp breath, I gain my balance and ease along the fence. The tracks beside me catch in a blink of sunlight then turn a dull grey once again, humming gently against the stained aggregate beneath them.

'A swan? Leave it alone. What is with you? What's wrong with us humans?'

She laughs as I grit my teeth, push my fingers through the mesh, and take another step forward. The fence sags beneath my weight and the branch I'd attached to the mesh springs up, whipping across the side of my face. Thorns slash at the skin. I scream.

'What is it?' Charlotte calls from the shadows.

When I turn and face her, blood dripping into my mouth, I see she's frightened. We look at each other like this a while. There's a moat of nettles and brambles between us, but that is all. The rest of the world is silent again. It doesn't exist. It can't see or hear us down here, but we can see and hear each other. We both know what the other is thinking. We always have, and when the air sparkles suddenly I can't help but think of God pouring glitter over the two of us, showering this fathomless moment with his approval, where we are the only humans left on earth. Charlotte, too, she's beautiful, I think, silhouetted like that in this strange kaleidoscopic light.

'You OK?'

'I'm OK.'

'We should go.'

Wind pulls at the trees, distorting the shadows between us. It breaks the spell. Sound returns. All around me leaves chant, swaying in the warm air, aware of my thoughts perhaps. I look up, not really sure where I am or what has happened. Time has left me straggling once again. The light changes. A blackbird chirps. Crows caw.

The swan is a female. They are smaller than the males, with shorter necks. It looks dead but smells alive, not of a corpse, even though there are flies swarming around its head. I swipe them away as well as I can and take a look around. There is no sign of a nest and the nearest water is on the other side of the tracks, over the bank by Ten Mile Dyke. Maybe it came from the Wildfowl Trust. I imagine it's possible to get to the back of the grounds along the cutting from here. Perhaps it had become disorientated, mistaking the silver lines of steel for the water in the dyke.

I look down the tracks, the aggregate digging into my knees through my jeans, and start to pull free some of the brambles around her neck. A bee hovers by my head. Nonchalantly, I swing out at it, the back of my hand connecting with its tiny body, and run my fingers gently through the soft white down beneath the swan's feathers. I remember clearly then, feeling the sun leaking onto my back like warm water, sensing a heartbeat push gently into the palm of my hand.

SIX

There's nothing in Charlotte's notebooks and diaries.

On the bedside table is an iPod, earphones dripping to the carpet. She would have taken it with her had she run away. I imagine Sly will have thought the same thing. Beside it is a photograph of Tom, her boyfriend from London, a wide excitable grin scored across his face. There is also a novel, thumbed in the bottom corner, and a glass of water. The water has already developed a thin silvery film. Thousands of tiny bubbles cling to the glass's side. The novel is *Volpone* by Ben Jonson. I remember Charlotte telling me once how Volpone tried to dupe his family and friends by pretending to be on his deathbed.

I turn to a noise outside in the corridor and carefully move to the bookcase on the far wall, my trainers light on the wooden boards. Charlotte's scent clouds around me as I run my finger over the spines: *The Bell Jar*, *Room with a View*, *The Accidental*. My bedroom door opens. I stand still and listen, teeth gritted. I don't want to be seen in here, although why that is, I'm not sure.

'Simon,' Dad calls out on the landing.

I don't respond. I stay where I am, filtering my breaths. The light flickers.

'There you are,' he says at last, opening Charlotte's door. 'I wondered where you'd got to.'

I look up but I don't answer.

'What are you doing in here?'

'I don't know really,' I say, 'just looking.'

He part searches the room, part watches me, as though he doesn't believe me. 'The police don't want anyone to come in here. I should have told you. Sorry.'

'OK,' I say and I walk past him out on to the landing.

He follows. Something changes. I don't know what it is. But something changes. I can feel it as a mist floating between us. A small bird, possibly a starling, a young jackdaw maybe, it's too quick for me to see, cackles from the edge of the domed roof light, black eyes peering in, before quickly scrambling away, scraping its claws against the roof tiles and heading off in the direction of the village.

We both look up.

The sun blinds us.

'What happened that night, Simon?'

I look to the floor and the diffused pattern of coloured lights on the bare boards, each shapeless and shimmering through the glass dome, struggling to remain where they are. He asks me again, firmer this time, but still I don't answer. I don't even shake my head. I just stare at the lights and think about seeing the boy that night, standing in the doorway to the laundry room, pale and lifeless, that distant smell of lavender, as I listened to them arguing in the kitchen. I hold out my hand and cradle one of the orbs of light in my palm. Was he also, I think, nothing more than the shadow of something that can't be seen?

Dad tilts his neck. 'Simon?' he says, directly prompting me this time. His feet shuffle, stiff and uncertain like a puppet's, then he says, 'What did she tell you, when she came to see you?'

'You've already asked me that.'

'And you still haven't told me.' His voice is fraught, as though wanting to shout, but he holds it back inside his jaws. I can see them moving against the weight of what's inside. His eyes narrow. His lips judder. My body contracts. I look at him from the very top of my eye sockets, then back to the floor, my wrist beating against my thigh, trying to block out the tension contaminating the air between us. It's hot and cramped and fractious, eager to burst. I don't like anger. I never have, not even my own.

'Bewick's Swans have long been kept in captivity,' I mutter under my breath. 'These are usually injured birds incorporated into waterfowl collections in Europe, but swans from the eastern population have also been sent from China and America. A wounded male survived for many years in Anjou during the latter half of the nineteenth century.'

'Stop that, Simon. Please.'

I nod without looking up, but I don't stop. I only muffle the words with my mouth.

'We need to focus,' he says.

My lips tremble as I speak. My wrist thumps into my side.

'Simon,' he snaps, shaking the light in the corridor. 'Will you please stop that.'

I half look up, desisting my little psalm mid-sentence.

'Where is she, Simon?' he says, just about pleading now.

'I don't know, Dad,' I say.

He grips his hair. 'Bloody hell,' he says and he starts to cry, shuddering like a child as he paces back and forth along the landing, in and out of the shafts of light, the floorboards creaking beneath him, releasing the decaying scent of the house. He moves ever closer, tilting and swaying, like an untethered barge.

I step back.

A cup or a plate breaks on the flagstones beneath us. The sound is sharp and sudden.

I look back to the floor, not certain what to do. A strangeness, like the aura, falls upon me, but it is not the aura. It possesses no mass, no depth, no scent. It is a feeling of complete hollowness. Within it I hear them downstairs in the kitchen the night she disappeared. They're arguing. Charlotte's shouting. She's swearing, telling them she can't explain or something like that. It's hard to hear the words, and when the door slams and she swears again violently into the icy darkness of the hallway, I turn quickly and go back to my room.

'Where is she, Simon?' Dad says again on the landing. A bubble of spit, like spume, is hanging over his lips.

'It was me, David. I'm sorry,' I hear Aunty Anne say from the kitchen door. 'I'm just clearing it up now.'

Dad looks up with a start, blinking as though having woken suddenly. He wipes his mouth. 'Never mind that,' he calls down the stairs and he holds my gaze for a fraction of a second longer than he needs to, I think to tell me that what I just witnessed up here was between the two of us only, then quickly he wipes his eyes and nose with his sleeve and heads down the stairs, his feet heavy and clumsy on the old wood. The front door smites as he leaves the house, creating another little void from which emerges the sound of the mantelpiece clock, dripping incessantly into the muted silence.

I can still feel my pulse beating in my neck as I pull the bedroom door closed. A bullfinch trills in the ash tree at the side of the house. I turn towards it, then go to the window. Sunlight pours over me. My hands are shaking. My throat is scorched and the rash on my neck is burning like

48

sand. I trace my finger around one of the frames. The glass is cold to the touch despite the glaring heat beyond, as though the space outside of it and the space within are separated by so much more than glass.

The search party has moved into the wheat field, spread out in a neat line like the marker buoys of a fishing net. I go to my desk and take out a pair of 30 x 50 Porro prism binoculars. One of the police officers is talking to Mr Burton. The officer points towards the copse while Mr Burton, scraggly grey hair and large sideburns, nods his head astutely but solemnly. His eldest son is standing a few feet behind, hands forced awkwardly into the front pockets of a pair of work jeans. My fingers alter the focus as I lift the binoculars towards the ancient clump of trees where the rose was found. Ivy covers their crooked forms. Birds speckle the sky above the copse's dark and bloated shape, endlessly dipping and wheeling, gulls scavenging about the carcass of a dead whale.

The village is full of activity. I watch a woman with shoulder-length hair the colour of the fields beyond holding tightly on to her daughter's hand. A policewoman is asking her questions, watched obediently by half a dozen or so other villagers, the names of whom I do not know, each waiting their turn, as restless as they are concerned. In the far distance kids are sitting on the low stone wall of the war memorial. Police are everywhere, knocking on doors or talking to people on the side of the road. There's almost an air of carnival about the place. A small dog, its lead trailing behind it, leaps across the street by the old post office, darting erratically through the legs of the onlookers and chased by a girl of about ten in a bright red summer dress. She runs through a small group of journalists who are keeping their distance without the risk of missing anything important. Closer to hand a smaller crowd has gathered. They are some of the village bell ringers. None of them are talking. Like the rest of the villagers, they are simply staring at our house, helpless observers. Each of them is wearing a cream linen jacket with an orange crest on the breast pocket.

I refocus the binoculars as Mr Hinton, summer hat cocked at an angle, checks his watch, whispers something to the man beside him, and together they turn beneath the marbled shadows of the Manor House's holm oaks and head back into the village.

Shadows from the cherry and almond trees lean clumsily to the east. Everything is bright and luminous in the hot sun: the glossy white paint on the windows of the houses, the pale green leaves on the trees and hedges. High on the apexes of almost every house in the village is a thatched bird. Mr Hinton's house has a hawk with a twig in its beak. Next to his there is a pheasant, then what looks like a kestrel, although it could easily be a falcon or merlin. Beyond that is a buzzard. Further along, although it's hard to identify them, there is an osprey and a cormorant. Mr Scott has a grouse carrying part of a nest. Mrs Neal has an owl.

There's a knock on my door.

'Simon,' Uncle Pete says, pushing his head into the room, 'how are you feeling?' He sounds mildly out of breath.

I shrug, putting the binoculars back in their leather case, folding the strap and placing them in the bottom drawer of my desk. He squints, wiping his forehead with his bare arm, and moves into a long salient of white light that has stretched itself across the rug. It glimmers on one side of his face as his eyes roam uncertainly around the clean white walls and the painting of the Montagu's harriers.

'Your dad's told me what you said, about Charlotte coming to see you.'

50

'I didn't say that exactly.'

'No? What did you say?' When I don't answer, his voice becomes stilted. 'Anyway, he seems to think that. Mary and Ned and that other kid were with her until just after ten. They'd been to the pub then went behind the bell tower. It's where they go apparently. She was back here around half ten.'

'She came to see me,' I say, 'after she'd been downstairs with Mum and Dad. They were arguing.'

'What did she want?'

'I don't know,' I say. 'I can't really remember. She said she wanted to tell me something but then Dad came in and she went back to her room.'

He shrugs, and I am just about to ask him if he thinks the police will want to speak with me again when we're interrupted by a loud screeching noise coming from directly over the top of the house. We both move quickly to the windows where a huge skein of geese, fifty birds at least, is flying so low over the roof of the house we can see the intricate patterns and shades on their bellies. Their shadows stream across the front lawn as they block out the sun, making it strobe hypnotically, before banking south, their slow grating calls like the sound of some enormous metallic winch on the other side of the sky.

'Egyptian,' Uncle Pete says, making a show of watching them for as long as he can.

'They're the first I've seen here,' I say, 'other than at the Trust.'

'Do you remember when Charlotte cut her face?' he says.

I don't answer this. I look into the sky where the geese have been. It's re-moulded itself, as blue and unaffected as before they arrived.

'We were so worried, Anne and I,' he says. 'We could hear her calling out but we couldn't see you. We couldn't see where you were. She was by the old beach huts. Do you remember?'

'Not really,' I say, although I do remember. I remember clearly, standing on the weathered asphalt just a few feet behind her, long blades of pale green grass growing through it like strands of hair. It scorched my bare feet. I remember, too, the lethargic smell of oil, the salt in the air and the distant fetid scents of the marshes and the sea beyond. Sand covered almost the entire hut, making the roof appear like a ramp, which is why Charlotte had decided to leap off it, a towel draped around her neck like a cape. I think I was supposed to have followed, but I didn't. In the instant she left the ground, the peeling apex of the hut creaking, warning her of something, I found myself on the same dunes but at another point in time. I was looking out to sea, enveloped in a fog of sulphur, an enormous black wave tumbling out of the flat horizon, heading straight towards me.

'She was always falling over,' Uncle Pete says.

As he says this, I find myself leaning forward on one of the plastic chairs lined up in a row along the edge of the long corridor at King's Lynn hospital. Mum is pacing up and down the linoleum floor, her shoes clicking like hail. 'And I still don't know why you didn't call me earlier,' she says, as though she had said something else before it.

I'm sitting between Uncle Pete and Aunty Anne. With outstretched fingers, Aunty Anne is balancing a cardboard cup of coffee in front of her, blowing the steam away. Some coffee has spilt over the back of her thumb. At the end of the corridor I see a man in a faded blue gown shuffling unhurriedly on his own into what I assume is another similar looking corridor with similar looking chairs and doors and windows. He's attached to a drip that glimmers

52

as it catches the strip lights, one of its wheels squeaking every few seconds, even as he steps out of view, as though a sudden rasping intake of breath.

Mum had caught the train from Liverpool Street as soon as she heard the news. She'd been on the phone all the way up, she said, "sorting out some work crisis in Paris". It's only six o'clock but already dusk is falling through the skylights, splashing the polished floor with a salmon pink sheen and making it appear smoother than it really is. Part of me imagines her as a raft spider skating over a pond, ripples drifting quietly away from each of her steps.

'I'm sorry, Beth,' Aunty Anne says, looking up from her coffee.

Mum sucks her lips. 'It's not your fault,' she says, as though it is her fault. 'God! How long are they going to be?'

We don't know the answer to this so we don't say anything. A while later, a nurse and a doctor walk out of a room. They're in the middle of a conversation, something about ordering a new X-ray machine. They don't know anything about Charlotte. 'You'll have to wait until a nurse comes,' they say and they go into another room, continuing their conversation.

'I should never have left them alone,' Uncle Pete says.

'No,' Mum says, looking across at me. 'You shouldn't have.'

'We treated you as our own,' Uncle Pete says at the window. 'You know that, don't you?'

'I know,' I say.

Mournfully he walks back into the room and picks up the photograph of the kingfisher from the bookshelf. 'Still got this then,' he says, trying to lighten his tone. 'You can hardly see what it is.'

'It's a kingfisher.'

53

He even manages a laugh.

'Aunty Anne said I should keep it.'

'Did she now?' he says. 'They found a kingfisher like this in Constable's The Mill Stream. For years it had been hidden, right in the middle of the painting under a layer of grime.' He sniffs, puts the picture back exactly where he found it and straightens the books. 'Listen, I'm going to knock on some doors in the village. See if I can jog any memories. I don't know what's going on here, but if she left the village, someone must have helped her. Someone must have driven her somewhere. She wouldn't have gone out on her own, not in that storm. It doesn't make sense.'

'What about the rose, Uncle Pete?' I say. 'The one they found at the copse.'

'Superstitious nonsense,' he says and he leaves the room.

They kept Charlotte in overnight. Mum stayed with her. She was lucky she didn't lose the sight in her right eye. I remember looking through the back windscreen of the Triumph Spitfire, squashed in the back like an overnight bag, as the town dissolved into black rain. The bright lights of the hospital flared behind us, muffled and tremulous, and in the watery darkness I watched the greens and reds and ambers of the traffic lights on the ring road slide back and forth along the thermal grid of thin orange lines on the glass.

When I turned around Aunty Anne was looking at me in the rear-view mirror. I could see only a section of her face, as though she was peering through a letterbox, expressionless against the dark road, and I couldn't help wonder what she was really thinking.

SEVEN

The smell of a beef casserole threads its way through the house. It makes me feel nauseous. I haven't eaten anything all day, but still I don't feel hungry, or tired, despite the hypnagogic blur of my vision. I just feel sick. Accepting something so habitual as eating feels wrong somehow, an act of betrayal. We should all be suffering, as Charlotte is suffering. My eyes bulging yet unfocused, I tidy my desk, straighten my duvet and pillow and unpack the bag Mum made me for hospital. Next, I straighten the rug, take out a clean pair of pyjamas, place them neatly on the edge of my bed ready for tonight and go downstairs.

We eat in silence, each of us aware of the fading light pressing against the long narrow window over the sink, softening the edges of the roofs beyond, the warped wooden fence, the boughs of the ash tree.

Steam gathers about the light fittings.

Uncle Pete clears his throat as though he's about to say something, but instead he half smiles and takes another mouthful of food, chomping as surreptitiously as he can before carefully placing his cutlery back on the plate.

Mum glances sideways. Her eyes are inflamed and bloodshot. She takes a long sip of water from her glass.

'The college sent your information pack,' she says, motioning towards the corner table where we keep the phone and family diary. 'You should go through it when you're feeling better. There may be stuff for you to sign and return.'

'Am I still going then?'

The edge of the glass glints in one of the spotlights.

'Why wouldn't you be?' she says, lifting her chin.

I let my knife and fork clink on to the plate and peer around the room.

'Try and eat something,' Aunty Anne says.

The glass hovers precariously by the side of Mum's head, the water rocking goadingly back and forth to the rim. Her eyebrows arch as we watch. It's clear she isn't going to back down so I look over my shoulder to where the forms are, catching Dad's eye as I do. Subtly he nods his head, indicating, I think, that I should continue with this forced display of normality.

'I'll look through them later,' I say.

There's a calendar on the wall by the phone with photographs of birds of prey. I guess this is what Mum is really looking at. Charlotte hates that calendar. I imagine Mum does too, but I know why she bought it. June has a photograph of a goshawk. Its wings are flared open, eyes staunch, emerald green and perfectly symmetrical. I imagine Mum studying the field of little white squares beneath it, each with an event scrawled diagonally across in pencil: birthdays, dentist appointments, haircuts, trips away, most of which will never happen. That calendar, I think, if Charlotte doesn't return, will become a metaphorical gravestone. I picture it remaining here forever, long after we have left, like the painting in the living room, faded from the sun, the corners warped and crusty, grey with damp, the goshawk poised indelibly in the emptiness we've left behind.

'You've not said a word since you came back from hospital.'

'Beth,' Dad says through his teeth. 'Not now. Please.'

'No, David,' she says, her voice dropping, and for the tiniest of moments I think I see the corner of her mouth twitch. 'I want to know what Simon thinks. I want to know what's going on in this house.'

'Nothing's going on,' Dad tells her.

'Really?' she says, her pitch lifting. Her neck tilts as she looks inquisitively at the rash on my neck. There's no concern or sympathy in her eyes, only scrutiny. 'Where were you all that time?'

'Beth.'

Aunty Anne lowers her head and starts to cry.

'Three hours,' Mum says, stretching forward over the table.

I swallow. My insides contract and burn, and with my lips moving furtively I go over in my head various disconnected sentences from *Bewick's Swan*. 'Bewick's Swans of both sexes are vocal throughout the year. There is no obvious difference between the two. Downy young have high-pitched squeaking calls when distressed.'

Uncle Pete looks at me and shakes his head.

'Beth, I won't have this,' Dad says.

Something scampers on the path outside the window.

'It'll be a dry night according to the forecast,' says Uncle Pete.

'Shut up, Pete. I know what's going on, OK?' At last she pulls her glare away from the wall, staring instead at the glass, eyes fixed like rods, as though attempting to break it with her thoughts, as though staring at the glass will blur everything that isn't the glass. 'They don't start searching fields unless they know something,' she garbles, holding back tears. 'You don't have to lie to me anymore. None of

57

you do.' She takes a large gulp and places the glass back exactly where it came from. Her fingers tremble. Concentration puckers her brow and I realise she doesn't yet know about the rose. They've been keeping it from her, allowing some wretched strain of hope a stay of a few more hours.

When the water spills onto the back of her hand, she does nothing about it. I'm not even sure she's noticed. She holds on to the glass with an outstretched arm and waits in the teeming silence that follows, waiting, I think, for one of us to say something, but we don't. We don't say anything.

Tentatively, Aunty Anne wipes her eyes then goes to get a cloth.

'Leave it, Anne,' Mum snaps, her stare tight and avid and set back on the glass. 'When are you going to tell me, David? When are you going to tell me what is going on around here?'

Dad doesn't answer. We watch her like this a while longer. Without really thinking about it, I recite more passages from *Bewick's Swan* under my breath. With each word my lip quivers. 'Up to eighty-seven thousand Bewick's Swans winter in China and Japan each year. Most of them nest on Arctic tundras.' As the words appear before me, I picture the swans huddled on the frozen ground, nothing before them but hundreds of miles of flat ice, an aching steel-blue sky, their only concern the protection of their young.

She's gripping the glass so hard now I can see the bones pressing though the skin on her knuckles and I think for a moment she's going to snap it, that the glass will slice through the palm of her hand and blood and water together will seep into the contour-like grains of wood.

'Beth,' Uncle Pete says. 'Please.' There's a mixture of fear and uncertainty in his voice. 'She's a sensible girl.

58

She's seventeen, almost an adult. She'll be OK. You know what she can be like. We don't have any news yet. We don't know anything.'

I look at the table. Behind me the mantelpiece clock raps its thin metal fingernail against the enamel surface of time. I listen to Mum's shallow breaths between each malicious tick. We stay like this for a few more minutes, just listening to the house, as glazed eidetically across my memories, I see the boy standing at the top of the landing. I see him staring out of my bedroom window that first morning, and in the bathroom, and all those times he stands in the corner of my room thinking I don't know he's there. He knows something I don't, as does the house itself.

Sagged by the sink, Aunty Anne has covered her face in her hands.

'Beth,' Uncle Pete tries again, his voice lighter this time. 'I know what you must be thinking but—'

'No, you don't, Pete,' she says sternly. 'How can you?'

This triggers another silence. From the corner of my eye I see Dad glance across at Aunty Anne. She turns and fills the kettle.

'Can I go to my room?' I ask.

Mum looks up. She doesn't look like Mum anymore. Tears are streaming down the side of her face. Everything's changing. An adamantine course has been set. It can never be altered, whether Charlotte is found or not. 'Don't forget those forms,' she says coldly.

I scrape my chair along the flagstones and, brandishing a final glare at the table, scoop up the envelopes from the corner desk, knocking a pen onto the floor. I make my way back up the stairs. I drop the envelopes on the bed and hurriedly, my hands unsteady, take two more Diazepam then stand again at the window, looking out to the copse in the dying light. I breathe in through my nose, out through my nose, just as I have been taught.

Branches from the ash tree scuffle across the roof tiles.

The search party has gone. The vans have left and the fields are once again still, their colourful hues sharp beneath the falling sun. Time has sped away without me knowing and we are no closer to finding her. If anything, I have pushed her further into the darkness. A long thin feather of white cloud hangs over the horizon. Caught in its slender edges are the faintest tones of dusk: pinks and creams and coppery greys that flay like the tentacles of some enormous jellyfish caught beneath the skyline.

The church bell chimes nine o'clock, sending hundreds of crows and rooks up into the sky, cawing loudly before settling in the sweet chestnut trees. Standing in the middle of the road outside the Red Rose pub is a group of maybe a dozen people. Tucked tenderly under some of their armpits are tankards or glasses that occasionally glint in flashes of dull orange light. They are, as far as I can see, silent, each staring down the empty street towards our house, unified in thought, beguiled by the stillness, as though observing the strange tranquillity of an eclipse. Long evening shadows stretch behind them. As the last chime echoes around the inside of my head, I think I remember hearing the church bell that night in the storm, a single pulse echoing through the village, although I can't be certain.

'Simon?' Dad says at the door.

I turn and nod.

'She didn't mean any of that. We're all trying to deal with this in our own way.' He looks to the envelopes on the bed and pinches the corner of his mouth, feigning something normal, something prosaic. 'You should fill in those forms sometime. Pete and I are going to drive around a bit, maybe go into Spalding and Peterborough. You never know.'

'She would never have gone out in that storm,' I say.

'I know,' he says, 'but she went out somewhere, didn't she?'

'I think I may have heard the church bell, at one o'clock,' I tell him humbly, pleased with myself for at last being able to contribute. 'That narrows it down a bit, doesn't it, if you found me at two?'

He thinks about this a moment, drowsily looking around the room, then down to the centre of the white rug where they found me that night. 'I'll tell Inspector Sly,' he says. 'Thank you.'

'Dad,' I say as he's turning away. 'Why didn't you tell Mum about the rose?'

'We just thought it best. It's probably nothing anyway. Kids mucking about most likely.' He looks at me a moment, his face partly hidden by the dimness of evening, as a silence far bigger than the both of us descends into the room from somewhere outside. The air chills. Birds scamper on the roof tiles.

'You think she's dead, don't you?' I say.

'Of course I don't.'

'But she didn't even take her mobile phone.'

He swallows and nods. The birds fly away in a sudden rustling of wings. 'I know,' he says and he looks to the window and the copse in the wheat field in the fading distance.

'What about Tom? Have the police spoken to him?'

'He's not heard from her,' Dad says, his eyes tired and undetermined. 'Now get some sleep.' His mouth twitches a little. 'And fill in those forms, hey?'

I wait for the door to close and for him to go downstairs before heading to the bathroom, filling my glass with water, putting on my pyjamas and getting into bed. I place the two envelopes on my lap in the lemony glow of my bedside table lamp and take a biro from the drawer. One of the envelopes is white, Simon Davis and our address printed on a label and stuck slightly off-centre on the shiny paper. The other is brown, the writing frail and uneven, the ink blue. It is much heavier than the white one, the contents inside seemingly too small for the size of the envelope. I weigh it in the palm of my hand and look to the door, a childish sort of thrill dilating inside me from somewhere long forgotten, an abandoned desire to not be caught.

Dad's car starts up outside on the road, the light skewing across the curtains before it's driven out of the village. An owl hoots somewhere out over the fields, most likely one of the tawnies that nest at the back of Mrs Neal's garden. Nervous now for some reason and finding myself looking up to the door and the Montagu's harriers and that dark empty space in the corner of the room where I sometimes see the boy, I carefully open the envelope, releasing into the air a sudden and distinct smell of age and mould. Even before I take anything out, I know my world is about to change.

I pause and breathe, in and out of my nose, then, bracing myself, pull free a thin crinkled book which looks as though it's recently been dried out over a radiator. A folded letter has been paper-clipped to its once white cover. Carefully, my eyes drawing constantly now to the door and the far corner of the room, I place it neatly on top of the white envelope at my side and hold the book up into the light of my table lamp. The pages, no more than a hundred of them I guess, are thin and yellowed with age. Typed in small letters in the centre of the cover are the words *The Naseby Horses by Nathaniel Woods*.

For a few minutes I just sit here, staring at the book, the world spinning blindly beneath me, my time and the time in the rest of the house inconsistent and misaligned. The gritted fabric of the darkness, half lit by the glow of the bedside lamp, edges towards me, welding everything together as one monocoque form: my desk, the chest of drawers, the edges of the painting of the Montagu's harriers, the corners of the room. Everything is black and insoluble, a switched off television set where Charlotte is lost among its sleeping parts. Extracted from its silent breath is the same damp musty odour I smelt that night. I put down the book, my thoughts whirling back without consent to Nial from my support group in London and talk of Ötzi the Iceman.

I pick up the letter instead. I unfold it. Inside is a feather. I study it in the light. It's old and seems to have been meticulously sliced in half. It's a goose feather, or part of one at least. That's clear enough, but it's not like one I have seen before. The shaft is almost transparent, the barb grey and brittle. I run my finger over its edge, trying to remember what it means.

Floorboards groan outside my door. I look up, the feather poised in my fingers, and take a few breaths, as though to regulate the flow of time, to separate my time from the time on the other side of the door. The footsteps disperse, one set going to Mum and Dad's room, the other back down the stairs. The feather is an ancient Fenland symbol, a sign of loyalty. It was used in the civil war. I remember, now, reading about the split goose feather for my GCSEs back in London. Any Fenlander carrying one was entitled to protection from other Fenlanders. It was a loyalty which ran far deeper than even that to country. It was how at the end of the war Charles I managed to escape across the Fens from Norfolk to Huntingdon.

Carefully I place it down on top of the book, nerves threshing beneath my skin. I study the strange items before me then pick up the letter once again. The paper is thick and clean, still with the crisp floral scent of newness. The address on the letterhead, printed beneath a coloured sketch, the object of which I recognise immediately, is of the Old Hermitage Retirement Home.

Dear Simon

I lived once in the house you now live in. Part of me lives there still. My intention is not to frighten you, but frighten you I must. The knowledge I possess I cannot let die with me for I fear I am all that is left.

Yesterday I was informed that your sister, Charlotte, was reported missing on the 13th of June, the same date my own son, Henry, was taken from me, a date which, are you to believe the content inscribed in the book I have bestowed you, has seen many such tragedies. Tragedies, it pains me to inform you, I don't believe will ever be resolved.

Trust no one, Simon. Trust only yourself.
With all my blessings and all my faith,
Ethel Roberts

EIGHT

The Old Hermitage Retirement Home. I'll go there tomorrow, I think, the blood in my body cooler than I have known it before, obstructed and immobile, awaiting instruction. I'll go there and find out what all this is about, if, indeed, it's about anything, and not some vile prank. Or maybe I should just tell Dad or Uncle Pete or the police. I could ask Emma Proctor, I suppose, but I don't really want to do that.

The Home is situated at the end of a long shadowy drive that leads off a slight curve in the road at the far end of the village. I have to walk past it on my way to the Wildfowl Trust. Ancient oaks, birch and yew trees tower over a high brick wall, warped and swollen from having held back a thick sea of ivy for however many years, its waxy dark green crest folding over the top like a wave. In the Second World War it was used as a prison. The residents pay now. Emma works there. Sometimes, at the weekends, I walk with her through the village. There's a chapel on the right-hand side of the drive which used to be a hermitage, from where the Home took its name. Its turreted white stone roof pokes through the tops of the trees.

I get out of bed. I turn on my desk lamp, carefully place the letter and the feather beside my laptop, then go to the window, the book clutched like a prayer book in my hands. The pages are dirty and stained, the corners frayed and velvety from being handled so much. There's a mark on the front cover which looks as though it could have been made with blood. I lift it to my nose. It smells damp and musky, and yet beneath this I can detect the odour of ink, the vanillary scent of the paper itself. Instantly they transport me back to my grandfather's living room in Cambridge.

Books line every wall. Clinging to the curtains and the dark floral wallpaper, two leather armchairs facing each other in the stuffy auburn light, is the woody scent of pipe-smoke. I am sitting in one of the chairs, staring at Grandpa. His eyes are tired and foggy. Behind him, a tall frilly lamp projects a single cone of light onto the ceiling. There's a moth trapped inside it, flickering violently against the thin fabric and releasing little percussive spits every time it hits the bulb. Its magnified shadow looms over us. It frightens me even though I know it's only a moth. Maybe, I think, the leather crinkling beneath me and sticking to my bare legs, that's really all my demons are: the dilated shadows of moths.

Grandpa leans forward in his chair. His face is puckered and clownish, and I feel a little foolish, sitting here like this, my feet swinging like a pendulum over the dirty red carpet, at having asked him such a question. He, too, looks at the moth. His eyes squint and he tells me keenly, that voice of his so soft and burnished it's as though it had long ago been lined with silk, that, yes, it's the shadow we need to be afraid of, not the beast itself.

His face quivers and fades into my own reflection in the glass of the window in my new bedroom in Glennfield. Then he's gone.

Still mindful of every move I am making, every touch, as though I am being observed from the corner of the room, I put the letter and the feather in the bottom drawer of my desk beside my binoculars, close it and go back to bed with the book, opening the inside cover and releasing again that hefty scent of rot and damp. Written by an elegant hand in green ink, the ink now blanched and yellowed beneath a makeshift copyright symbol and the year 1969, are the words *Dear Ethel, Forgive me.*

In the middle of the book, crudely photocopied, the edges of the original pictures visible as long dark margins, there are photographs of portraits of Edward Montagu, Oliver and Richard Cromwell, Charles I, Sir Thomas Fairfax and Colonel Pickering. I recognise the names, some of the portraits even, from my GCSEs. There are more I don't know, the reproductions black and smudged, a print of the village crest, three sheaves of wheat pinched with twine, beside some gothic-looking symbol with what is unmistakably a pentagram in its centre. Taking up two pages is a photograph of the painting in our living room. The wall behind it, as far as I can see, is papered with what looks like a flock of crows. On the next page is a sketch of someone called Albert Fox. He poses flamboyantly in a wide-brimmed hat, and there follows a number of images of paintings of a mother and daughter, Frances and Elizabeth Johnson. Long flowing hair frames Elizabeth's narrow face. Her stance is rigid; deep circular eyes looking restricted, as though she is intending to look miserable. Looking dapper and saintly is Lord Gibbins, 2nd Viscount of Boston. The family still owns the Manor House in the village. Rupert Gibbins brought a case of wine round a few days after we arrived here.

At the back is a collection of deeds and pamphlets, each with almost indecipherable lettering, a number of scans of photographs of children and a printed list of about fifty names. Each has a date hanging at the end of a faded line of dots. They span from 1646 to 1967. My chest tightens as I skim through them, memorising as well as I can the pattern of the letters. The date for each entry is 13th June. The first simply says Morton, the last Mark Richardson. Beside some of the names are various handwritten scrawls.

I trace my finger over them as I try to think. Beneath the last name, written in green ink by an elegant hand – the same hand that had written *Dear Ethel, Forgive me* – are the words *Charlie Montagu, Coppingford Manor, 1973*. That is the last entry.

When I turn the page, however, there are another four names written in blue ink in Ethel's quivery hand, each with the same date, 13th June, inscribed beside it. The last name is *Holly Thompson*, beside which she has written the word *Chaplin*. I remember seeing Holly's face on the news a few years ago, as we stood in a long fall of summer light in our kitchen in London: me, Dad, Charlotte and Kika, our nanny. 'It'll be someone she knows,' Dad had said profoundly, not taking his eyes off the screen. None of us responded. I think because, maybe, we each agreed with him.

Hesitating, a taut pull of apprehension reeling through my body, I rest the back of my head against the headboard, and in the edgeless sphere of dull amber light seeping from the lamp beside me, carefully let my finger draw over each letter on the front cover. The page is chalky. I glance towards the window, exhale a long composing breath and begin to read.

THE NASEBY HORSES
by Nathaniel Woods

Foreword

The story I am about to tell is taken from words handed down by the worthy, hard working men and women of the Fens. Words are all they are. Understand this before proceeding. Words in themselves do not warrant the truth. They are mere tools employed with equal proficiency by both philosopher and raconteur; used with comparable rights. It is how one chooses to interpret them that matters. These are not my words. They are words that have, over centuries, been whispered around campfires, by fathers and mothers, brothers and sisters, sometimes, I imagine, with a certain theatrical verve, sometimes, as darkness would have settled over the flatlands of East Anglia, the sounds of the unknown world creaking mysteriously above the heads of their children, with great urgency and caution. They are, sadly, words that have since been coated with incredulity and suspicion, mockery even. As an historian I have to accept that. There is no evidence the tragedy you are to hear of ever occurred, and yet circumstance leaves me no option but to believe it did; that on the night of the 13th June 1645 in a wood behind the small village of Glenn Gate, Cambridgeshire, now the picturesque English village of Glennfield, the following event did, indeed, occur. The words have not changed. It is only by stepping away from them and looking beyond the specific drama they narrate that a true story reveals itself.

If it is facts that are required, as, paradoxically, are so often demanded when dealing with matters beyond the realms of the common acceptance of the boundaries of our existence, then all I offer are these proposals, garnished, perhaps, with the sagacious words of the great Sir Arthur Conan Doyle. "When you have eliminated the impossible, whatever remains, however improbable, must be the truth."

These stories are without protestation: the unknown whereabouts of the Naseby Gold and the unexplained disappearances of a large number of children around the world occurring on the 13th June; an enduring atrocity that I believe has been hidden beneath a cloak of secrecy for over three hundred years. Chapter Nine looks into the unofficial words and beliefs of certain personnel of the Cambridgeshire Police Force whom I have interviewed off record. They have insisted on remaining anonymous, thus, I accept, rendering their suspicions and thoughts obsolete beyond my word. They each concurred with me, however, that Scotland Yard has had a file on the disappearances since its inception in 1829.

These two mysteries are bridged via a young Englishwoman, Frances Johnson, and her daughter, Elizabeth, who disappeared on the night of the 13th June 1645, the night before the Battle of Naseby commenced on the sloping fields outside Market Harborough. Frances Johnson was maid-in-waiting to Marie, wife of Charles I, daughter of King Henri of France. She was last known to be residing at Sandringham stables, a renowned hideaway for royals and their acquaintances predating the Prince of Wales's (later Edward VII's) stately home. It is well documented that Frances and her daughter left England for France with Marie under the guide of French agents, on the direct orders of King Henri himself, for fear of reprisals from Parliamentarian advocates; yet no physical trace or sighting of them was recorded.

Let me deal with more facts. According to accurate accounts (Pic. 9) from the treasurer of the stable, the King's stable manager, Albert Fox, personally prepared a chest of gold for carriage on the night of the 13th June. Its destination was unknown. Albert Fox, according to the roll call of the dead

(Pic.10), died on the battlefield on the 14th June 1645. He was mentioned in dispatches for saving the King's life, and consequently awarded a celebratory and long-standing reputation at the museum at Sandringham. I firmly believe this to be a fabrication, that he died the night before, on the 13th June, as the story that follows suggests, and that his name was added to the list of the dead by conspirators attempting to hide the truth behind this deleterious tale. Albert Fox is not listed as a soldier or carrier or service officer in any of the King's regiments, yet he was named as a fallen soldier. How, we should ask ourselves, did this man appear to be in two places at the same time? At the Sandringham stables preparing the gold and, concurrently, with the rest of the Royalist forces camped at Naseby.

It is worth noting (as indicated in Drawing 8) that a track, known as the Bukehorn, albeit a route not known to have been used since the 1620s due to the instability of the land, was in place at the time. It ran from Sandringham to Naseby via the village of Glenn Gate, making it geographically viable that the route taken by Albert Fox was, indeed, the route depicted in the story. Farmland has since replaced woodland. Nothing else has changed.

There is the behaviour of a young nobleman and loyal friend of the King's, Edward Montagu, to be considered before our story begins. He was well acquainted with Frances Johnson through his regular visits to the King's homes and his wife Jemima's friendship with Marie. What part Edward Montagu played in this tale of deceit and murder was historically unknown until now, although it has been widely accepted that he was a spy for Charles I. Lord Montagu was a fine young officer with an excellent new infantry regiment tied with Colonel Pickering and Hammond of the New Model Army. He was set up on the west flank on the morning of the battle. Although his line broke when the Royalist infantry advanced, he later proved himself in combat with great distinction. In

1652, as a reward for unbridled loyalty to his country, he was conveyed Coppingford Manor in Huntingdon by Samuel Johnson, returning the estate to its rightful heir.

The bathroom door opens and closes. Quickly I close the book and slip it under my pillow. I get out of bed and go to the window nearest my desk.

What I have just read is clearly fantastic, conceived, surely, by the innovative murmurings of some wannabe author or charlatan feeding off the grief of parents, although to what possible end I can't imagine; or the writer was genuinely insane, assuming, as I am, he is now dead. Yet all the while, lacquered across the fringes of my thoughts as a shadow, is the image I saw that night, the horse's head forming as a real entity out of that wild violent sky, felt not only by me but whoever painted the picture that hangs now, as it did for Ethel Roberts, in our living room downstairs.

Aunty Anne knocks on the door. She pops her head into the room. 'You're still up?' she says.

'Just looking,' I tell her.

She smiles. 'Get some sleep.'

'Aunty Anne,' I say, turning my head. 'When you were younger did you ever hear the story of the Naseby Horses?'

She arches her brows and releases a sardonic little snort from her nose. 'Blimey,' she says. 'I haven't heard of them for a while. Why?'

'It's nothing,' I say, 'not really. I just wondered. That's all.'

'A silly story,' she says fondly and she smiles again. 'Now, come on. Try and get some sleep.'

I go back to bed and with panic and fear and all those things I usually accept with silent grace crashing down in the room beside me like the wings of some giant maligned bird, I continue to read *The Naseby Horses*.

This book suggests the gold was indeed aimed for Naseby to be used as bribes for the captains of Cromwell's forces, and that Edward Montagu was the man charged with their distribution. As a close comrade of Sir Thomas Fairfax, he had ample opportunity to coerce the uncertain captains out of fighting for generous monetary award. He was a fickle statesman at the best of times, as examined in the journals of Richard Cromwell: "He was the perfect spy; eminent and untouchable."

What is indisputable is the following. A wooden chest, packed with gold and jewels, a remnant hoarding from the War of the Roses encrusted with the Apothecary's Rose of the Lancastrian forces, as well as Frances Johnson with her daughter, Elizabeth, was never seen again after this dreadful night. As history clearly reveals from the outcome of the battle itself and its political repercussions, the bribes were never issued.

There are no written accounts of this sacrosanct mystery: a point in itself of great importance and where I, too, fall into its pages. The story of the Naseby Horses is one wrapped so tightly in secrecy it doesn't seem, at times, to have the opportunity to exist beyond the gently blowing whispers of the Fens. It is as though for centuries a conspirator's eraser has followed its evil path. There is but one written reference of any repute, a passage by the disgraced cleric Balfour from his renowned 1691 St Margaret's pamphlet.

Balfour was a forthright and ethical churchman residing at St Margaret's church, Kings Lynn, during a spate of child disappearances across the East of England. Following a whirl-wind of rumours, panic and fevered claims of actual sightings of horses flying through the skies, stirring iniquitous talk of devil worship, the Horses of the Apocalypse, the Breaking of the Seven Seals and the Seventh Trumpet, the area from Norwich to Peterborough and up to Lincoln was declared a "haven of evil" by the church. Balfour declared this omen to be

73

nothing shorter than "the Devil himself riding the beasts of hell to collect the children of the damned freely at his disposal." (Pic. 19)

This was a belligerent period in England, a time obsessed with the power of the Devil and the existence of witches, many of whom were unjustly burned or hanged following unfair feudal trials of ordeal. Balfour, himself, was found hanging from his bell tower days after the publication. He was not only deemed a heretic, but posthumously convicted by the church of murdering some of the children himself as part of a cult of East Anglian Devil worshippers known as the Hecate. He, the church wrote, in his last moments and with God's pre-eminent strength, had conquered the spirit inside him in order to allow him to resort to a guilt-ridden suicide. The parchment still belongs to the Kings Lynn library, although it has not been on display for decades, it being the last written word on this subject for over three hundred years.

In 1965, I wrote a paper as part of a doctorate whilst at Cambridge University. Despite my previous works on the paranormal all making it to print, to somewhat commendable acclaim, this article was denied publication, denied acceptance from the university, denied acknowledgment, even by some of my closest friends at the time. I was, days later, sent down. Two years after, on the same day I presented my story to a leading national newspaper, my house was broken into and my research stolen, confirming indubitably to my conscience that my beliefs on the clandestine cloak which covers this eerie tale were indeed veritable. I suspect it will also seal the fate of this book.

DAY FOUR

NINE

Yawning, I watch the last of the night's stars return to space. I'm not sure how long I slept in the end, if, indeed, I slept at all, and I find myself feeling a little foolish standing here, barefoot in my pyjamas, in the grainy half-light of dawn. My mouth tastes stale and is sticky from sleep. My eyes are resinous. My reflection glares back at me. It tells me I'm seventeen years old and that part of me has seriously been considering the possibility that this curse could be real. However ridiculous, at first, it sounded, however fatuous, overnight Nathaniel Woods's story had managed to ingrain itself into my thoughts. And it is only now, in the brutish honesty of morning, watching the fields and the low hedges and the copse in the distance gradually extracting themselves from the night, that I realise how naive I have been to allow its unrestrained narrative to convince me so unquestionably.

Disturbed only by the occasional hooting of Mrs Neal's tawnies, I spent most of the night reading the book and researching at my desk in the harsh blue glow of the computer screen. Wind keened in the boarded-up fire-place, occasionally dragging the branches of the ash tree across the roof tiles, but mainly I sat in uninterrupted silence, accompanied only by the still breath of the house, its thin aluminium heartbeat which, at times, I even contemplated as my own.

There was, it turned out, very little information about the Hecate online. As with many cults of its age, it had died out towards the end of the seventeenth century. Its symbol was of Greek origin, a pentagram encircled in a wheel. Woods, however, had clearly uncovered a great deal more information, I guess by searching endlessly through stacks of history books, as I remember Grandpa used to do. The cult's origins, he claimed, were spawned not simply from a constitutional belief in the dark arts, but as a deliberate recrimination to the marauding of the livelihoods of local men and women: the trials and tortures that at the time were draining not only the land, but the ancient ways and customs of the Fens themselves. Its inception was, he writes, both politically and religiously motivated, far from being an organisation evolved crudely out of the fears of those suffering in East Anglia, but the cognitive designs of educated men of power, linked directly to the Crown itself, or what was left of it at the time; to Richard Cromwell and Charles II. Lord James Gibbins from the Manor House, he claimed, also played a part in its initiation, following the brutal death of his father on the fields of Naseby. Its name, Hecate, was taken from Shakespeare's *Macbeth*, Shakespeare himself, according to Woods, having been historically suspected of harbouring a keen interest in the occult.

He concludes the book stating that what has been proposed, both by himself and past archivists, is merely what at the time of writing are deemed to be facts: names and dates and events. Not all historical expositions are to be trusted, he insists. Without evidence proving otherwise, he admits he cannot dismiss the notion that the Hecate are still in existence and are in some way responsible for the disappearances, as certain personnel of Scotland Yard have informally proposed to him. But he cannot accept it either. His investigation into such a claim has been thorough and persistent, he states, yet has unearthed no reasonable evidence supporting it.

The proposition is not if, but why such an elite and eminently clandestine body such as this Hecate would desire, still, three hundred years beyond its inception, at great personal risk and endeavour, to follow with such considered precision the exact narrative of the story of *The Naseby Horses*, if, indeed, its existence had not perished in the latter years of the seventeenth century as with other agencies of similar repute. As Chapter Twelve has ascertained indisputably through in-depth research of meteorological records obtained from the National Meteorological Library and Archive, of the forty-six suspected disappearances (Appendix 1), thirty-eight of these have occurred, worldwide, on nights where electrical summer storms have ravished the vast, unguarded skies of East Anglia. Is this, we must ask ourselves, the corollary of desires and rituals performed by men and women here on earth, or the enterprise of elements far beyond our understanding of earth, of life itself, of nature and the universe? Until that is decided, I fear there can be no resolution to this cruelly neglected mystery.

The browser of my laptop opens automatically to my Wildlife Explorers forum, informing me of two new messages: a sighting from Gull Girl and someone calling themselves The Swan Lands. I close it without reading them, open Google and type *Coppingford* into the search engine, but I'm met with nothing more than threads for the village: local garages, houses for sale, church meetings and a company manufacturing doors.

Frustrated, I drop my pencil on the desk. It lands with a thin crack. I don't believe in curses, I remind myself, so what am I doing here? I don't even believe in God. Nor does Charlotte. I should just tell Dad about the letter and be done with it. Like he said, she's probably in London, and as I think this, I picture her slumped on some fawn-coloured sofa, maybe in Tom's friend's flat in Balham, crinkled shirt, bare legs, a joint in her fingers, watching the soft white smoke curling seductively about her. They may even be laughing at me right now.

I type *Naseby Horses* into the search engine. Maybe this is all I need to do to expunge any possible chance that my brain may even for a moment be offering this any lucidity. Maybe the answers are spelt out on some poorly designed curse website alongside Tutankhamen and Ötzi. Maybe its inclusion among such conspiratorial nonsense is all I need. As I think this, however, part of me shudders, not because I'm frightened of curses all of a sudden, but for a moment I am sitting on a bench in the snow with Nial from my support group, and I am remembering what it was he said to me the last time I saw him.

The page offers nothing but links to the battle and the civil war, some properties, a farm, numerous riding schools and a gym. There are no references to the curse, and when I type *The Curse of The Naseby Horses* I get not a single thread. It's as though the internet has simply not yet been informed of such a story, that these words, *The Naseby Horses*, have never been written on a website before. I guess if the book was never published, which clearly it wasn't, it could easily have escaped the internet, but even so, someone must have written about it in the last twenty odd years; unless it really is as vacuous an idea as all other curse stories, its narrative limited only to the fanciful whims of this Nathaniel Woods, and poor Ethel Roberts, of course, indoctrinated by his words, believing, even, her son lies not dead in a field somewhere, but lost, wondering the transcendental planes between life and death.

Without realising it, I have adopted a praying stance. My hands and fingers are pressed together as a steeple, the top corner of which I appear to be kissing as I go over these points in my head. I quickly remove them, take out a sugar-free cola cube from the top drawer of the desk, place it in my mouth and try searching Nathaniel Woods. But after another hour of going through however many links, I soon realise the Nathaniel Woods who wrote this book is also strangely absent from the internet. I feel cold, even though the sun is starting to leak through my windows. I go to my chest of drawers, take out a green Wildlife Explorers hooded top, put it on, sit back at the desk and run my finger over the coarse spine of the book. It's grainy and tangible, and yet part of me still feels as though I'm in a dream, although I'm not in a dream, or in the aura, despite the oily surreal texture of the light. I would know. There are signs. I'm awake. I'm conscious. I'm here in my bedroom, in this ancient insipid house, in the middle of nowhere, with not a single sighting or message from Charlotte for three days.

The floorboards creak outside my room, the muted light beneath the door rippling as though caught in the wake of a passing ship. There are whispers and muffled sobs. A door closes, softly. Footsteps go down the stairs to the steady lament of the mantelpiece clock. I wait until they have disappeared before turning back around on the stool and, a little reluctantly, type into the laptop *Charlie Montagu 1973 Coppingford Manor*. This time the page fills with options. I glance over to my closed door, my eyes drawn to the Montagu's harriers and the far corner of the room, then click on the first link.

I feel both intrusive and impelled as a grainy black and white scan of the front page of a newspaper appears on the screen. It carries a photograph of a boy. He has a wide smile that digs into the far corners of his cheeks as though his face is not yet big enough to contain it. He would be the same age as Dad now, I think, folding my arms around the back of my neck and calculating it in my head. All those years of growing up and college and jobs, starting a family, simply never happened for him. Time just stopped, when for everyone else it continued.

I roll what's left of the cola cube around the back of my teeth and read that Charlie was the first son of William Montagu, a farmer in Huntingdon who still owns Coppingford Manor. It was on the morning of 14 June 1973, during a year-long archaeological dig at the estate, that he was discovered to be missing. He was thirteen years old. The police found no evidence of an intruder and it was initially suspected he had tragically wandered off, possibly, even, in his sleep. He was apparently prone to sleep-walking. They searched the grounds, the lake, neighbouring farms and the village, later extending their efforts across the entire county, but no sighting of him emerged. There were a dozen archaeologists on the grounds at the time, all of whom were interviewed. Nothing suspicious ever rose its head.

I read a number of reports saying the same thing until finding an article in a Sunday newspaper from 1993. It covers the twentieth anniversary of Charlie Montagu's disappearance. His mother had since left her husband. She speaks of the pain that shadows her every move. She goes on to explain that sometimes she is not even sure any of it really happened, that she can't be certain of what is real and what is not real anymore, that her life since that day is shared equally between reality and a make-believe

82

parallel existence where Charlie is still with her. The more she thinks about it, the more tangible that world becomes, the less believable the material world seems. Really, she explains, she cannot distinguish between the two. They're as palpable as each other, both beginning and ending in sleep. She now rests, she claims, as often as she can, sometimes wasting entire weeks at a time in the hope that one day she may wake to discover the last twenty years belonged only to some merciless nightmare and Charlie is asleep still upstairs in his bed.

When asked about the rumour that silhouettes the speculations behind her son's disappearance, of the warning heeded by one of the archaeologists that night, she replies simply that she can't recall such an event, it is mere fantasy. She later goes on in the article to describe the unfounded yet impermeable mistrust that developed between her and her husband, eventually leading to their separation. Bill, she explains, has never left Coppingford Manor, not for one day. He has taken up every floorboard, knocked down walls, been through the ancient drainage system and excavated half the grounds searching for his son.

Above the suppressed sounds of the slowly waking house, I spend the next hour or so looking for any clues as to what these speculations may be. However, I find no mention of anything mysterious in any of the newspaper stories, just that Charlie was found to be missing on the morning of 14 June 1973 and no word of him has since been heard. Nor do I find any other such mysteries, and I am beginning to suspect this tragedy has been no more than rather callously tethered to the Naseby Horses by Woods solely on the basis that Charlie was descended from Lord Montagu, 1st Earl of Sandwich, who happened to be fighting at the battle that day.

I think of Mum and Dad downstairs and consider what could be the worse outcome of Charlotte's disappearance: knowing their daughter is dead, or sustaining the rest of their lives coaxed by the inexorable hope that she isn't, that she may just walk through the door at any time. I suspect they will also eventually leave each other and this house, and I will be at university in Cambridge, or wherever I end up. On the rare occasions we will get together – Charlotte's birthday or the commemoration of the day she disappeared, a dispirited Christmas with few decorations – we will each be too afraid to talk about her. We may even blame her for whatever paths our lives subsequently take.

I stare blankly at the screen, my reflection staring back at me through the image of Charlie Montagu as though it wants to tell me something, as though, in a way, we are the same person. But it doesn't tell me anything. It just stares back at me, saying nothing.

TEN

My support group was held in the basement room of a hospital in South London. Old pieces of equipment were stacked up at one end like a poorly assembled climbing frame. Once a month, Dr Chatterton, who preferred to be called Tim, set out a dozen plastic chairs in a wide circle. There were always a dozen chairs even though there were only seven or eight of us who ever turned up, and in that windowless room beneath people dying and being born, we discussed how we were coping with our varying degrees of epilepsy.

Synthetic light glared through little squares in the ceiling. I would position myself so I could see the door. Two thin rectangles of meshed glass flashed white, green and blue as people hurried past. Behind me the heater murmured, jetting out hot counterfeit air. We often talked about the aura at the meetings although I never mentioned what I sometimes saw inside it. No one did.

One afternoon, Dr Chatterton introduced a boy called Nial. He was tall with a thin face and huge brown eyes that looked as though they were about to fall out of his head. He was from Croydon, he explained in a low voice that seemed far too entrenched and morose for his age, and he didn't really want to be here. He didn't say another word until six months later, one sharp November afternoon, a few days before my fourteenth birthday.

'Déjà vu?' he said behind me as I stepped through the revolving doors.

I squinted, pulling the flimsy hood of my anorak over my head against the cold, and when I breathed in, I noticed, floating above the fossilised scents of London, the distinct smell of lavender.

Nial studied me with those large bulbous eyes. 'You don't say much, do you?'

'Nor do you.'

He laughed a serious sort of laugh like he knew something I didn't. 'I don't have to,' he said and he walked on, arching his neck towards the sky as a plane appeared out of the swollen grey clouds. 'It's going to snow.'

'How do you know?'

'It was on the news,' he said, and he laughed again.

When the plane disappeared, Nial kept looking up. 'What do you see in the aura, Simon? You never talk about it. People who don't talk about things, know things.'

I shrugged.

He smiled as the plane reappeared. 'They used to call it the falling sickness. Did you know that?'

I did know this, but I felt the conversation would progress further if he thought I didn't. The red plastic bench in the bus stop was cratered with cigarette burns.

Somewhere behind the hospital a siren wailed.

'They used to think we were possessed by demons, that we were cursed. Do you sometimes think that?'

'You sound like Tim.'

Nial stuck his hand out for what seemed like a long time. 'See. I told you,' he said, grinning.

When I looked up, thick feathery snowflakes were

spiralling out of the sky, lingering uncertainly in the cold air before melting on the tarmac by my feet.

'See this,' Nial said, showing me an iron ring on his middle finger. 'My gran gave me this. It's supposed to help ward them off. Can you believe that? My own gran thinks I'm possessed by demons. What chance does that give me?'

'I bet she doesn't,' I said.

'You don't know my gran.' Nial leant forward to see if any buses were coming. He seemed anxious, I thought, although whether this was because he wanted my bus to come or not to come, I couldn't tell. 'You're not cursed, Simon. Whatever you think you see in there, or hear in here,' he pointed at his own head, 'you're not cursed. It's just your miswired brain. It's too big, you see. In evolutionary terms our brains are still in the Jurassic period. They've only just reached land. What really goes on in there we'll never know, not for thousands of years. Have you heard of Ötzi the Iceman?'

'No,' I told him, pulling my hands out of the cold and pushing them inside my anorak pockets.

'He was a five-thousand-year-old skeleton found somewhere in the Alps. Everyone who was involved with uncovering him died that same year, all through mysterious circumstances.'

'I don't believe in that stuff.'

'It was 1992,' he said. 'This wasn't like Tutankhamen. It really happened. Ötzi had been shot with an arrow before having his head smashed in, and was left to die in an unmarked grave. He wasn't meant to die, you see. If people die before they're meant to die, they don't die completely. Something stays behind.'

I stamped my feet on the ground to warm them up.

'The body hasn't quite absorbed the spirit, see? That's what life is, Simon. You're born, then gradually your body soaks up your spirit. That's all your body is, really, a sponge. It's inanimate. When it's full, you die. Simple, but if you die before that happens, a little bit is left behind. It makes perfect sense. Only the dead disappear. My gran told me that. Anyway,' he continued, 'what if, before he died, and knowing he was going to be brutally murdered and unfairly robbed of life, Ötzi cursed those who were about to kill him? What if he believed it so much, all his hatred and frustration somehow turned into a real thing that stayed inside his body after he died? Or maybe it leaked into the ground, like a virus made from the vengeful thoughts of this one man. It would have needed somewhere to go, you see, to hibernate. It needed a sponge. When the archaeologists dug him up all those thousands of years later, it was released and fed on the nearest living organisms it could find. Them.'

'It's impossible.'

'Why?' he said. 'It would be like a disease. That's all.' He looked over his shoulder towards the hospital. 'We know all about diseases, don't we? Their sole purpose is to cause harm. They're not malicious. It's just what they are. They don't know any different. It's completely possible. Have you ever wished anyone dead?'

I blinked, my gaze drawn to a pigeon swiping across the sky. It landed on the corner of a tall brick building and shuddered, as did I. The snow was settling now in odd shaped patches, on the edges of buildings and the roofs of cars. It had turned everything and everyone quiet.

'When you do, your blood boils, doesn't it? It's infected with your thoughts, see. That's how it gets out. It starts in your head and ends up in your blood.' He peered down the road. 'Your bus is here.'

The bus hissed to a stop. The roof was already white and swollen, as though packaged in polystyrene. A man got off, on two crutches, looking up into the grey sky before hobbling his way towards the hospital.

Nial tapped his ring. 'Possessed by demons,' he said, grinning. 'I'll see you next month, hey?'

But I didn't see Nial next month. He had a clonic seizure the following morning at his grandmother's house, and died before his body had a chance to drink his spirit completely.

After Nial died, I did think it was possible to be possessed by the Devil, and to my detriment I started to read a good deal about it. I even read parts of The Bible, The Book of Revelation mainly, good old-fashioned adolescent stuff: *and when the Lamb had opened the seventh seal, there was silence in Heaven about the space of half an hour.* That sort of thing.

It transpired that, historically, epilepsy was cured not with medicine, but divine intervention, its inducement being not of the body, but of the soul. Of course, deep down, I knew this was not true, but that didn't stop it becoming an obsession, and for years each night, in the small sweet-smelling room with the animal wallpaper and the alphabet poster I shared with Charlotte, I would clench my palms together and secretly pray I would not be taken by evil spirits; I would not be made to do things I didn't want to do.

The clattering sounds of South London would pass by the open window. Cans would be blown across the road. In the distance, there would be shouting and I would turn over and watch Charlotte as she breathed gently and thoughtfully beside me.

The book in my hand, pressed reverently against my chest, I go back to the window and look at the copse and the fields, the icy notion of devil worshipping once again boring its way through me like a resurrected nightmare, when in a sudden rush of activity, as though the earth has simply been turned upside down, thousands of starlings fall into the sky. They twist and gyre in the low morning light and make me think of God dripping ink from a pipette into its dense watery surface.

I breathe through my nose and try to imagine what the landscape would have looked like on the night of 13 June 1645. Possibly starlings danced in the sky that night too, watched on by the monks, maybe even from this window. Thick woodland would have fallen away from the grounds of the Manor House. The earth would have seemed darker, more compact. I see the still waters of the marshes to the south glimmering in the moonlight, smooth reflective shapes beset with reeds. Geese fly over their own reflections. None of the houses on the road would have been here. There would have just been the Manor House and the pub and the old stone cottages circling the Green. And the abbey, of course. I picture fires burning in wooden huts, smoke weaving in thin grey ribbons into the night. Farmhands, husbandmen and drainage men would have been huddled with their families, talking of the war that was threatening their ancient way of life.

The starlings turn in one smooth swift calculated movement, as though a single form, a devilish phantom that coils itself into a long geometric shape, a Möbius strip of life with no beginning and no end that gradually slips away into the distance. A chill passes through me. I don't believe in the Devil. Not anymore. That's not it. That's not what is making me feel so uneasy. It's the names in the back of the book, Charlie Montagu and Holly Thompson, who I had seen on the news with Dad and Charlotte and Kika in London. They were real, as is Ethel Roberts. She lived here once, with her son, Henry. It was in the letter. He, too, was real.

I glance into the far corner of the room, where I know he sometimes stands, then down at the white rug, before hurriedly flicking through the pages at the back of the book. 'H R, '50,' I say out loud. *Henry Roberts, June 13th 1953.*

'Morning,' Mum says behind me. Her voice is dry and emotionless.

By the time I've turned around, she's already standing in the centre of the white rug, standing where Henry Roberts had once carved his initials. More than ever I feel his presence, to the point, I think, of guilt, as though I am in some way responsible for his death, if that's what it was, for having ignored him all this time. I look away from Mum into the corner of the room, half expecting him, as though on my command, to simply step out of the wall and stand there as he does, pale and waxy, a cupola of neat black hair parted to the left, those dark hollow watchful eyes.

Mum follows my gaze. 'What is it?' she says. She's wearing slippers and pyjamas beneath a thick red cardigan Aunty Anne knitted for her years ago. She looks down and picks at the sleeve, trying to push her thumb through a hole she has made. Charlotte used to do the same thing until Mum threatened not to buy her any more clothes.

'How long have you been standing there?' I say.

'Did you sleep?' There's something hypnotic about her, something crushed yet acceptant, as though she's sleep-walking, simply waiting for all this to splinter into daylight. Looking down to her sleeve again and holding a long thread of cotton about a foot away from her wrist as though she's not really sure how it got there, her expression pinching, she moves to the window. 'I don't think she ever really liked me,' she says. The morning swims towards her, the fresh indigo blue of the light making her seem older than she is. 'I've not been a good mother,' she adds. 'I know that.' She tilts her head to the glass, half expecting me, I think, to respond. But I don't. I allow this odd moment of serenity to glide through us. 'Is that a thrush?' she says.

'You can hear them from around four o'clock most mornings.'

'We had them at Polders Bridge,' she tells me, and for a moment we listen together to the song thrushes and the blackbirds calling to each other across the morning.

'Did Grandpa ever tell you a story about a curse when you and Aunty Anne were little?'

Her breaths fog the glass. Her eyes taper as she thinks. 'He was always telling stories.' She half laughs at this and I notice her head lifting slightly, as though for a moment she may have even believed he was here in the room with us.

'The house wasn't far from here, was it?' I say.

She turns and smiles and sits on the edge of the bed, smoothing out the pillow and the duvet. I look away to the painting of the Montagu's harriers, the scorched yellow light spread across the cold December sky as it was that day at Lakenheath, my wrist finding a gentle rhythm against my side. I look about the room. I have almost nothing materialistic to show for myself, I realise. I have my bird books and my school books and my box of feathers. Hidden away, I have my clothes, CDs I'm not even sure I have ever listened to, a few rolled up drawings beneath the bed – but that is all. Other than my thoughts, Charlotte is the only thing I have really owned.

Mum straightens *Bewick's Swan* on the bedside table, moves the glass of water a fraction of an inch, opens my drawer, rattles my bottle of pills and says, 'We have to be honest with each other.'

92

A car misfires out on the road.

'Why did you keep that painting?'

'Painting?' Mum says, her tone dropping.

'It's the view from here,' I say. 'I told Dad, but he didn't seem to care.'

She gets up from the bed. She stands beside me. Her cardigan smells of the house, fusty and damp. 'Have you been taking your pills?'

I frown. 'Of course. Why wouldn't I?'

'I don't know,' she says. 'I'm just asking.'

'Don't you think it's weird,' I say, 'leaving a painting like that behind?'

Mum leans forward, towards the glass, seemingly oblivious to what I just said, her eyes narrowing as she spots something on the windowsill. 'Not if it's a view from the house, no,' she says impassively. 'I think it's always been here.' She takes a tissue from her sleeve, wipes a dead fly from the ledge and drops it into the bin beside the desk.

I run my fingers over the rash on my neck. It feels hot and dry. 'Do you know what it means?' I say.

'It's just a painting, Simon,' she tells me.

'What happened to them?' I ask. 'To the family that used to live here?'

She doesn't answer, and together we spend the next few minutes looking out across the fields, our silence far more conspicuous than either of us would ever concede. The copse is now almost fully defined against the horizon, where a single fray of bright red cloud has floated up from the other side of the earth. A muntjac, gaunt and sandy brown, appears from behind a hedge at the top of the farm track, by the edge of the rape field. It stops dead, as though it has spotted something in the distance, or is, perhaps, aware that it has been spotted by us, and waits absolutely still for a few seconds, legs bandy and awkward, before darting off. Across the fields, pinkish in the quiet glow of dawn, birds are stirring over a distant wood, scarring the air as though the last remaining flakes of night.

'He died,' Mum says. 'She was moved to the old people's home eleven or twelve years ago, I think, but still owned the house. It came up for sale last year.'

'The Home here in the village?' I ask, even though I know the answer.

'I think so, yes.'

'Did they have any children?'

She scowls at this, although I'm not sure she knows she's doing it, her lip crimped irritably in the corner of her mouth, eyes lean and fixed on the copse. 'I don't know,' she says, as a train passes on the tracks behind the house, moving the light in the windows and carting me instantly and without warning on to a train on the London Underground.

I'm cupping my face in my hands against the dusty dry smells of other people, cheap perfume and fast food, listening to the machines of the earth toiling laboriously beneath me. Charlotte is sitting opposite. Tom is beside her, straight blond hair and angular nose. He's holding her hand, but looking sternly ahead at his thoughts stretched and distorted before him in the glass. Behind Charlotte, I watch my own reflection, pale and blue and comical, a cartoon figure melting on the screen, the dirty black veins and arteries of the earth zipping endlessly through me as though I wasn't there.

Charlotte leans forward, encouraging me to do the same. I glance at Tom and do as she asks. Odd shaped patches of dried-up chewing gum cover the metal floor at our feet.

'I need you to do something for me,' she says quietly. 'Tomorrow night. Is that OK?'

The bathroom door opens and closes. I blink and turn as Dad comes into the room. He waits a moment, watching us together at the window.

'How is everyone?' he says, his voice strangely light.

'We're fine,' Mum says. 'Simon was asking about the painting. The one in the living room.'

'Right,' he says, screwing up his face. 'And what was he asking exactly?'

'About why it was left here.'

'I don't know,' he says, looking at Mum, not at me. 'It just was. Now listen, I've been thinking. We should do a national appeal. Sly mentioned it before. I think we need to make this public, go on television. I'm going to phone him now.'

'If you think so,' Mum says.

'Is that alright with you, Simon?'

'Fine,' I say and I allow my eyes to be once more drawn into the far corner of the room. 'She's still alive.'

They both look at me.

'Who's still alive, Simon?' Dad says.

'Ethel Roberts,' I say. 'The woman who used to live here.'

ELEVEN

By lunchtime I have read most of Woods's book and have amassed nearly half a notebook full of notes. I learn, beyond what I knew already, that East Anglia in the early seventeenth century was a place both geographically and institutionally distant from the rest of England. Most of the land was under water, a mysterious and feared place that until this time had largely been left to its own devices, its own spirits, its own gods.

As war unfolded, many drainage men went on to form foot regiments. Adopted Fenlanders on the newfound farm-lands were the first to be recruited in Cromwell's new Regiment of Horse. They were garrisoned at Huntingdon and Cambridge. Woods writes of one such horseman, John Morton.

He had been injured at Newark and had returned home to his wife and family. Their house was a stone cottage in a line of four other stone cottages on what is now Farm Lane. Mary Murphy lives there now. Morton was a Puritan, having conformed to this extreme adaptation of the Christian faith alongside other men in his unit; a movement quietly wel-comed by the residing priest at Glenn Gate, Charles Yeaman, on hearing every day of hushed rumours of an insurgence into the old ways.

The phone rings.

I put my pencil down neatly by my notebook, take a sip of water and go back to chapter six in the book, where Woods recites exactly what happened here in the village the night before the battle.

Two weeks later, word had found its way to Glenn Gate. Royalists, having lured Sir Thomas Fairfax and his Parliamentarian forces to Leicester, were heading to Oxford under the prominent and celebrated generalship of Prince Rupert. Fairfax had already set out to meet him, engaging in clashes with Royalist outposts near Daventry. Lord Gibbins, on receiving the news, immediately began making ground with a small and eager force of local volunteers, leaving his estate in the hands of his eldest son, James.

By the afternoon of the 13th June, Prince Rupert was camped on the undulating ground between Market Harborough and Naseby, ready for battle. The King was close behind with a strong army of his own, yet fearful of the rising strength and number of Cromwell's forces, he sent a messenger, a Fenlander named Henry Sturgess, to meet with the Royal stable manager, Albert Fox, at Sandringham. Sturgess, according to Albert Fox's last entry in the royal accounts, offered a split goose feather on his arrival accompanying a sealed message of grave urgency from the King himself. Albert Fox, a wily and loyal servant to the King, was to arrange a chest of gold to be sent as King's bribes to be rewarded to certain inconstant Parliamentarian captains. It was to be met by Lord Montagu. This news, however, most likely by way of Lord Montagu himself, fell also upon the ears of John Morton, whose allegiances, as ever, remained faithful to Cromwell.

Glenn Gate sat directly on the route the Royal coach was intended to travel. Thick woodland surrounded the village to the west, marshland to the south and east. To the north stretched newly developed farmland. With the order of great haste, Morton sent his eldest son to Naseby to pass on this news to Fairfax. Yet fearful he would not make it, Royalist troops dominating the eastern side of the battleground, he called a secret meeting in the church.

The church at Glenn Gate, the church of St Mary's, was originally of Anglo-Saxon design, later reconstructed in Norman times. It was, and still is, a simple structure, comprising a rectangular nave with north and south aisles, a chancel and small vestry. Morality paintings adorn the walls. A bell tower was added in the fourteenth century housing five bronze bells still used today. Candle flame would have licked at the cold stone walls that evening as the men and women of the village gathered in the nave beneath gently flickering tapestries. It was their duty to God, Morton proposed, standing on the steps leading to the chancel, to intercept the coach, to at last rid the country of Royal dictatorship. The future of England depended on it.

Not all agreed. Some, they say, slipped out of the meeting to reassemble in the tavern. Most, though, stayed, incited by the passion of Morton's words, and moments later, armed only with farming scythes and forks, hammers and knives, they set off along the Bukehorn, the abandoned road that led through the woods in the direction of Naseby.

A large hole was dug. The men worked hard and fast. Some were experts in such undertaking and knew how to buttress the muddy walls using felled trees. The women held torches, the flames dancing beneath a thick canopy of leaves as the sky quickly darkened above them. From out of the watery trap lifted the oily stench of the marshes: rotten trees, dead fish and reed. Wet, tired and cold, they laid branches over the top, then covered them with leaves and dirt. The women damped their torches. Stars pushed through the night sky. They waited in the silence, only the sound of their breaths to accompany them, the odd rustling from an inquisitive animal or hoot from one of the owls that nested there. Many of the villagers would have feared for their lives. If there were troops accompanying the coach, they would not stand a chance in a fight.

First came the sound of hooves, the coach appearing in what moonlight could find its way through the gaps in the trees. The driver, Albert Fox, wore a brimmed hat as he hurried six huge black horses towards the villagers and their ambush. A King's guard sat at his side, the handle of his sword glimmering in the blanched light. Still, the villagers waited, their hearts beating to the frantic drumming of the horses in the near distance. In the dark, with trembling hands, Morton loaded a flintlock pistol. The men beside him gripped what meagre weapons they had. Frightened and uncertain, the women stepped further back into the shadows. Crows and rooks squawked in the darkening sky, spattering the air above the coach as the horses ripped through the damp stillness of the wood. The earth pounded. The villagers waited. The thundering of hooves echoed in the trees behind them until at last, twelve dark eyes formed out of the deep archway of trees. Wispy grey clouds billowed from the horses' mouths. Wheels clattered. Albert Fox's whip cracked in the thin air above their manes.

There was a terrible crashing sound as the coach dropped into the trap. Splinters of wood and wet earth surged through the trees towards the villagers. Then, from out of the dust and the settling quiet, came the lurid cries of injured and dying horses.

Morton, the flintlock pistol clasped in his hand, was the first to approach. Before him, squirming and kicking in the crudely dug basin they had gouged into the earth, lay six resplendent creatures, horses that would have once carried the King over the cobbles of London and Dunfermline, once been adorned in the Royal Colours. The coach lay upside down, half in the ground, half crushed against the trees, a single wheel spinning achingly to a halt. Albert Fox and the guard were dead. Both their necks had been broken. Rain began to fall as Morton's pistol cracked and flared in the cold darkness. Five times he reloaded with ball and powder. Six shots in total. With each one the wood fell quieter and more remorseful until a deep quiescence fell about the silent villagers. One by one they emerged from the black gates of the wood to gather around the upturned coach. The smell of blood and black gunpowder stuck in their throats as ghostly white skeins of smoke and soot residue lingered in the night air.

Morton pulled on the handle. As the door came free, a bloodied arm dropped at his side.

In the distance, thunder broke. Urgently the men and women looked skyward, yet all they could see were stars. They began to pray, but only more thunder came, growling its displeasure across the Heavens. Rain pitted on the leaves and against their clothes. A fraught and inconsistent wind tugged at the trees as the men laid the body of an elegantly dressed young woman on the ground. Her frame was slight, one side of her face darkened with blood.

Morton found the chest and placed it on the side of the hollow beside her. Still, no one said a word. The chest was a foot in length, coated in gold leaf, the curved lid decorated with a red Apothecary's Rose made from the finest rubies. It was undamaged.

Then they heard a voice.

The sky above rumbled. Lightning cut across the faces of the frightened villagers as Morton held his torch back inside the carriage. Lambent flames found shapes in the crushed remains, moving over the twisted corpse of a captain in the red tunic of the King's Lifeguard of Horse, before resting on the flickering, bone-white face of a young girl. As they laid her beside the dead woman, rain began to force its way through the gaps in the trees; large, heavy drops connecting with the

100

muddy ground in thousands of little explosions. The girl was fifteen or sixteen years old with long, flowing red hair. Her white embroidered gown was torn and soaked in blood where a piece of gilded wood had pierced her heart.

By now a storm had gathered overhead, swallowing the night's stars. Huge, steel-grey clouds swirled above the trees, the air thick with their phosphorous breaths. Wind pulled at their clothes, scattering leaves and branches high into the air, the sharp, metallic rain glittering among them. All the while, the young girl did not once lose sight of one of the horses lying dead at the edge of the pit.

Morton started towards it, bent against the wind. With wet, trembling fingers, he reloaded damp powder into the flintlock. Blood dripped from the smouldering gunshot wound he had already made in the centre of the horse's forehead, yet, still, one of its eyes, black and misty and locked open in death, was staring directly at the young girl.

Morton turned towards the villagers. They were huddled together, cowering beneath a spiralling serpent of wind that seemed to reach as high as the Heavens. It crackled and fizzed with electrical energy, its buckling tip just yards from the tops of the trees. It was God's work. There was no doubt. God's or the Devil's. Beside them, the girl's and woman's gowns danced errantly about their bodies. Still the girl stared at the dead horse, as though nothing else mattered, as though they were connected somehow, communicating through thought.

At the back of the group, one of the women began to chant. She sank to her knees in the wet mud and spoke in tongues; wild, grating words with no meaning. No one shut her up. They just stared at the girl and the dead horse, mesmerised, aware of their own mortality perhaps, that they were to be punished by God himself for this dreadful act of sin. With a fierce crack, lightning struck one of the trees. Flames whipped around its branches only to be sucked into the twisting cone of wind like

101

rags. Then, in the briefest moment of calm, they heard the sound of the church bell. It tolled a long single chime, its mellifluous note juddering through the darkness. Terrified, the villagers each turned to the pastor, Charles Yeaman, who, fighting against the wind, proceeded to pull a large key from beneath his robe. He held it aloft in the rain and, with a look of forlorn despair, crossed his chest with his other hand. Hurriedly each of the villagers copied, but it was too late. As Morton's shot cracked into the horse's skull, thunder ripped open the seal in the sky, lighting up the awful scene around them in a brutal flash of incandescent light.

The eye was still open. Quickly Morton reloaded and turned to the villagers, his face scorched in fear. 'The battle is lost and won,' he shouted across the wind and the rain, and as though it was the most unerring moment in his life, he raised the flintlock pistol to his own mouth and fired.

Legend states that Morton witnessed a vision of the curse in the eye of the horse that night; that it was invoked by the young girl moments before she died; that she called upon the horses to seek revenge on each of the villagers who had caused her death, to rob them of one child each year until she could be at rest. Her ghost then lifted from her body to be taken by the storm.

Morton's child, a boy of twelve, was the first to go missing. It was the same night the following year, the first night of the summer storms.

Cantering with military finesse, two horse riders are making their way down the bridle path that leads to the back of the Manor House. At their side, the long narrow dyke, cushioned between pale green banks of grass, scours through the earth, gleaming and shimmering beneath the high sun towards the foot of the most enormous sky I have ever seen. It just seems to be waiting there soundlessly in

102

the distance, like some huge shutter temporarily sealing off the darkness beyond.

They are not searching the fields today. There is just a single white van parked a little to the north of the copse from which, all morning, people in puffy white boiler suits have been coming and going.

I focus the binoculars back on the riders. They dilate in the lenses. It's Rupert Gibbins and Emma Proctor. I knew that anyway. I've seen them before. They're talking to each other, red faced and animated, seated primly on their mounts as though at a dining room table. On other days I have seen them galloping, racing each other along the path that runs adjacent to the one they're on now. I adjust the focus as they disappear from view, re-emerging, as expected, directly in my line of sight in the stableyard of the Manor House. The sun, arched high over the tops of the holm oaks, has scored serrated shapes across the cobbles. An old man, bulky and unhurried and wearing a black polo shirt, takes the horses without a word, other than to the horses, and leads them away. Their backs steam. Their tails whip.

Rupert kisses Emma on the cheek then stands and watches her, as do I, as she makes her way across the stableyard, through a brick arch bound in clematis, into the forecourt and out of the main gates. She crosses the road without even a glance, aware, perhaps, there is little chance of anyone knocking her over here in Glennfield. Her riding hat swings loosely at her side, long buoyant steps striding across the tarmac, her hair almost white in the morning glare.

She waves at Mrs Neal standing by her gate.

I put the binoculars down as Mrs Neal smiles up at my window, looking both ways down the road before beetling her way towards the house with a casserole dish held in her hands. I like Mrs Neal, even if Mum and Dad don't. The lines in her face are hidden beneath a thin but persistent layer of make-up, her hair as white as chalk. I like the fact she is a busybody. We didn't get busybodies in London, where strangely the houses seemed so much further apart than they do here. There's an owl house fixed to a large walnut tree at the back of her garden. She showed it to me when we first arrived. We had walked back together through the village. It had been raining. The air was damp, the road steamy, the sun sometimes catching the light at the edge of the village and revealing to us both the intrinsic colours of the world. I had helped her with her shopping and she offered me a glass of water.

Her husband acquired the owl house in Malta as a merchant navy officer, she told me. It's shaped like an owl's head, the eyes abnormally large and used for doors by the pair of tawnies that live there. Occasionally, when I'm lying awake in bed, I hear the female setting out for a night's hunting. I picture her gliding silently over the fields, lit only by the moon, before flying back to the home that looks like a giant version of herself.

'I suppose you've heard the stories, then?' she said that day, tearing up pieces of bread and dropping them rather clumsily onto the bird table at her side. The little wooden roof was dark and bloated with rain. Without looking up, she said brightly, 'Here they come.'

'What stories, Mrs Neal?'

Two chaffinches landed on the roof of the bird table. When they shook their feathers, a thin arc of light glimmered in the air. One of them chirped.

'Shh,' Mrs Neal said to the birds, glancing up in the direction of the Manor House. 'Or they'll hear you.'

The chaffinch tilted its head, curiously, picked up some

bread, and together the pair flew off through the wet leaves of the walnut tree, out over the fields. She looked at me firmly and made a derogatory sound in the back of her mouth as though I should have already known this.

'What stories, Mrs Neal?' I repeated, interested but looking back to the house at the same time, as though to suggest I wasn't. Mrs Neal's house stared back at me, bright and white and perfectly symmetrical, more like a dolls' house than anywhere someone may actually live. The thatched owl on the roof glared keenly into the village, as did the other thatched birds on the other thatched roofs, as though all waiting for the same thing. Water dripped unevenly onto the patio from bright red geraniums hanging below the windows. Everywhere, the rain and the sun had brought out the rich fragrances of seed and flower, rock roses and hellebores, snowdrops and purple iris. Beyond her fence, the more ponderous scents of wheat and rape, barely formed, were drifting in from the open fields. Through the damp air, the church bell sounded muffled and distant, and for some reason I felt frightened of it.

'Oh, it's a silly thing really,' she said through poppy-red lips. She handed me some bread to break up for the birds. 'I remember being told when I was just a little girl. We all were. It was my brother, Paul, who told me.' As she said his name, her thoughts seemed to take her away to another place. 'What was it he used to say? The light thickens and the crow makes its way to the rooky wood,' she said with a half-aborted laugh. I can still hear the dry rasp of her breath, even as I stand here now, watching her in a different moment walking back to her house, as her gaze had sharpened to a point.

'Wretched things,' she said.

*

105

Tottering and unhurried, she reappears moments later with a large wicker basket hanging under one arm, which, with a slight shuffle of her shoulders, she carries out of her gate. Mr Hinton is waiting for her at the entrance to the Manor House. He's wearing his cream summer blazer with the bell ringers' crest on the chest pocket and a boater, which he doffs rather ceremoniously, and together, a strange sort of glamour about them, they walk into the village. They pass Reverend Spragg outside the old post office, briefly exchanging words before he crosses the road beneath the webbed shadows of the holm oaks and heads towards the house, his gait slowing as he spots me up at the window.

TWELVE

With a sudden sense of urgency, a fear that time in the place Charlotte has been interned is moving faster than my time, I go back into her room. The same scent of perfume meets me there. It's resonant and aromatic, and I'm thinking it's rather callously washed away Charlotte's own scent when I catch a waft of her passing across the room from left to right and find myself turning as though having caught myself unawares in a pane of glass.

She is standing by the window. It's hallucinatory, I know, but still a surge of exhilaration runs through me, sending me off balance, and I have to hold on to her chest of drawers to steady myself, even as her image begins to fade. I look about the room, thinking back to that night standing on the landing. The ghost of Henry Roberts is watching me from the gleaming vent of white light at the end of the corridor, that redolence of lavender crawling seductively along the walls before him. Was he warning me? Did he know Charlotte was in danger? Have they somehow been entrapped in the same place?

I turn back to the window. The cold inside me is almost glacial, fostered, I think, from what can only be the emergence of terror. It numbs my thoughts. My breaths mist the air. I don't know what's going on here and I don't know the answers to these things, for I don't yet know if they are even things, not merely the shadows of things. I only know that Charlotte is not dead. I feel it within me. I feel her heartbeat next to mine, as I always have, the echo of my own. She is with me still. She is near. I have to save her, for that is all in life I have ever been required to do.

The room is unchanged from the last time I was in here. The bed is cast still in the chaotic mould of someone who didn't realise they wouldn't be returning. It feels both hopeful and tragic at the same time. A single beam of sunlight points out the books on her desk. I go to them and, with my hands shaking from what I guess is both fear and conviction, sit on her chair and study the sketch I made of the swan by the railway lines and the words she'd written beneath it. *Silence in Heaven about the space of half an hour*. I squeeze tightly the bridge of my nose, trying to focus on the now, keep my thoughts and memories under rule. The quote is from the Book of Revelation. I'd read it extensively after Nial died, and without any warning I find myself unaccountably in a busy room among the stifling smells of old suits, cheap tea and instant coffee.

Split between two times, each one thin and crystalline, I wade through the low cagey murmurings of people I vaguely know: silver-haired men with sallow mottled faces, wearing dark jackets that no longer fit them correctly. Women in navy blouses and tweed shawls with fur collars. A silver brooch catches the grainy flaxen light coming from the standard lamp. Rain skims across the window by the table where plates of sandwiches have been laid out on a crisp white tablecloth. I hear a woman say, as she nervously cradles a cup of tea on a saucer, 'Well, it always gave me the creeps. It was just one of those places, wasn't it? And those poor girls.' She shudders as she catches my eye in the quiet bustle and looks rather fearfully down to her tea for a few seconds, ignoring her friend's response.

Through the kitchen door I see Charlotte. She is talking to Aunty Anne. A dull sort of light, like grey paint, leans across her. Her hair, mousey brown then, like Mum's, is draped purposely over the scar that now accentuates her face. She turns and looks at me through the crowd, smiling thinly, letting me know that part of her will always be aware of where I am.

Back in my room, I see the photographer hunched forward on the bench by the village sign. He spots me, but he doesn't take my photograph today. His camera is sitting idly beside what looks like a lunch box and a flask. People are gathering again outside the old post office, close enough to see the house but far enough away to not be prying; to be seen to be concerned but not invasive. In the far distance a helicopter shadows the fields, and closer to hand, over the copse, turning effortlessly in a great circular motion, are maybe two dozen crows and rooks. They blotch the sky like ink.

I go to my desk and open the book at the photograph of the painting hanging in the living room, releasing once more that fusty scent of age and mould. I think of Grandpa studying his own books on the desk that now sits in Charlotte's room, that conspiratorial glint in his eyes. Somewhere in my memories there is a radio on. It's coming from the kitchen, a live commentary on the cricket. The sound is muddy and distant. 'All we have to do is peel the shrine like an onion,' he says keenly, 'and we will be with the King himself.'

Still in my thoughts, that smooth voice of his reverberating in my head as a guide, I study the grainy image: the horse's head thrusting its ghostly form through the very fabric of night. It's contorted and malefic, an entity as real as it is illusory, as abhorrent as it was that night, teeth baring, eyes the size of lakes. Woods has written a name beneath it in block capitals. Still, so smudged and tiny is the print, I have to take out my magnifying glass from the centre drawer of my desk before being able to decipher it properly.

ARTHUR BRADLEY CIRCA 1875.

Without delay I open the laptop. I take a sugar-free cola cube from the desk drawer and suck on it as the laptop powers up. I ignore the messages on my Wildlife Explorers forum and, with that thick swirling image of the clouds I saw the night she disappeared braiding itself resolutely through my thoughts, type into the search engine *Arthur Bradley 1875*.

Arthur Albert Samuel Bradley (28 January 1835 – 13 June 1879) was an English sculptor and artist. As a young man growing up in East Anglia, he worked as a farmhand during the early realisation of the industrial revolution, a time when much of this newly reclaimed land was being, in his own words, "dissected and opened to unbidden exposure". Influenced by the concept of windows, and painting only a handful of commissioned scenes in East Anglia that could be visualised exactly in the canvas as though seen through the naked eye, he insisted by contract that the works were never moved from their original sites; that they were, by their definition, windows. "Moving them would move the landscape itself," he wrote before his untimely death. "That is not our right. We are merely observers even if the consistency of what we see through the same glass is not always compatible."

Although something of an enigma, as Bradley himself proved to be, his paintings are still regarded as notable pieces of work. In his one and only correspondence, he claimed his art was governed by translucent symbolism, the artistic decadence of theosophy and western esoteric traditions. Arthur Bradley did not reap the rewards of his now highly regarded ideas. A gaunt and odd-looking man, infirm and suffering increasingly from seizures, he was frowned upon by the authorities for his hedonistic lifestyle and his suspected involvement in the dark arts, explaining to the Art Society in 1878 that, "The mind when numbed only by religious morality cannot see beyond the veiled walls of existence". The following year his life spiralled rapidly into scandal, culminating in the tragic fire that destroyed his family home, the prestigious Glenn Gate House, killing him, his wife and young daughter, Elizabeth.

Reverend Spragg is in the kitchen. He's talking to Mum and Dad. Aunty Anne is in the living room. I can hear the taut whine of the hoover, smell the hallway scents of polish and dusters.

'Simon,' Reverend Spragg says. His voice is soft and cautious, fawning almost, as though he has been dreading this conversation since our arrival. His eyes, magnified through round-rimmed glasses, appear in the sharp light the umber of old oak, glazed and yellowish, like living specimens. 'Why don't you sit with us?' he says, offering his hand.

'What's happened?' I say, not sitting.

Dad motions to the chair beside him. 'The Reverend's here to talk. That's all.'

The kitchen seems like a different place from last night, as though someone – Aunty Anne, I assume – has frantically attempted to bleach it of all those malevolent thoughts, and for a second I have to think back and remind myself it really did happen, that Mum really did look at me that way, as though she doesn't trust me, that ensnared among her thoughts there bides a coarse and tarnished voice telling her I'm lying to everyone; that perhaps, even, I have caused Charlotte harm.

Sieving through the gaps in the branches and leaves on the other side of the long narrow window, sunlight, white and inert, has made mosaic shapes over the silver taps and the curved spine of the kettle, lacquering the edge of the fridge. Everything shines. Even the lupins on the windowsill.

Spragg regards me, his spectacles catching the light in little celestial flashes that appear, I think, almost as angels bespangling the air around him. I half laugh at the image, pushing my thumbs behind the straps of my backpack, before eventually walking over and sitting on the edge of the chair furthest away from them. I don't really know why I hate religion so much. I'm not even sure I don't believe in it fully. Maybe it's not even religion I hate. Dr Chatterton liked to blame my uncommunicative behaviour on a fear of authority: parents, school, religion, politics – anything that lay beyond my direct control, but he was wrong. I'm just intrigued, that's all, as to what would have happened to the world without such an intrusion, how potentially composed or apocalyptic things may have turned out if this latent and inconsequential little ripple in time had simply been over-looked. I wouldn't have spent all those years believing it really was physically possible for a demon to crawl inside my thoughts and control my actions. I had been institutionally made to believe in the Devil as the Hecate believed in the Devil. If they really are still in existence, I think, then this is the fault of religion, not individuals.

I leave the backpack on my back.

Behind me, the mantelpiece clock ticks thinly and precisely. Each scant second it throws away seems like another grain of sand dropping from an hour glass I'm beginning to think may never be turned over. That it will metaphorically build up in the hallway, grain by grain, before sculpting its way up to the landing, blocking out the windows until the house resembles one of those abandoned beach huts at Brancaster.

Reverend Spragg nods his head. He leans back in his chair, stirring his tea with a spoon held in long anaemic fingers, and scrapes his teeth across his bottom lip. Never once does he take his eyes off me. He places the spoon on the table with a thin clink and smiles politely. His face is pockmarked and ruddy. A full head of thick grey hair has been combed rather unsuccessfully to one side.

'Are you going somewhere?' Dad asks, eyeing the backpack.

'To the Trust.'

He looks at Mum. His arm is stretched across the table, his hand covering hers and I try to remember the last time I saw such a gesture, before noticing a fresh bowl of fruit on the table that wasn't there yesterday. I lean over, take an apple, sit back and savage a large bite, crunching it noisily in my mouth.

'Carry on, Father,' Mum says quietly, slipping her hand away from Dad's and cradling it in her lap.

Spragg pivots forward, holding the mug as though it were something that had answers. The apple rolls around my mouth as I watch him move the mug away, just by an inch or so, keenly mindful of his own movements. Then, and still concentrating hard, he pulls it back to exactly where it had been before. 'God is with you at these times, even if you cannot hear him,' he says, a little pleased with himself.

'God is silent,' I say across the table.

Mum and Dad both look at me.

I take another bite from the apple. 'It's from a film.'

'This isn't a film, Simon,' Dad says firmly. He turns to Spragg. 'Sorry. Carry on, please.'

I shift about on the hard wooden chair, partly regretting what I just said. 'I know it's not. I'm not saying that.' I swirl the words around my mouth with the apple. 'I'm saying God is silent. He won't find Charlotte. It's not up to Him. It's up to us.'

Spragg coughs. He looks down to the mug again. His smile is slow and measured. 'Simon is right,' he says, his voice irritatingly sagacious. 'I won't pretend differently, but please do not think for a moment He is silent.' He pauses and smiles inwardly and moves the mug an infinitesimal amount towards him, focusing deeply, as though, perhaps, this time attempting to line up a direct connection with God himself, and says softly, with such profound conviction I almost want to believe him, 'He speaks, if we allow him to do so, through our hearts and in the faith he bestowed upon us in our creation.'

'What do you know about the curse?' I say, my tone deliberately facetious.

'Simon,' Dad snaps, firing me a look.

'It's OK, David,' Reverend Spragg says. His lips purse. His eyes sink down in their glass containers towards the table, away from the conceit of my glare, the slope of his shoulders morphing his appearance into that of a frail and vulnerable old man; but it doesn't stop me. It only fuels my resentment.

'What does the church say about such things?' I say. 'Does it acknowledge them? Does it exorcise them as it would a haunted house? What?'

Dad stares at me, eyes lean and admonishing, shaking his head in that tight calculated way he sometimes does, as though he genuinely believes people nearby can't see

114

him do it. 'Sorry, Reverend,' he says. 'We're all finding this hard to comprehend, as you can imagine.'

Reverend Spragg doesn't respond; not to Dad anyway. He just looks at me, the rough pale skin around his mouth creasing with what I assume, at first, is a reflection of nervousness, I can't be sure, so subtle and discreet is its movement. 'It's only natural Simon should ask such a thing,' he says slowly. 'God is not here to fix things. That is up to us. What He can offer, though, is hope.' He clears his throat. 'By their very nature these tales and myths suckle on our fears. That is when we need Him most.'

'So how do you explain them?' I say.

Dad thumps his hand on the table, startling at once both me and the reverend. 'For Christ's sake, Simon,' he spits. His frown is fierce and unforgiving.

'It's OK, David,' Spragg says again. He faces me. 'Curses and spells are not recognised by the church, not in such unambiguous terms. They are the products of fiction. However, this is not the time.'

'But ghosts are?' I say, interrupting him. 'Ghosts are recognised by the church? Is that right?'

He looks at me.

I turn to Mum. She's hunched like a pupa in her chair. She's been so quiet and focused, I'd almost forgotten she was here. 'Mum's house when she was younger was haunted,' I say. 'My grandfather used to tell us the story. There was a boy there who wouldn't let her or Aunty Anne leave their room. The church sent a priest to exorcise it. Why would they do that if they didn't recognise such unambiguous threats?'

The reverend lifts his hands from the table. He folds them neatly in on themselves, glances at Mum at his side, and lowers his voice. 'Maybe this is not the time for such a conversation. What your parents need now,' he appeals, bowing slightly, as though in his pulpit, 'is your support, and, if you allow it, the goodwill of faith.'

'The goodwill of faith,' I say, almost laughing now, and it's as I'm looking away that Mum meets my stare and starts to cry. Like part of a glacier breaking off into the sea, her face creases and deforms. At the same time my stomach contracts. It discharges a guilt that clots my insides, causing physical pain as her body begins to rock inanely back and forth on her chair.

'Where is she?' she pleads, her voice so meek and entreating I almost feel like crying myself, but I don't. I sit and I watch her, as do Dad and Reverend Spragg, numbed and uncertain of how to react to this pitiful little psalm dripping from her lips. When eventually I stand, I do it too quickly. Blood rushes to my head and in the dizziness I find myself partly in our kitchen in London. It's raining. The skylight sounds like a mob of demons have thronged together in the dark, banging their long greasy fingers on the glass. Mum is sitting at the table with Charlotte. She is crying as she is now, each narrative a shadow of the other, a concurrent reflection of the past and the future. I let my school bag fall to the ground as I, too, start to cry because I know what it is she's going to say. We've been expecting it. In an instant, my body, as Mum's is doing in another kitchen somewhere in the future, feels as though it's collapsing inwardly on itself. Grandpa once told me that places change when people step into them; they begin to occupy the physical and mental space which, until that moment, had previously been taken by others, whether they are welcome or not. I guess the exact opposite happens when someone dies.

'Simon,' Dad says abruptly, breaking the memory like a stick. 'Did you hear what I said?'

'Yes, Dad,' I say even though I didn't, and I turn around and leave the kitchen.

I had sat alone that evening in the small Exhibit Cinema in Balham, the deep leather chair crinkling and squeaking with each subdued move I made. I drank Coke through a straw, the straw hardly leaving my mouth I was so absorbed in the film they had made me watch. I was in the front row, directly beneath the projector's beam, dusty and coruscating with the silent ghosts of what was on the screen before me, fringed between furrowed curtains, neat folds in the darkness. The only colour available to me was the muted green of the fire exit sign. Silhouetted faces loomed from the seats behind me, fusing into the darkness as I watched a ghoulish figure playing chess with the Devil for his life amid the sweet scents of popcorn and red wine and fresh coffee. Tom had chosen the film as he had recently applied to film school and, he had assured me, it didn't contain flashing lights and wasn't too noisy. His friend's flat also happened to be nearby.

Afterwards, he and Charlotte met me outside. They were holding hands and stamping their feet against a sharp December cold that froze the black air and the breaths in our lungs. I couldn't help but think of them as Block and his wife from the film I had just seen, set against the dark background of Balham instead of medieval Europe. Charlotte didn't say much. I had the feeling she was frightened of something.

When Tom asked me what I'd thought of the film, I said without hesitation, picturing the pattern of the small white subtitles on the screen, 'And when the Lamb had opened the seventh seal, there was silence in Heaven about the space of half an hour.'

Tom smiled at this. The sharp white light of a passing car sliced across his face as he rather clumsily kissed Charlotte on the cheek. Charlotte and I didn't speak as we walked home. There was something up with her, though. That much I knew. Something had changed inside her. The moon was as blurred and as milky as the street lamps over our heads. Snow whirled inside them. It made the tall houses on our street appear bulky and bigger than they actually were. Windows hung in the darkness like modern canvases. Christmas trees flashed red and green and blue. I couldn't see the stars. They were hidden.

'Did you tell Tom we're leaving London?' I asked her.

She didn't reply, not at first anyway. Instead, she looked down to her feet, watching them making fresh shapes in the snow. She nudged the back of my hand and I noticed for the first time the faintest waft of perfume caressing the air around her neck. Her fingerless gloves scratched my skin, her fingers slipping fluidly into mine, and even though I couldn't hear any words, I knew exactly what her thoughts were saying because they were the same thoughts as mine.

THIRTEEN

I walk out into the hot sun, pausing by the gate a moment to see if I'm being watched, but other than the photographer slumped on the bench, looking as though he's waiting for a bus he knows will never come, there's no one here. The spectators have gone. The village is empty. So, too, is the sky, and the fields beneath it, trembling in the heat and reflecting its silvery glare like enormous solar panels. All I can hear is a metallic tapping sound, like the ticking of someone's watch, but there is no one nearby, other than the photographer. There is no wind and there are no cars. There are no dogs. There are no people. There's nothing. The village is dead. It's alive, I think, only in my thoughts. The air is colourless and static, as thick as formaldehyde, embalming this strange counterfeit place and all its secrets like a dead animal.

By the village sign I notice daisies and wild purple orchids clumped together in neat little cliques where the grass hasn't been cut, I suspect deliberately, to incorporate them as part of Glennfield's welcoming entree, as though it was a stand at an exhibition: *Glennfield twinned with Saint-Bonnet-lès-Allier. Please drive carefully through our village.* Hopping mindfully between the clumps of flowers are two birds. I can't see what they are. Coal tits or blue tits. Marsh tits perhaps, although they don't seem small enough and we're possibly too far inland. The photographer catches my eye, nodding his head incisively, as if he knows me. Grey hair sags over his face like straw, which he runs his hand through, quickly, as though feeling the need to do something other than simply watch me and the house and this empty insipid village.

The birds flitter away.

I draw into my lungs the scorched air, composing myself and allowing the glutinous scents of dry wheat and rape to fill my nostrils. I haven't been outside for days, I realise, other than to get in and out of Uncle Pete's car bringing me back from the hospital. It feels strangely claustrophobic.

An opened-back truck with wooden side panels splutters into the village from out of the haze. It fills the air with the smell of diesel. The driver, a large and haggard-looking man wearing a weathered flat cap, nods at me, a little knowingly I think, as he drives by in the wrong gear. I cough. The acerbic bite of the fumes claws at my throat, the rattle and glimmer of the beer barrels he's carrying reverberating through the shattered stillness. Out across the fields the air has blurred. The edges of the sky are smeary and distant, as though part of a dream, but this isn't a dream. I'm not even certain it's the aura. It's vertiginous and frightening, but it doesn't feel as though it's being generated within my head. It's outside my head, a real thing, beyond my control. It's coming from the sky, or from the other side of it. I'm not sure. Part of me can even sense a small vibration in the ground, which is when I see them, huge but faint ripples of colour crinkling across the surface of the sky as though it were a liquid, as though someone – God, again – was peering through its thin delicate meniscus, watching to see what I will do next. The pavement keels and tips. The air glistens and for a brief second I can see clearly every particle and molecule within it. Millions of lines of interconnected atoms are linking up before me, forming a vast perpetual honeycomb in the sky, and it occurs to me for the first time that what I have been seeing all these years is not merely a symptom of electrical surcharges in my brain, but some sort of map.

It's fatigue, I tell myself, breathing through my nose. Lack of sleep and too much medication and the strain of everything that's going on. It's hardly surprising my brain feels like the plasma ball on the bookshelf in Charlotte's room, or that the aura I felt that night in my bedroom has yet to fully recede. It hasn't had a chance. The light is as thick as the air. It hangs in the corners of space, foggy and tarnished, like an old photograph; and linked, perhaps, via the haze of time, I find myself back in Grandpa's living room, but Grandpa isn't here. Only his scent is here, ingrained in the leather armchairs and the hundreds of spines of old books leaning over me as I sit on the floor, going through various boxes.

'Uncle Pete will take the books,' Mum calls from the kitchen. 'How he ever found anything, I don't know,' she adds tiredly. The radio is off and the house seems small, enclosed in brick, where before it always seemed to go on forever.

'We can keep some, though,' I say, turning my head and noticing an old cardboard box tucked away in the far corner of the room by his desk, and it occurs to me now, in another time, that maybe it had always been there, hidden in the darkness all those occasions I visited, all those times I went through his books and asked him about his finds.

I walk over to it, dragging it noisily into a large gridded square of daylight by the window. It's heavy. Dust sprinkles the air as I open the flaps, releasing a sudden waft of age. I peer inside. There are maybe a dozen books of all sizes. A tiny brown spider scampers across the spines and down one edge, where hundreds of sheets of paper have been crammed into wilted cardboard folders. I tilt my head and read the titles of the books: *Britain's Lost Homes, The Origins of English Villages, British Surnames, Devil Worship in Britain, The Question of Lucifer* and more whose titles by their very nature send a shiver through my body, both here in the brutal glare of the morning and back in Grandpa's empty living room. I flick through some of the books, quickly absorbing the multitude of roughly torn strips of lined paper stuffed inside them, and look up with a start into the glittery brightness of some other moment not yet established, a semi-translucent patina covering my vision as I take a marker pen from the coffee table, write LONDON on the box and seal it up.

'Do you need help?' Sly says.

'No,' I tell him, but I accept it anyway, steadying myself on his arm as gradually colours condense, the sulphuric tinge of the air being replaced by the earthy scent of the fields beyond. I focus on the BMW parked on the road directly in front of me by the lamp post. It's an early nineties model, I guess by the shape, and bright white. I imagine it's something he takes great care of. Its chrome edges sparkle under the high sun.

'You sure you should be going out anywhere?' he says, reluctant, I think, to be offering such familiarity.

I stare ahead, not answering, waiting a little longer for time to catch up with itself. The sky shimmers back into place, becoming once again blue and stratospheric. The air thins. In the angled reflection of the car window, a magpie forms out of the darkness of our roof. I look up at exactly

122

the same time as the reflection meets the bird, making it appear, for a moment, kaleidoscopic, before it cuts sharply to the right and lands on one of the chimneys of the Manor House beside a stone statue of a raven. It rattles out its call, its head arched skyward.

From the corner of my eye, I see Sly salute it. He doesn't know I saw him, but as though to compensate for such a frivolous gesture he clears his throat and raises his eyebrows, expecting me, I think, to move off the path, but I don't. I watch the magpie perched on the chimney, as still and as motionless as the statue beside it. The chimneys themselves are grey and pillared. There must be a dozen of them, ribbed and guttered in stone and looking as though at some time in the past the ruins of an old church or cathedral had been carelessly discarded on top of the house.

'I used to go to the Wildfowl Trust as a child,' Sly says, spotting something up in the sky behind me. He shields his eyes. 'I understand it may be closing down.'

I don't answer this. He's only being courteous, picking at my guard before asking me something more direct. I study the Manor House instead. There's a flagpole over the front façade, but no flag. I picture the Royal Standard hanging there, limp and wrinkled against the bright June sunshine of 1645. In my mind, as today, there is no breeze to pageant its garish colours for the men readying themselves to parade through this quiet reticent village, never to return.

'Does the name Hecate mean anything to you?' I say. 'It was a cult set up here in the village in the seventeenth century by Lord Gibbins.' I point my head in the direction of the Manor House. 'I think the man who painted the canvas in our living room was also part of it.'

Sly's face gently contorts, curious at first, amused even, letting slip a puckish sniff before squinting against the

123

unsparing glare of the sun. 'What is that?' he says.

I turn my neck, ignoring that he has purposely not answered my question, and follow his gaze up to a sparrow-hawk circling over the top of our house. Its head is pointed down, its neck kinked in the clear light, stark yellow eyes fixed on something on the main lawn at the side of the house. As though being spun around on a long piece of string, its shadow orbs hypnotically on the grey slates.

'Sparrowhawk?' he suggests.

'Yes,' I say. 'What about Holly Thompson?'

He pulls away his look from the top of the house, his stare at once sharp and unsettled. 'This has nothing to do with Holly Thompson,' he tells me flatly.

'She went missing on the same date,' I say. 'And what does the rose mean at the copse? Has that happened before? Is that what this is? Some sort of ritual?'

Reluctantly he acknowledges this, the sun creeping into the folds under his eyes and chin, forming minute little shadows like the contours of a map. I notice Mrs Neal peering through her downstairs window. When she sees me, she looks up, pretending to do something with the curtain, before disappearing back into the room.

Sly, too, spots her. He exhales, clearly incensed at my last comment, picks a hair from the cuff of his jacket, inspects it a moment and drops it to the ground.

I watch it float to the pavement, noticing a crushed snail by my trainer. Bits of shell have stuck to its grey jelli-fied corpse. Its trail runs almost to the end of our wall, where insects are pitting frantically over wild ivy and bramble. I pull at my collar. It's damp and feels itchy against the rash. On the grass, burnt with heat and thirst, a starling is shuttling around the stump of an old oak tree, reminding me of one of those plastic wind-up toys with the stiff flat feet that used to waddle aimlessly across our kitchen floor in London when we were small, bumping into a cupboard then, unperturbed, continuing to walk contently on the spot until it ran out of life.

'You're an intelligent boy, Simon,' he says at last, 'clearly more so, I imagine, than you're letting on. But this is not in any way a game. Do you understand? This is about finding your sister. She's been missing now for four days. We are taking this very seriously. We are extraordinarily worried about her.'

I swallow, humbled by the stony note of his voice. The village is empty, save for Mr Chaplin cutting his hedge. 'Where is everyone?' I ask.

'They're searching the fields to the north of the village,' he says. 'They are also concerned, Simon. This is a good community. Remember that. Now, has anything come back to you from that night?' He looks over my shoulder, eyes peering diligently back up to the sky over our roof where the sparrowhawk had been, but really, he is avoiding my stare, giving me time to think.

I shake my head even though I know he can't see me. 'They were arguing in the kitchen,' I tell him, still trying to gauge the sternness of his look, the meaning behind those tiny but measured pinches of his cheek. 'Mum and Dad and Charlotte. I was on the landing. I wasn't feeling well even then.'

'And what were they arguing about? Do you remember?'

'I didn't hear, most likely about her being late back, I guess.'

He cups his eyes, still looking into the space over the house, not at me. 'Was she happy here, do you know?'

'She was Charlotte. She was never happy.'

This time he looks directly at me. 'I mean,' he says firmly, 'has something happened recently that may have caused her to run off?'

125

'No.'

'What about this Tom from London? Do you think she may have gone to see him?'

I sniff. 'No,' I say. 'They finished before we came up here.'

He nods his head thoughtfully. 'And you haven't seen any evidence she may have been bullied or picked on or anything like that?'

'No,' I say. 'She was Charlotte. She was weird but people liked her.'

He looks briefly back to the house, carefully chewing his next words around the inside of his mouth. 'And what about at home, Simon?' he says, attempting to disguise any suggestion in his voice.

I look to the floor.

He waits a moment then prompts me. 'Is everything OK at home, Simon?'

I tell him it is, the astringent light of the sun scorching my thoughts and temporarily moving me, as a conveyance, from one time to the next.

'Would you like me to take you inside?'

'I'm OK,' I say, drowsily looking into the village, not at Sly. Mr Chaplin's hedge cutters catch the light. They dazzle me. In the haze I see a policewoman walking out of the drive of the Manor House, her face stippled in the shadows of the holm oaks, and once again, as though it had never not been there, the sound of a helicopter out over the fields.

'Did you hear what I said?'

I don't respond.

'I asked if you were happy here.'

'I am happy here.'

'And Charlotte?'

'And Charlotte.'

126

He pauses and smiles. 'You look after yourself now, Simon,' he says steadily, 'and do send my best to Arthur Skinner, won't you? I'm sure he'll remember me.'

I kick the snail into the gutter, turn and walk down the pavement, not to the Trust, but to Emma Proctor's house.

When I was very small there were rows of huts half buried in the uneven tiers of sand at Brancaster, each bonded together with marram grass. I used to think of them as the daggerish eyes of whiskered old giants and that there were hundreds of these giants hiding in the dunes, waiting for something to come out of the sea. They have all gone now.

Charlotte is behind me, playing a game, her singing gradually getting thinner and thinner until it is no longer there. Sandpipers skitter back and forth along the silver channels of water. To my right are the marshes, the sky above them so speckled with gulls and terns it's as though from out of its glassy texture are emerging the very first flakes of snow. The sea lies ahead, a thin grey line on the horizon, from which is crawling like a mist that ethereal and now distinctly familiar stench of sulphur. All signs are indicating I am about to have a seizure or am already having one. However, I find myself trying to fight it, trying to look directly into the reeling space before me. It's exactly what I have been told not to do. Besides, it's beautiful the way the air sparkles and glitters like this, as though two worlds, two moments of time, neither of which I really belong to, have been laid on top of each other like sheets of ice. I can still taste the salt in the air. I can feel the sting of the sand against my cheeks, but everything is different. The wreck and the beach and the marshes are in sight, but they possess no depth, no distance, as though I am looking at them through the wrong end of a pair of binoculars.

127

Then I see it. A wave as black as space is heading towards the beach. Gulls and terns flee inland, soaring low over my head, mewing frantically. To my left, families run, screaming. In the far distance, I can hear Aunty Anne and Uncle Pete calling my name. I can't hear Charlotte. I only know she is nearby. She always is.

The wreck and the marshes are soon engulfed. When eventually the wave hits the shoreline and collapses on top of me, everything vanishes.

FOURTEEN

Through the frosted glass I see Mrs Proctor's muffled form falling into focus in the bright hallway. I step back, to be met by an austere and solicitous smile shaping itself across her sleek and narrow face.

'Simon,' she says through a low exasperated breath, her shoulders dropping exhaustedly. 'No news, I hear. Gordon spoke to your father this morning. He's doing all he can. We're all doing all we can.' She sighs deeply, I suspect more for Gordon than for Dad, and shakes her head. 'Your poor mother,' she adds, 'I just can't imagine.'

'Is Emma in?' I say.

With a furtive glance over my shoulder, she ushers me inside. The hallway is bustling with the scents of dried flowers and polish and what is possibly lavender from a scented candle, although I can't see one. The house is as clinical as a showroom. Upstairs the shower is on. I look up. A pristine beige carpet unfolds its way to a small landing where a mahogany table filled with little china cats acts as a centrepiece. The hallway and the stairs are cloistered with pale green wallpaper. A venous pattern of embossed flowers, lilies I think, with tiny white buds give the impression they are floating dreamily up the stairs towards the sound of running water, and for the briefest moment I am back in my own house, on the landing, in the dark.

It's freezing cold. My breaths drift across the brittle air as a phosphorescent light. I'm staring at the bathroom door. Inside, the tap is dripping, but I'm too scared to go inside and turn it off because I know he's in there. And yet I have to go inside. My pyjamas are soaking wet and my legs are stinging. To my right, at the far end of the landing, the laundry room door is open, a bright white rectangular shape suspended in the darkness. I shiver, listening to the echoic peck in the sink on the other side of the door. It's slow and methodical, in perfect rhythm with the mantelpiece clock beneath me. The house is dying, I think. Its last drops of blood are seeping into the porcelain. It doesn't want us here anymore. He doesn't want me here. He doesn't like me being in his room. He's made that clear.

Birds scurry about on the roof tiles by the domed light. I look up but I can't see them. I can't see anything. It's too dark. The night is black, and when I look back to the door, I see that it is open. Henry Roberts is standing there in the harsh white glow of the bathroom light, watching me like a reflection. His face flickers. His eyes twitch, and for a moment I almost think he's about to smile, but then I step back, into the present, knocking into a small desk near the door where the Proctors keep a visitors' book. It's pink with a pale green bow and looks as though it's never been used.

Clumsily I straighten it, and the pencil at its side, noticing a small sepia photograph of a band of bell ringers standing in front of the church tower. They are all men, some with lavish moustaches, each dressed in cream blazers. Written in white ink are the words *The Three Sheaves Bell Ringers 1922*. Their names are scribed beneath: *G. Hinton, W. Chaplin, J. Scott, J. Howe, G. Thompson, C. Proctor (Bell Major).* I recognise some of the names from the back of the book.

'Oh, Simon,' Annie Proctor says. Her voice is plumed. 'All this must be so hard for you to understand.'

I don't answer.

'Would you like a glass of water?' When I don't respond to this either, she glances up the stairs and smiles. 'She won't be long,' she says. 'Why don't you come and wait in the drawing room?'

I, too, steal another look up the stairs as she guides me with long gentle fingers through a glossy white door and sits me down in one of the armchairs, leaving me with more hoax fragrances: cedar from a small green vase, potpourri, and something lemony. Beneath it all I can smell the cat. The room is spotless. Every surface gleams in neat parallelograms of sunlight that have squeezed aside curtains delicately pinched at the waists with factory-clean tasselled ropes, like mannequins in wedding dresses in London shop windows. I turn to the door, hearing the tinny motionless trill of a pop song coming from a radio in the kitchen. Mrs Proctor is trying to sing along to the words. In the fireplace is a vase of fresh white roses.

She reappears in the doorway, the cat slinking guilefully into the room beside her, where it walks across the carpet and rubs itself against my leg. I fidget awkwardly in the grip of the chair, trying to get it away from me as subtly as I can. It's large and white and purrs conspiratorially, as with a rehearsed grace Mrs Proctor sits herself in a matching armchair positioned directly opposite me, on the other side of a glass coffee table. Magazines are laid out in one corner in a neat fan: *House and Garden, Horse and Hound, Tatler.* She crosses her legs, folding her pale summer dress delicately over her knee.

'Ignore Samson,' she says, looking at Samson, not at me. Samson curls himself around her feet, blinking at me conceitedly with runny green vertical eyes. 'Your Uncle was around earlier. He seems nice,' Mrs Proctor says, noticing a speck of something on the table at her side. She licks her finger, frowns and picks it up, flicking it nonchalantly over her left shoulder with a little satisfied pinch of the mouth. 'Must blind the Devil,' she says through a smile. 'Gordon tells me the police think she's in London. She had a boyfriend there. Is that right?'

'They're not together anymore.'

She doesn't respond to this. She waits for me to speak, but I don't. There's a brooch pinned to her cardigan. It's a silver sheaf of wheat, the same as on the village crest. When she sees me staring at it, she stands, brushes down her dress, her mouth twitching inwardly, and says, 'I'll see if Emma's ready, then, shall I?'

I watch her leave. Samson follows.

Over the door is a glass cabinet with a folded bell rope inside. The sally's once bright colours, the diagonal red, blue and white stripes I recognise from books, are faded and marked. Beneath it is a golden plaque. I walk to the door and read it, half aloud, half in my head: HENRY PROCTOR, TOWER CAPTAIN, 1958–2006. PRESENTED BY THE THREE SHEAVES BELL RINGERS, GLENNFIELD, JUNE 13th, 2006.

'Gordon's father,' Mrs Proctor says proudly, appearing back in the doorway. 'It's been a family tradition for centuries.'

'Not for all of us,' Emma says, bounding down the stairs. Her hand slips smoothly off the bannister and down Mrs Proctor's back. 'No news, I hear,' she says in that low gravelly voice of hers.

I look to Mrs Proctor. 'Did they ring the bell that night, do you know?'

Her eyes narrow for the briefest of moments, then she half laughs. 'We don't ring the bell at night anymore,' she says. 'Why do you ask?'

'It's nothing,' I say. 'I thought I'd heard it, that's all.'

Emma's wearing a long black skirt and formal jacket, a white rose in the lapel. 'I saw the police on the Burtons' farm this morning. What were they doing there? Rupert seemed to think they were forensic scientists. What's going on?'

'They're not forensic scientists,' I tell her, my tone hardening, seemingly of its own accord. 'The police think she's in London.'

Mrs Proctor smiles kindly.

'So why were they there?' says Emma.

'It's just routine, darling,' Mrs Proctor says, adjusting the rose. 'Isn't it, Simon? Now, tell your mum and dad we're thinking of them, won't you? All of us, the whole village. We're praying for her. God gives us strength at such times.' She smiles again and walks to the kitchen where, once more, she quietly sings along to a song on the radio.

Emma steps forward and hugs me. 'You poor thing,' she says, her body pressing into mine as though I were a pin-art frame. I look away towards the kitchen, trying not to think about her touching me. Mrs Proctor is putting on an apron, still singing to herself in a long slant of white sunlight that has leant against the side wall like a mirror. She turns, almost dancing, smiles when she sees us, turns again and folds two long blue straps around her back, bringing them round to her front and tying them in a bow. Emma's hair is damp against my face. It smells of coconut, which as quietly as I can, I draw into my lungs.

When eventually she releases me, I swallow gracelessly and shuffle back towards the desk by the door. 'Can you take me to the Home?' I say.

133

Emma leans over me. She takes a key from a board that is hanging at my side. It is painted in that distressed rural style Mum used to like in London, but not so much here. The word KEYS is painted across it in case there was any doubt of its purpose. On it, I notice, is an archaic looking key with a flimsy brown label. TOWER is written on it in faded blue ink.

'So why do you want to come to the Home?' Emma says, turning briskly on to the pavement.

'There's someone there I want to speak with,' I tell her.

She walks on. 'The police were all over the place yesterday. Caused a right fuss.'

Her polished black shoes click smoothly ahead and I'm almost having to double step to keep up with her. Once again the heat is blurring the air, making it move like water. It's drawing sweat down my back, sticking the thin fabric of my shirt to my skin, and I become acutely aware of the smell of my own body. I pull at my collar as I walk. I fold my sleeves one more turn, exposing my white elbows to the sun, noticing as I do a dead hatchling lying on the pavement beneath a small sycamore tree. Its prehistoric looking claws are stretched apart as though it had been trying to grab hold of something as it fell to its death. Flies pick at its grey hairless body.

'So can I come then?' I ask.

Her pace resumes, long willowy steps increasing the gap between us. 'That might be difficult today,' she says, without turning around.

I continue to walk behind her as I think. When we were younger, on those long breaks in Norfolk with Aunty Anne and Uncle Pete, Charlotte and I used to play games of hide-and-seek either in the house or, sometimes, along the ivy-covered paths that ran from the road all the way to the beach front. I would run and hide, and Charlotte would find me. It was always this way round in our games. I would hide. Charlotte would find me. Heroically she would then pull me out of a burning aircraft or rescue me from sinking sand, or the marshes themselves, dragging fallen branches from the half-buried pine trees made smooth by the sea and stretching herself out on the ground, the wind scratching through the marram grass beside us, the sea a dark score in the distance.

In order for her to find me, I would first send her my position. I would clear my mind of thought and, with my knees pulled up tight into my chest, making myself small behind a dune or entanglement of bramble or one of the beach huts there, I would repeat silently in my head exactly where I was, and she would find me. Always she found me.

I look about the village and the slowly gathering villagers, overcome with a profound sense of loneliness. We don't belong here, I think. No one really knows us. No one really cares. They join the searches in the fields and they put up posters in their windows and they speak with genuine concern to the police officers with their bright white shirts and their clipboards, but they don't really care. If Charlotte never returns to this place, life, although temporarily scarred, will continue as it always has. Each day the tender sky will sharpen and fade. Each month the fields will change their shape and colour. Each year the winds will sag and fight, and I will not anymore be able to tell her where I am, for she will be silent within me.

Emma turns. 'Everyone seems to think she's in London,' she says, almost sounding annoyed.

When I don't answer, she smiles sympathetically and continues to walk ahead. There's a decidedly piqued note

135

to the rhythm of her shoes now. Partly hidden beneath an over-sized beige boiler suit, Mr Chaplin is cutting his hedge. He stops when he sees me, the blades of his shears catching in the sun and hiding the deep lines in his face. He looks at me, expressionless, and nods.

'Why are there so many police officers about then?' I say after her. 'And why is everyone searching the fields? Why did they even look in the copse in the first place?'

She stops and holds my arm, a little too tightly, eyes flaring and transparent in this savage light. 'Because we're worried about her,' she says, ignoring Mr Chaplin's greeting. Defiantly she continues, her strides carving across an old bed sheet that has been neatly laid out on the pavement to catch the cuttings. It momentarily dampens the sound of her shoes. I follow, the acrid tang of yew catching in my throat and mingling with the powerful scent of Mrs Yearsly's roses next door. They're bright white, heads slumped, half asleep in the sweltering heat. As she glides into view, I offer her a wave, but she doesn't seem to notice. Mr Chaplin's cutters tap out little off-beats, and for a moment I'm not entirely sure where I am. Somewhere up ahead I hear the clattering sound of metal on tarmac. To my right someone is playing a violin, and all around me, high like walls, the clean sand-coloured stones of the houses glow bright and spurious against the flawless sky as though it was nothing more than the blue screen of a film studio, an empty canvas to be furnished with any memory or thought my subconscious mind desires.

As I think this, in another time, Charlotte's fingers link through mine and it is not Emma walking ahead, but Mum, and the sky is low and grey and discharging rain we can see behind us, scraping itself across the gently rippling surface of the fields, dark and gauzy, the cloak of some vile demon. 'We have to protect each other,' Charlotte says, turning her head against the wind to face me. She laughs impassively. 'You understand, don't you? No one else will, not out here. It's just you and me.'

Her image suffuses into the light. I blink, unsure whether that was the memory of a dream or something that actually happened. I don't remember it happening, but I don't remember dreaming it either. The only time we've walked into the village with Mum was when she made us visit the church soon after we arrived here and tried to persuade us to do a brass rubbing, as though we were still children, as though she was making up for all those years she missed when we actually were.

The roofs on the houses are silvery and harsh in the heat, glimmering like the hides of animals, and I notice even more thatched birds, ones I'm not sure I have seen before: a swan, an eagle and a peacock, its dark tail closed and guarded.

'He alright?' someone shouts across the road.

A dandelion floret drifts by my head. To my left is the Red Rose pub. The landlord looks up and nods his head inquisitively. The barrel in his hands flashes beneath the glare of the day.

'It's alright, Fred,' Emma calls across the street. She holds my arm again and guides me forward. 'They went in there that night,' she says disapprovingly. 'Dad told me. Then they went down behind the bell tower. It's where they go, near the old rose garden. Listen, Simon, I can't be late today.' She pulls me across the Bukehorn, the long straight road that heads east to Norfolk. In 1645, according to Woods, it would have run through the village along what is now Farm Lane out to the copse and the marsh path towards Naseby. The level crossing is a hundred metres out, just before where the road bruises a little over Ten Mile Dyke. It's how I got back the day I found the swan.

'What about Holly Thompson?' I say. 'She went missing not far from here, didn't she, and on the same date?'

Without looking at me, Emma guides me into the shadows on the other side of the road, where behind the high brick wall of the Old Hermitage Retirement Home, trees stretch tall above us, rusty and contoured. She stops at the gates, eyes widening as she looks up, reverently almost, I think, into the stippled roof of leaves and branches. 'Mum and Dad knew her parents,' she says seriously. 'They used to farm around here.'

'So what happened to her?' I say, my voice quieter than I had intended.

From the Trust, geese scatter their calls through the gaps in the trees, sounding like the mad frantic wails of prisoners. Beech and oak trees lean motionlessly over the gravel drive. The hermitage, I know, is on the right-hand side. I can't see it from here. It's tucked back in the trees and the shadows, but I can just see the arched roof of the wooden lychgate. At its base are two stone vases filled with white roses and lupins. Ground ivy crawls out of the under-growth towards them. By the main doors of the Home, standing solemnly on the wide stone steps, I can see maybe a dozen people of all ages, snared in a long spear of dusty lemon sunlight. They are all wearing black.

'What is it?' Emma asks. 'Are you having one of those things?'

I ignore her. I'm not. Something's just occurred to me. The notion races through me, leaving a strange and hollow feeling in my chest. 'Ethel Roberts,' I say, half pointing down the drive. 'Is that her?'

Emma looks at me for a long while, her frown puckering the high swathes of her forehead. 'I thought you knew that. I thought that's why you wanted to come here. What is all this, Simon? What's going on?'

'I don't know,' I say drearily.

She places her hands on my shoulders and finds my gaze.

'She lived in our house,' I tell her.

'I know.'

'Did you ever go there?'

'Why do you ask?'

'There's a painting. It was there when we arrived. It belonged to Ethel Roberts. Her son went missing on the same date Charlotte did, and Holly Thompson. The same date the curse was set.'

Her face widens, her eyes gleam, and in the foggy stillness that follows, she tells me it's just a stupid story, that she really has to go, that I need to look after myself, Charlotte will be fine, she's probably in London somewhere, as everyone seems to think. But Charlotte wouldn't have gone to London without telling me. I know she wouldn't.

I watch Emma walk down the path, the verdant darkness beneath the trees distending into the empty space she leaves behind her, hear the lamenting groan of the large wooden doors opening as Ethel Roberts's coffin is carried out and placed into the back of the hearse. Their faces pressed tightly against the tall narrow windows set over the door, as though peering up through ice, Ethel's contemporaries, each graciously awaiting their own death, look on, wide-eyed like ghosts, as her life is shrunken before them to the size of a box.

FIFTEEN

There's a car in the Trust's car park. It's an old Mini, navy blue and rusty, one side almost flat on the ground. It's parked at an odd angle by the picnic benches. Other than that and Mr Skinner's two-seater Mercedes hidden beneath an old canvas cover encrusted with bird muck, the car park is empty. It's been empty almost every day I've been here, its inhabitants large jagged dandelions pushing out of the swollen cracked tarmac, and thistles and ragwort and bright red poppies standing two feet high, each dazed and vacant under the exposed sun. Insects stir the warm air where two lamp posts stand bare and redundant. Cones lie scattered in the shadows of tatty looking conifers shielding the car park from the grounds of the Home, and spewing out of a hawthorn hedge, brambles and nettles, spiky caltrops of hedge-mustard, have taken over what, I guess, was once a picnic area.

I pick up an empty can from the verge. It's weeks old, its logo almost entirely worn away by the sun. Black water drips from its lip as I walk up the wide concrete steps, my reflection meeting me cautiously in two large glass doors. I knock and, without waiting for an answer, go inside.

'In a minute, Simon,' Mr Skinner calls from the office. He sounds flustered.

I walk to the side of a curved mahogany desk, drop the can into an empty bin and peer in through the open door. 'Whose car is that?'

His head appears around the side of a huge photo-copying machine. 'Accounts,' he says, scowling at a swollen brown envelope in his hand. 'Mrs Skinner's work, really.' He puffs air into his top lip and looks around the cluttered room for somewhere to put the envelope, dropping it, in the end, nonchalantly, on top of the photocopier. 'Didn't expect to see you today. Any news?'

'They found something at the copse.'

'So I hear,' he says scornfully, coming out of the office and standing behind the desk, where his attention is drawn to the doors, his weathered chin lifting contently as though expecting people to start making their way inside. When they don't, he looks down, a little sadly, and with long bony hands, veins blue and conspicuous like old rope, repos-itions a large diary, places a few pens in the drawer by his waist and inspects a half-drunk mug of tea. Printed on the mug is the same blue and green logo that hangs drearily behind him in large sun-faded lettering. The first T of TRUST is missing. Between the other letters spiders have made webs, and coating almost every surface is a layer of dust, yet despite this blatant air of neglect there remains, as always, an organic scent of wildfowl, as though it has, over the years, become ingrained in the woodwork, in the mould spreading across the ceiling, in the empty glass cabinet on the desk and the box of grey feathers by the phone; in the peeling walls, even. Framed certificates do their best to cover a patch of mildew shaped, I think, like a map of London. There is also a bleached photograph of Mr and Mrs Skinner with a Mayor of some era, taken on the steps behind me when the roof glimmered in the sun and flags caught the breeze like sails.

141

'Do you want to see how she is, then?' He scoops up a brown paper bag from the corner of the desk and takes me through a large fire door that sticks unyieldingly to a magnet attached to the wall behind it. 'Police were all over the place yesterday,' he says over his shoulder. 'Made a right mess.'

'What does the rose mean?'

He laughs deeply.

Down a long concrete corridor painted two shades of green there is the fused smell of birds and feed and dust and straw. The only sounds of wildfowl, however, are coming from beyond the glass doors at the far end, where a distorted square of sunlight lies dormant across the floor. The rooms leading off it are all empty. 'Just folk, that's all. Means nothing,' he says. 'It's got nothing to do with Charlotte running off.'

Mr Skinner waits as I kneel before an open cage, the sharp musty scent of the Bewick's Swan soaking through me like warm air, filling my nose and chest with a dry and redolent memory that takes me back to the bedroom in London I used to share with Charlotte. Lights would cut across her sleeping body, her breaths shallow and somewhere else entirely. I often used to imagine myself as a bird when I was younger, a harrier or eagle or hawk, smaller more common birds too, finches and blackstarts, pipers and martins. But mostly it was a kingfisher. At night, swathed only by the muffled sounds of London, I would have lucid dreams of soaring high in summer skies, over fields and meadows and villages, always waking to the same sour smell, my arms curled beneath me like wings. Charlotte was always a swan, white and majestic and graceful.

The morning before my seizure at Pensthorpe last summer, I had told Aunty Anne about the dream I'd had the night before.

142

'I could fly,' I tell her between mouthfuls of toast.

Aunty Anne clears away the breakfast things as I explain how I had been dipping and weaving masterfully over the tiny model-like streets of London. The river below was a long curling strip of metal. The sky was mine. There were no other birds flying, none perched together on the rooftops or sitting pensively on the wires that neatly dissected the streets below. Closing my dorsal wings, I had dropped towards the concrete, darting in and among the smartly dressed men and women as they made their way to work. I'm not sure why, but I began pecking each unsuspecting one of them on the back of the neck with my long beak. It was a glorious and serene experience, I explain to her.

Aunty Anne smiles at this.

'The people I struck just fell to the ground like puppets,' I say. 'Bodies lay everywhere.'

She smiles again, only a little more thinly this time, suggesting it wouldn't be a bad idea if we leave early for Pensthorpe as it's the Bank Holiday.

I'm standing at the edge of the wooden viewing area when it happens, when a cold gust of wind slips guilefully over the wide silvery pond, spraying tiny molecules of water across my face and dragging with it that unmistakable reek of sulphur, the silent breath of an incoming tide. I put down my binoculars, letting them hang loosely over my anorak. Fragments of day flicker in the high sun as I hold out my fingers, numb and bleary, half smiling at the strange and persistent tranquillity the aura seems to bestow on me. I squint and lean forward. My head sinks into the glistening air as though it were made of sand and I think for a moment I can actually see through it, I can see through the walls of the aura, into the black world beyond it.

Slowly it opens up, the malicious screaming of gulls and sandpipers, redshanks and buntings filling my head as white noise. Mallards and pintails bob their heads in the water, seemingly unaware of the world fast tipping over on its axis. I widen my legs and look around for Uncle Pete. The taste of copper floods into my throat. The edges of the universe are blurring, closing in. The wind rushing violently through the willow trees at the far end of the pond is making them bend and groan and shake. They lean over the twisting earth, chanting incantations, grey and lethargic, degenerate priests sending ripples through the water towards me. Ducks take flight. Swans rise in wide glimmering arcs of spray that catch the sun, hurling themselves clumsily up into the sky like great white shadows. Moorhens squeak. Rails cry. Everywhere the indiscreet and pitiless stench of sulphur pours. It's taking me. It's pulling colours apart as though they were no more than spools of thread and it's just as I'm getting myself ready to sit down on the wooden platform and curl into the recovery position that I see it. Perched on top of a half-submerged fence post is a kingfisher. It's staring at me from inside the aura. From the other side of the universe.

I can still see it now, that kingfisher, flying low across the water towards me, its long beak piercing my subconscious mind as though it were lancing bacteria under a microscope. As I blacked out, I'd seen it fluttering in the darkness. It was looking directly at me from the inside of my head, inside my own mind, a sharp viridian blue, wings blurred anemones of colour as it hovered there a moment before disappearing into the distilled depths of my brain. There are moments, still, when I can hear its thin high-pitched call coming from somewhere inside me.

*

144

The swan is curled up on a bed of straw.

'Careful,' Mr Skinner says behind me.

I breathe out and let my fingers push gently through her feathers. They are coarse and oily, in places coated with a brittle grey film that looks like a fungus. Her head is looped wanly around her neck. Not once does she move, or react to my touch. She is as still and lifeless as she was that afternoon, nearly three months ago.

Carefully I trace my finger down the scratch that follows the supple curve of her face. The skin beneath her right eye is smeared still with a pinkish stain where the vet had to stitch her. As I look up, the overhead light flickers and hisses and, as though having stepped outside from one place to another, I feel the breeze of that afternoon flowing through me.

The air is barbed and dry. I start to snap away at the helix of brambles with my fingers, drawing blood that runs across the back of my hand as a delta of external veins. What just happened there? I glance ahead to where Charlotte had been standing. We'd spoken to each other again, like we did when we were younger. Maybe that's why she left so quickly, leaving me here on the tracks alone. We'd broken our voiceless pact, our unwritten treaty to conceal at all times the extent of the bond between us.

When her neck is finally free, I stand and look down the tracks. Eight boundless steel lines waver in a glimpse of sunlight. The scents of yew and elderflower drift over the hard stones, and from somewhere I can smell wild garlic and the toxic leaves of giant hogweed.

Ahead, from the grounds of the Wildfowl Trust, the heron yaps its call.

*

'Simon,' Mr Skinner prompts me, turning off the tap and passing me a clean brown towel.

I stare at my wet hands and allow time a few short seconds to adjust itself. 'Did you know Ethel Roberts?' I say. 'She used to live in our house.'

'Let's go outside,' he says. 'Get some air.'

We sit on a wooden bench, shaded beneath a low copper beech tree, a wide kidney-shaped pond falling away from our feet. Reflected in its tinted surface, the sky and the shapeless sun look like a photographic negative of the universe. At the far end, beneath the tired lethargic limbs of a willow tree, perched on a twisted branch, is the grey heron. I take off my backpack, offer Mr Skinner a cola cube, which he declines, put one in my mouth and stare out across the pond, its fetid earthy scent drawn out from its depths by the heat of the day.

'She died,' he says eventually, looking skyward and dabbing his brow with a large faded handkerchief.

'She sent me a book,' I tell him.

Squinting, he takes a handful of feed from the brown paper bag and throws it into the water. It patters on the surface like rain, enticing towards it a small flotilla of coots and moorhens, their tiny wakes rippling behind them. He makes a grating sound in his throat and looks over his shoulder to the Old Hermitage Retirement Home. Its blackened walls are three floors high, veiled behind trees and a sea of brambles that cover a large overgrown area of land beyond a tall mesh fence. Crows and rooks bicker along the slate tiles between four stone turrets.

'How long do you think you'd survive in there?' he says. He sounds forlorn. 'They're nice enough, surely,' he adds, turning back on the bench and taking another handful of feed from the bag, 'but there's only one way out of there and that's in a box. Mrs Skinner wouldn't want that for me,

146

would she?' He pauses to think a while, the paper crinkling in his lap, before scattering the feed into the pond.

'What do you know about Glenn Gate House?' I ask.

'It burnt down,' he says, a reluctance to his voice. 'They built the Home on the same ground.' He sighs deeply. I watch his face, the sun catching in its wrinkles as he thinks. 'Nathaniel stayed here one summer,' he says. 'It was the year before all the trouble started, 1972.' He looks up to the sky as though something up there may help jog his memory. 'He was involved with a study on whether certain birds were able to communicate with each other through telepathic energy. He was into all that stuff. A bit of a hippy really. Archaeologist. You know the type.'

'My grandfather was an archaeologist.'

'Yes,' Mr Skinner says, and he throws more feed into the water.

'What happened?'

'It was the following summer. He was on a dig at Coppingford Manor.' He turns and looks at me. 'You know about that, too, I assume?'

I straighten. 'Something happened that night, didn't it?' I say. 'Before Charlie Montagu went missing. One of the archaeologists warned them something was going to happen. Was that Nathaniel Woods? I tried to look it up online but couldn't find anything.'

He rummages in the bag for more feed. 'You won't find anything on the internet,' he says roughly. 'There's nothing there. No one took him seriously, see? His book had come out, or not come out as it transpired, a few years earlier. Kicked up a bit of local fuss, even so. Got him thrown out of Cambridge too. People thought he was a bit short of it, and in a way he was.' He throws the feed dispassionately into the water. 'When Charlie was found to be missing the next morning, they assumed, naturally I suppose, that

Nathaniel had something to do with it.' He shakes the bag. 'They finished him. Accused him of being involved in a number of terrible things. Made his life a misery until a few days before Christmas, 1980 I think it was, he walked out to sea at Brancaster.'

I take the book from the backpack and hand it to him.

Mr Skinner raises a sceptical eye, hunches forward on the bench and waves it back in my direction. 'I'd hoped never to see this again,' he says, but he doesn't give it back. He studies it a while longer, turning over the first page and reading the inscription written to Ethel, having to move the book back and forth in the bright light to focus correctly. 'Ethel,' he says remorsefully and he turns another page and pulls free the feather. 'This is dangerous stuff, Simon,' he says, holding it up to the light and running his finger along its edge. 'This book has caused nothing but trouble. Give it to the police and be done with it. Charlotte will have run off somewhere, that's all. I'm sure of it. A girl like that was never going to fit in here.'

'It's been four days,' I say. 'Something's happened to her. I know it has. The police are everywhere. They know more than they're letting on.'

He hurls the last of the feed into the water. 'There are no curses, Simon,' he says darkly. 'You know that as well as I do. There is only us.'

I sit back and watch him for a moment, watch his glare harden over the book, his fingers gripping it so tightly I think he may throw it into the pond, but he doesn't. Without looking at me, he passes it back.

'Did you ever go to our house?' I ask.

A freight train passes, heckled by a crane perched at the western end of the pond.

'Cold, damp place it was,' he says. 'Mrs Skinner used to cook her something occasionally.'

'There's a painting there. Did you ever see it?'

He shades his head from the sun. 'We kept telling her to sell it, or keep it in storage at least. It's not a nice thing, is it? But it's pretty valuable, apparently. I offered to look after it for her, but she wouldn't have it. Mrs Skinner wasn't too keen to go anywhere near it either. Said it had a malevolence about it.'

'It was painted by the man who lived in Glenn Gate House,' I say, looking over my shoulder towards the grounds of the Home. 'He was part of a cult that worshipped the curse.'

Mr Skinner, too, turns at this. He looks me straight in the eye, his grey hair clumped in little tufts around his ears, his skin mottled and dry. 'Give the book to the police, Simon,' he says.

I wait for him to leave, take a long sip of water, close the lid on the bottle and place it back in my backpack, all the while looking at the pond, and the coots and the ducks and the moorhens returning to the reeds at the far end, their wakes kneading the water and making shapes like old faces pressing through the darkness below, and I think about what Grandpa used to say about having to peel back the shrines like an onion to find the King.

SIXTEEN

The moment my fingers sink into the wire fence separating the Trust from the dark grounds of the old people's home, the sound of the church bells peals across the sky. They are vibrant and loud, and clatter obtrusively in my ears as I press my face against the warm metal lattice, the acerbic bite of nettles catching in my throat, and look across the brier at what must have once been the grounds of Glenn Gate House, where Arthur Bradley and his wife and daughter died.

To my left, I can make out parts of a high wall. To my right, yew trees have bunched resolutely together and there is what appears to be an interior area of trees, no more than carcasses now, swollen with thick lesions of ivy, bramble and knotweed. I guess from their size they could have been apple or pear trees. It's hard to tell, but together they form a square enclosing what must have been a decorative lawn. A larger structure, bulbous and more robust in shape, pushes up from its centre. It, too, is smothered in ivy, dotted with hundreds of faint yellow flowers. In the far distance, like some indefinable shoreline, lies the Home itself, its edges hidden in shadow, the wreck of an old warship, teeming with ghosts and secrets.

Towering above the far corner of the Trust is an ancient horse chestnut tree. Its thousands of hand-shaped leaves appear withered and rusty with disease. An enormous wheat field lies beyond, thick and greyish-white in the hot sun, soft and inviting and so different from the dankness I feel in here, as though belonging to another place entirely, a place disconnected in every way, with a clear and definable man-made border. There's a gap in the fence where a low branch has been allowed to grow through it, discarding it to one side like a broken fingernail.

The moment I step through, the gloomy viridescent air before me shrieks with the sound of corvids. They're up on the roof of the Home and in the top branches of the trees, shaking the thin spears of sunlight propping up this wide canopy like suspension cables. I look back over my shoulder towards the Trust, to try and berth myself to something concrete, as gradually the birds settle, their cantankerous jarring replaced by the pastoral psalms of the church bells overhead, and carefully make my way over the corner of the stone wall and across the brier, my mind unable to discard thoughts of Ötzi the Iceman and how his impaired revengeful thoughts had lain where he'd died, undisturbed in the ground for all those years.

The dampness of the earth leaks through my trainers. It soaks the bottom of my jeans as, simultaneously, the sun disappears and I am standing in a graveyard in the gloomy Cambridge rain.

Beside me is Charlotte. The rain beats rhythmically onto the umbrella she holds over the two of us, gathering in its flimsy metal spines before dripping onto my shoulder. Wind bends the yew tree at our side, red berries littering the earth like spilt pins. Inside my school shoes my feet are wet and cold. I stamp on the sodden grass to try and warm them, as the church bell wails a deep lament into a saturnine sky of blacks and blues and greys that make me think an enormous wave is about to crash down onto earth from Heaven.

As Grandpa's coffin is committed, I wonder whether or not he has left any thoughts or memories of his own that may one day be exhumed and reborn into someone else. As though on cue, the priest shouts over the sound of the rain, 'We therefore commit his body to the ground; earth to earth, ashes to ashes, dust to dust; in the sure and certain hope of the Resurrection to eternal life.'

Aunty Anne falls onto Uncle Pete's shoulder and starts to cry.

Charlotte takes my hand. 'I don't want to go to Glennfield,' she says quietly, without turning her head.

Rain gushes down the green tarpaulin covering the mound of earth that will soon entomb Grandpa, one of its corners flapping vigorously in the wind. Some of the funeral party turn towards it, staring accusingly as it spits out its angry deflating breaths. I look away, across to the street framed between the high brick columns of the cemetery entrance. Cars are pressing against each other, headlights diffused, rain misting beneath them. A bus passes, spraying a huge fan of water through the railings and soaking the graves neatly lined up along the stone wall, as a young woman with a pram runs past, squealing in mock panic with her child at being caught out by such a presiding downpour.

'It'll be OK once we get up there,' I say.

'I want to be with Tom,' she says seriously, the wind quickly stealing her words away as though it doesn't want me to hear them.

Rain drips steadily onto my shoulder. The sound is terse and methodical. I look straight ahead, into the hole where

Grandpa lies, not at Charlotte even though I know she is looking at me, which is when the sky lights up without a sound, flickering like a camera flash and exposing the bright white veins and arteries that feed the universe. They curve over the town as though the most enormous cobweb, stretched and intricate, a net keeping one world safe from the other. It catches my breath.

'But what about me?' I say.

Somewhere in the distance, a horn blows. My leg twists, snarling in a thick loop of bindweed and almost knocking me over, but I manage to support myself on the large structure positioned in the centre of the trees. It's pressed against a holly bush that has grown up its side, the hard waxy leaves scratching at my fingers. The rash on my neck stings and all around me the air is seething with dust and the smell of rotten fruit. There's a bees' nest high above, but the bees haven't noticed me. I crane my neck and watch them zipping eagerly in and out, breaking the stillness with their minute vibrations that sound like distant aircraft. The structure is so overgrown I can see no stone, just a mass of ivy clutched so tightly around its frame it's as though it had long ago choked to death whatever lay beneath it. The grass is as thick as wheat. It comes up to my waist. The blades are sharp against my bare arms, entwined with thistles and dandelions and nettles nearly the height of me.

The house groans as a boiler starts up somewhere inside, spilling thin grey smoke out through the leaves of a blackened holly tree. I wait for it to settle, for it to compose itself, the smell of burnt oil drifting through the fruit trees, before starting to pull away at the ivy. The roots are, in places, as thick as my arm, but I don't give up. Despite the thrumming in my head, I pull and I tear at the boughs. The answer is here, I tell myself. Whatever the answer is, it is here.

With the sun slipping quietly west, I eventually manage to remove enough that I can see what appears to be an inscription. I wipe my face with my bare arm and rub at the letters with my fingers, picking at the stone with my fingernails and scraping away the long veins and arteries clinging to it like skin. The smell of mould and rot catches in my throat as flakes of dead vegetation and stone spit into the air. A spider races across my arm, disappearing deep into the foliage above. Soon my fingers are raw and bleeding. My skin itches, not just on my arm but all over my body, and my throat is burning. Still I carry on and it is only as I see the word develop, as though this has all been carefully scripted, that I realise the church bells have stopped ringing and not a soul in the world, except maybe Mr Skinner, knows I am here. I could have a fit right now and die and no one would find me.

As though in response to such thoughts, the taste of copper drips insidiously into my mouth and I am over-whelmed with a forceful sense of detachment. For a second the earth tilts. Distances stretch, then condense. I close my eyes and try to wait it out. There's nothing I can do anyway, not here. When eventually it recedes, I realise I've bitten my bottom lip. I spit a bright red globule of blood onto the glossy surface of an ivy leaf, watching it delicately slip off, then take a few breaths and rinse my mouth with the last drops of water from my bottle, put it back in the backpack and read the letters. 'Acheron,' I say into the falling dust. Pit of Acheron. I feel at once both terrified and strangely thrilled at seeing this. It's a quote from *Macbeth*, from Hecate.

I can't make out any of the letters beneath, although there are at least another two lines. They are blackened with mildew and pressed so tightly behind the main bole of ivy, I would need an axe to move it, but it doesn't matter because I already know what they are. I step back, exhausted, my arms hanging limply at my side, and roll my tongue over my lip, desperately trying to work out what all this means, which is when I hear the sound of a car crackling down the gravel drive of the Home.

Crows heckle from the roof, getting more and more agitated as I listen to the polite groan of Inspector Sly's BMW. The door opens and closes with a smooth clicking sound and I hear a faint crunching beneath his shoes before the front door opens and he goes inside. The birds scrape their feet across the roof tiles, cawing incessantly. They're angry. They're bellowing at me. They're shaking the trees. They're telling me I shouldn't be here, that this place belongs not to me, but to them. It's in their blood.

I manoeuvre myself back on to the path I have made, reciting over in my head the quote from Hecate.

> *And at the Pit of Acheron,*
> *Meet me i' th' morning: thither he*
> *Will come to know his destiny.*

Acheron is one of the rivers of Hell. Fear rushes into me as pure as it was all those years ago as I read of the Devil in that room with the animal wallpaper and the alphabet poster. It numbs my senses. It smothers my thoughts with its wings. This place is wrong, I think. It has an essence, a coldness, a malevolence. It belongs only to the past, to the dead and the revengeful thoughts they have left behind in the earth. Trees spin. Birds scream. Light implodes as my foot catches against something solid, something made of stone. Then they come.

Filling the bright air with a deafening rushing sound that almost topples me, a huge flock of corvids swarms:

crows and rooks and jackdaws. They deluge through the trees like black water, blocking out the light, brushing against my body and clawing at my head, shrieking and bickering, desperately trying to close any gaps with their frantic rustling of wings, until I am standing in complete darkness. I am all alone but for the screaming birds.

But I'm not alone. Dad is with me.

He's leaning over me. He's shouting, tears dripping down his nose and onto my face. 'They're coming!' he bellows. So vivid and savage is the memory, it pierces as a blade into my side. My body twists and buckles beneath him. His hands are on my shoulders. He's looking directly at me from a place I recognise only as my past.

'Hold on!' he pleads. 'For Christ's sake, Simon, hold on!'

SEVENTEEN

The police have set up some sort of crisis centre at the far end of the Green, by the gate to the church. I'm not sure how long it's been there. A crisp white gazebo has trawled in maybe two dozen villagers, each of them red faced as much from a sense of subdued excitement, I imagine, the implicit swagger of a community in disaster, as from the sun. They look at each other knowingly, unified in breed, a hand resting on an aged thigh, clutching a free bottle of water as though they've just come in from a charity walk. Children rock silently back and forth on the swings, observing with interest this chaotic yet thrilling infringement on their daily routine. Even the grass has been cut for the occasion, the thick impermeable air steeped with the green scent of jasmonates. A handful of police officers, each dressed in a short-sleeved white shirt and carrying a clipboard, gather among the villagers like the porters of an ocean liner as, hazily, I cross the Bukehorn.

The space before me is abnormally distant, glimmering and unsteady. One of the officers is standing adrift, I notice, silhouetted in the aqueous heat and this strange indistinct glow. She wipes her brow, stealing a curious glance at the sky, her shoulders dropping as though disorientated by the sheer size of it all, when at once dozens of birds, hundreds of them, detach themselves from the darkness of the trees behind me, forming a wide shadowy pall of dark matter that blocks out the light over the Green. It folds itself, stained and tattered, over the roof of the church, where one of the birds caws disdainfully, stirring others hidden in the arms of the sweet chestnut trees. For a few seconds, the air judders with the discorded barking of corvids. It consumes all other sound. Everyone stops what they are doing, even the police officers. They each look to the bellowing sky.

Everyone but Daniels. He is leaning against the lychgate, arms folded and looking keenly across the suspended activity on the Green. He spots me instantly, as though he has been waiting there all this time for me to appear. Penitently I look away to the row of houses curving the unmarked road circling the north side of the Green. They are each painted in quaint pastel colours: grey and pink and white and blue, their gardens foaming with purple bellflowers, delphiniums, lavender and bright white roses that can't quite obscure the indefatigable redolence of sulphur. It's everywhere. It's in the heat and the light and the gaps between them, staining this world as it has its own.

Terry Baldock is watching the birds from his door, purple ivy climbing vivaciously about the glimmering white bricks above him. Sometimes I see him at the Trust with Mr Skinner, rummaging through folders in the office. I think he used to be an accountant. He looks at me, sombre and cadaverous, before turning quickly towards the churchyard. Two doors down, in front of a large pink house, are a group of maybe a dozen other villagers, each doing the same thing: looking at the sky, but watching me. The bell ringers are among them. All but Gordon Proctor

158

are wearing their cream blazers. His is clutched impatiently in his arms. I should feel guilty, I suppose, that my family has broken the lucidity of their lives, dented the untarnished pith of the village itself, but I don't think I do. I feel only anger and scepticism. I don't even trust them, not any more.

In the distance I hear the helicopter. No one looks up. The heat bears down. A single chestnut leaf pirouettes cloddishly down to the pavement by my feet, the breathless air not strong enough to keep it afloat. The crows and the rooks cease their chanting, dust filling long spikes of sunlight sieving through the leaves and branches, as I hook my thumbs behind the straps of my backpack and carefully walk on. My face and head are bruised from the birds. My eyes are stinging from the ivy. Shapes and colours are misaligned, slipping from their canvases like oil, the sound of seagulls screeching from somewhere cold and dark within me.

Coming from the bus stop, lingering in the air like the strings of abandoned beach kites, each tied to the same rock, are three neat ribbons of blue-grey smoke. All three of them are in there: Mary, Finn and Ned, dark and shadowless under the high wooden roof. Panic folds around me. There are so many questions I need to ask them, but part of me doesn't want to do that. Part of me doesn't trust them either. It wants me to lower my head and walk home and sleep, let everything flow pitilessly over me, let time sort this out on its own, but I don't. I have to see this through, I tell myself. I have to find her. I'm the only one who can, and so I clear my throat and start to cross the road, which is when, once again, a sudden and overbearing sense of disconnectedness surges through me. My body disengages with my mind. There's a jackdaw picking at the ground by the edge of the bus stop just as there had been

159

before. It's a déjà vu, only I can see myself standing by the lamp post, pale grey shadows sweeping across my face as though being projected onto a screen.

The sky throbs. The air quivers and ripples, carrying with it that indomitable stench of sulphur. It's so thick I can almost see it, black smoke rolling in before the flames. It smothers me. It chokes me. It invades my lungs. It blocks out the light. The earth trembles. I feel dizzy and uncertain. Millions of molecules of air break their bonds. They scatter in the heat, scintillating as though the wings of angels, and for a moment I almost believe this is what they are, but then the world divides and in one abrupt movement, as though the strings holding me up have simply been cut free, my leg buckles and my weight slides away from beneath me.

'You OK?' It's Ned Morton. One hand is gripped tightly around my forearm.

I stand for a moment, slumped and listless in his arms, unable to support myself. His shirt smells of cigarette smoke. The road sways beneath me. I stretch my eyes as wide as they will go, letting in as much sunlight as I possibly can, I think to try and extinguish, once and for all, the shadows in my brain that conceal the aura, if indeed it is concealed in my brain at all, and not out there beyond the light. I don't know what to think anymore. The sun scorches my pupils. I feel sick, but still I glare at it, hungrily, panic sacking any sense of logical thought.

'What happened to you?' Ned says, trying to pull me away.

Blood is dripping down the side of my face.

'He's having a seizure,' Mary says seriously, and before I know it they have guided me off the road and sat me down on the wooden bench. As the brightness disappears, a cold murky compound surges into every recess in my

160

body. It's like acid in my belly. I shiver. Someone says something in a muffled and hurried voice then puts my head between my knees, which is when this dark matter – whatever it is – the antimatter of my thoughts rushes back through me out on to the pavement in an oddly sweet-smelling mess of dirty green liquid.

Mary shuffles away with a small shriek.

I groan and spit out long viscous streaks of saliva. Daylight flares.

'We need to get him home,' Mary says.

'No,' I say. Clumsily I wipe my mouth with my sleeve.

'What happened to your face, Simon?'

'Do you have any water?'

A bottle appears before me. I take off the lid, swill some round my mouth, spit out more fluid and take a huge gulp, almost finishing the bottle. I lean forward again, still not certain if I am going to have a full seizure. The light around me shimmers, and through glazed eyes I watch ants scampering in the cracks in the pavement, racing away from this sudden and unaccountable eruption, seemingly uncertain of which direction they should be heading. I pour the last of the water over the mess on the pavement, watching it run under the seat beneath me. Upturned ants kick their legs as they're carried away, the sun rapidly siphoning off the outer edges of the puddle and leaving a stain and a foul stench that almost makes me want to be sick again.

'What's going on, Simon?' Mary says, moving back beside me. She pads the side of my face with a tissue.

I close my eyes against the sting and release a long breath. My mouth tastes disgusting. 'Where is she?' I say, the words dirging from my lips. 'If you know where she is, you have to tell me.'

'We don't know,' she says. Black eyeliner has scarred both sides of her face. On her wrist is a bangle exactly like the one

I saw on Charlotte's table, with the ring attached to it by a black chain. It's so vampire-ish and infantile I almost shake my head at the banality of it, but then I remember that morning right here at the bus stop. Mary was sitting where she is now, a copy of *Macbeth* on her lap and a brown paper bag. She wasn't wearing it then. I look up.

'Did you buy Charlotte the same bangle?'

'It was a gift,' she says, clearly holding back tears.

I don't bother telling her Charlotte must have taken it off almost as soon as she got home.

She turns to Ned.

'We've told the police everything,' he says. 'We went round the back of the bell tower. That was all. Then we went home.' He pauses and frowns and studies my face. 'What happened to you?'

I ignore him. 'You didn't go to the copse?' I say.

'No,' he tells me. 'Why would we have gone there?'

'They found something, a white rose, on the stone circle. What does it mean?'

'I don't know,' he says, scrunching his lip and shaking his head.

Finn laughs from the back of the shelter. An unbending sneer digs into the corner of his face. A single quiver of black hair hangs over his eyes. The rest of his head is shaved. He's wearing a black t-shirt, black skin-tight jeans and huge boots he hasn't zipped up. It's almost inconceivable, I think, that we're the same age.

'Where do *you* think she is then, genius?'

'I don't know,' I say, trying to match his tone. I'm too tired to pretend anymore. I turn to Mary and Ned. 'She came to see me that night,' I say. 'She wanted to tell me something. If you know what it is, you have to tell me.'

Mary looks at Ned briefly. 'We don't know anything. I promise.'

I scratch the back of my head with both hands, thousands of tiny white dots still patterning the light before me. 'What do you know about the curse?' I spit again, still not looking at them, I guess as a way of retracting such a statement, making myself seem less ridiculous.

Finn cackles.

By the base of the village sign, a starling, stern and speckled in the watery heat, is staring directly at me, its sharp beak pointing like a needle, making little gurgling noises that sound impossibly distant. 'It was at the copse where the curse was invoked, wasn't it?' I say. 'Is that why there's a stone circle there? Is that why someone took a rose, on the date it was supposed to have happened?'

'It's just a story, Simon,' Ned tells me sternly. He shakes his head and releases the foundations of a laugh. 'It's got nothing to do with where she is. She's our friend. What, you think we're all part of some cult or something, that we dressed up in gowns and marched out to the copse in that storm? And then what? What are you suggesting here?'

'So where is she?'

'She went to the church,' Mary says.

The starling flies away.

'When was this?'

Her broad ingenuous face, ashen white foundation cracking over flecks of red, creases as she thinks. 'That afternoon,' she says quietly, 'when we got back from Peterborough. She'd been acting weird all day. I think she was going to pray or something.'

'That's right,' Finn says, indignation sculpting his tone. 'Charlotte went to pray.' When I glare at him, the anger inside me narrowing my eyes to a point, he laughs contemptuously. A hole in the roof of the bus stop has drawn a mark across the side of his face. 'She went to the church to pray the Naseby Horses didn't come and get her.

163

Or maybe that we didn't come and get her,' and he laughs again and calls me a prick. 'If anyone knows where she is, it's this freak,' he adds, flicking his half-smoked cigarette out onto the road.

Mary starts to cry. 'We thought she was in London. She said she wanted to be with Tom, but he hasn't seen her either, has he? We don't know anything else. We really don't. We don't know why she hasn't called. We just want her back, the same as you.'

'She went straight home,' Ned says. 'It was raining. It was about to chuck it down.'

Mary looks to the ground. 'It was supposed to protect her,' she says.

'What was?'

'The bangle.'

'From what?'

'It was just a charm, OK?' Ned says for her. 'We're all worried about her. We want her back as much as you. The whole village does.'

I don't look at him, though. I look at Mary. 'Protect her from what, Mary?'

She grits her teeth and sucks in air. 'We just want her back,' she repeats, looking up at a sudden and rhythmical knocking on the side of the shelter.

'Simon?' Daniels says, his voice rising as though he hadn't expected to find me here, even though I know he saw me earlier. He looks down. His face changes as he sees the mess on the pavement and the blood on my cheek. Quickly he moves his shoes away. 'What's happened?'

I wipe my mouth.

He offers me a hand, which I take, noticing as I do the crest on his silver ring, and, with Mary and Ned's help, I stand up and get my balance. The earth re-aligns. My face stings. My head aches. The rash below my ear feels as

164

though it's swelling, spreading down my neck like burning fat as, simultaneously, Brancaster sun blurs the air, sand folding over my bare feet, pricking the skin as though formed from needles.

Everything's numb and distant and struggling to fall into place. Fragments of light and colour and scent hang resolutely in the air, debris spiralling from one moment of time into another. Charlotte is screaming. She's nearby. She's hurt. She needs me to save her. I have to save her. Nothing else matters. I won't ever leave her, I tell myself. She knows this, for when one of us dies, the other dies. We are tied eternally. We have been all our lives, from that one little moment that belongs only to us, that first glimpse through the warm syrupy carmine light, that indubitable coalescence of our tiny unique embryonic forms, that silent vow.

Uncle Pete and Aunty Anne are calling for her, and for me. They sound frightened, and then, as though time had simply receded, Aunty Anne is standing directly in front of me, her face magnified in the heat. She's shaking my shoulders. She looks down to my bleeding hands.

'I didn't do anything,' I say.

Mary puts an arm around me. 'No one said you did,' she whispers, and as she says this, she stares across the road at a huge crow sitting on top of the stone wall curling around the corner of the main road and the Bukehorn. It's old and bedraggled, eyes like stones, and possessing such a look of distaste the both of us feel the need to turn away. 'I tried,' she says quietly before Finn ignites from the back of the shelter.

'Watch this one, Detective,' he says. 'Ask him how Charlotte got that scar on her face.'

There's a brusque pause before Ned says, as a way of distraction, 'What are they looking for at the copse?'

Daniels's mouth twitches, keen eyes set on Finn at the back of the shelter, and for a moment I think he's about to respond, but he doesn't. He turns to me and lowers his voice and says, I think with genuine concern, 'Come on, Simon, let's get you away from here, shall we?'

Without speaking, Daniels and I cross the road and head along the pavement on the east side of the village. Opposite the war memorial, I notice a group of kids leaning against the white stones of the house on the corner of Farm Lane. When they see me, they stop talking. One of them, a boy of about ten, his scattily cropped hair almost white in the sun, taps his friend on the arm and whispers something in his ear. The other boy laughs. Lying forlornly on the bottom step of the war memorial is a single white rose. I look at it accusingly, and at the boys, as though both it and they have been intentionally placed here for my benefit, the props of some forbidding dream. Beyond, the farm track has been cordoned off with a single strip of blue and white police tape.

Daniels's shoes click with an irritating precision as I try to think, try to put things in order, but it's almost impossible in this heat, and with the seemingly endless throb of the freight train passing along the tracks by Ten Mile Dyke, muffled and defiant, like a heartbeat. Mr Chaplin has removed the bed sheet. A few cuttings are still scattered on the pavement. As we pass his house, I can hear a radio in the garden and smell the orangey scent of his sweet peas. Mrs Yearsly regards me through her kitchen window, as do those villagers not gathered on the Green, standing mutely in their doorways, as do the police officers in their white shirts. Ahead, Reverend Spragg

166

swings out of the entrance to the Manor House. Respectfully he bows his head to Daniels before scurrying through the shadows of the holm oaks, his shoes tapping incessantly on the baking tarmac and making a sound like the cracking of glass.

'What happened to your face?' Daniels asks.

'I fell,' I tell him.

He supports me with his left hand and peers skyward for a long while, seemingly unaffected by the glare of the sun. 'Do you believe in God, Simon?'

I ignore him but the words don't go away. They tread water in my head as the train clatters laboriously away from us, as the heat of the sun swells within me. 'She was at the church that afternoon,' I say, 'when she got back from Peterborough with Mary.'

'So we understand. Why do you think she went there?'

'I don't know,' I say.

'She wasn't going to pray?'

'No.'

'How do you know, Simon?'

'I just do,' I tell him.

He walks on. 'What about you? Have you ever been to the church?'

'Just the once.'

'And did you go there to pray?' he asks, his tone as incredulous as it is dismissive.

Sly drives slowly past, parking outside our house. He gets out of the car and waits for us, but Daniels slows and stops by the low stone wall. He waits for the train to finally pass, then turns to me. The photographer has gone. Further along the road, past the village sign, more policemen and women are getting out of a white van. They're wearing high visibility waistcoats over their white shirts. None of them seem to be talking.

'We know she went to the church,' he says with a flat voice. 'What we don't know, yet, is what happened in the hours between her getting home and coming to see you and your parents finding you unconscious on the floor of your bedroom.' A vague little smile falls across his lips. He looks up to Charlotte's room then across to mine. The sun blazes in the windows.

When I look away from the glare, I notice a chaffinch lying dead on its back a metre or two away from where we're standing. It wasn't there when I left the house this morning. Its eyes are open, its head tilted to one side, as though admiring the thing that killed it.

EIGHTEEN

When I go inside, I see Aunty Anne sitting on the bottom stair, swaddled in an inner silence so severe it distorts the air around her, and for a brief moment the long hallway stretches and contorts and she appears no bigger than the size of my thumb, just sitting there, staring blankly into the green baize of Dad's office door.

'What's going on?' I say.

Sly and Daniels step around me, Daniels catching my eye with a sleek and deliberate sideways glance suggesting I already know what is going on.

Aunty Anne looks up as they pass. Her face is pinched and awkward. When I get to her, she stands and hugs me, wrapping her arms around my neck as though for the last time. She's trembling. Her skin is grey and cold and she's been crying. Behind me the house breathes and ticks. It feels wintry, its essence, that sallow and fusty scent of age, that air of ascendency it has held over us since we arrived, seeping into our lives as though we didn't belong here, as though we should never have come in the first place. I look to the top of the stairs, picturing the ghost of Henry Roberts among the thickening orbs of coloured light left stranded there from the glass dome. He's so clear in my mind it's as though he's really there, layered like a piece of laminate over this restless indefinable point in time. He was there that night. He could have warned me. His smile is measured, shaped with conceit, as though he knows something I never will. His skin is china-white. His lips are blue, hair combed neatly to one side. Maybe one day Charlotte will join him here, I think, reborn into these inimical shadows just as he was, that he won't anymore be so alone.

Aunty Anne flinches.

Mum is at the kitchen table, in the same chair she had been sitting in earlier. She doesn't look up when I come into the room and it occurs to me that, maybe, she hasn't once moved from that moment, anaesthetised as she is with medication as much as she is fear, and, perhaps, the stark realisation that these courteous few days of hope bequeathed to her by time have at last run their course. Uncle Pete and Dad are also there, as is the police constable. She stands as Sly ushers us all inside. He looks at Dad briefly beneath heavy foreboding brows and closes the door on the gently beating house.

'Traces of blood have been found at the copse,' he says straight away, almost relieving the tension in the room. 'There are also signs of disturbance in the soil. Our forensic team is down there now.'

In the bloated stillness that follows, time flowing as a blur between us, Mum bends over the table, clutching her face in her hands. A mug drops to the floor. It cracks on the flagstones. The silence is unbearable. Where before it was pounding like a drum in my head, it now seems clear and precise, strained to breaking point, a resonant and high-pitched distress signal capable of breaking glass. Within it, I watch as whatever obdurate pride has been keeping Mum afloat shatters inside her. Her face contorts.

Her frame contracts. Her body slumps as a long grating sound, like the sound of a metal crane buckling, courses from within her.

It fills the air.

She falls to the ground.

Uncle Pete pulls her up into his lap and holds her tightly as, stiff and juddering, as though suffering a seizure herself, she locks her jaw and groans. I watch and I listen. Beside me, Aunty Anne goes slack, releasing in the back of her throat a tiny sound of her own.

'She would never have gone out there,' I say. 'Not on her own.' My voice seems sluggish, and for a moment I'm not even sure it's strong enough to carry, but Sly nods his head, seemingly in concurrence.

He's careful with his words, finding Dad's eye before speaking, although Dad makes no response. He just sits there, gaunt, staring intently into nothing, Mum's punctured body lying inert beneath him in Uncle Pete's arms, a dead hatchling.

The police constable kneels beside her.

'There's a possibility she didn't go there willingly.'

Uncle Pete looks up. 'What are you suggesting?'

The words catch in Sly's mouth. 'It's a possibility,' he says beneath the wailing.

Uncle Pete swears. He stares up to the ceiling, his lips moving frantically as though in prayer. Behind him the light glimmers over the marble work surface. The sky, blue and depthless, presses its face against the glass in the long narrow window over the sink as the ground begins to tilt and, at last, almost as a release, as euphoric as it is terrifying, the air shatters, swirling into a vortex of colour and sound from which deluges that vulgar stench of sulphur.

Aunty Anne takes hold of my shoulder.

171

I shake her away and grip the corner table instead. From the wall calendar above, the goshawk beams at me.

'It's important you prepare yourself as a family for whatever news may now develop. Constable Witt will remain with you at all times. I'm very sorry,' he adds, his voice humble, as though veering off-script. 'Charlotte has not been seen or heard from now for four days. We have to assume other parties are involved.'

I turn away from Daniels's glare and shrug someone's arm away. Aunty Anne has laid out cushions on the table. 'They've taken her,' I say, my garbled words at once swallowed into this disordered whirlpool of sound and colour.

'Who's taken her?' someone says, but I don't know who it is. Everything's disappearing, one world vanishing as another opens up. Gulls and terns flee inland. The sky over the sea-line is as black as space, rushing towards me as a wave.

'Why don't you sit down?'

'Can't you see it?' I bellow, although the words, I suspect, have broken up in my mouth long before I even release them. 'Can't you see the Horses have taken her?'

My head crashes into the cushions. A hand loops behind my back as I half close one eye, biting into my lip as I do. Blood drips into my mouth and down the side of my chin. Pain shoots up my back. My right leg gives way. Daniels pulls nervously at his tie. I look at him gormlessly, partly in the heat and the chaos of the kitchen, partly lying on the floor in my bedroom the night Charlotte disappeared.

'Simon!' Dad screams through the darkness. His face is just inches from mine, metallic in harsh slashes of bright white lightning, his expression wild, his breaths sharp and urgent and muddied with the stench of fear. Behind him, the sky is moving in chaotic swirls of black and viridian

172

green. It twists and turns like the ocean. It spates the smell of sulphur.

'What's happening?' I scream, and without warning, my back spasms, my legs and arms twitch and dance beneath me, as though belonging to someone else, and I see before me only lines of light, a bright network of three-dimensional shapes geometrically fighting each other for position. Slowly and methodically they form a colossal grid that seems to be bending, straining at its peak, across the outer reaches of the universe, and it's as my body cracks and my bowels release, the blackness beyond pouring into me, spewing ravenously from one world to the other, that I see it, as I always do, there in the black matter, quivering and aqua blue like a distress signal, the kingfisher.

I don't know how many hours passed but the thin square of sky in the bathroom window is uncertain whether it belongs to day or night. I sit entombed in still water, infused with the artificial scent of lavender. Tortoiseshell patterns dance on the ceiling. Through the window, out in the fields, I hear Charlotte's name being called.

Aunty Anne knocks on the open door. She sits on a small wooden stool beside the bath.

'I'm sorry,' I say. 'Did you have to…?'

'It's alright,' she says.

I manoeuvre my arms over my middle. Water slurps around the back of my neck. 'How's Mum?' I say.

Aunty Anne doesn't answer. Instead, she looks across the landing into Charlotte's room. 'She always used to beat me at chess,' she says.

I ignore her. 'Aunty Anne,' I say, watching the honey-comb patterns of light on the ceiling, 'what is a curse? You know all about this stuff, don't you?'

She releases a drowsy breath. 'Come on,' she says kindly, tapping the edge of the bath. 'We're not talking about that. Not now. No one really believes in it, not even you.'

'I'm just asking,' I say. 'You not believing in something doesn't mean others don't, doesn't mean it isn't true. Isn't that what we're told, to respect people's beliefs whatever they are?'

'You're being pedantic.'

'I'm asking you what a curse is.'

She sits forward on the stool, rests her face in her hands, fingers pressed firmly into her eye sockets. 'A curse is a jinx or a hex,' she says reluctantly, 'the wishing of ill-will onto someone or something. But that's not what's happening here.' She pauses and releases her hands. She faces me. 'Listen, Simon,' she says, 'if there's anything you need to tell me, you need to do it now, OK?'

'What do you mean?'

She looks at me sternly, as she used to do in Norfolk when I was playing up, not reprimanding me, not sympathising either, just retaining me in her stare, letting time pass between us. 'If you've remembered anything from that night.'

'No,' I say. 'And does it ever work?'

'Does what work?'

'The wishing of ill-will on to someone or something. Can it have an actual affect?'

'Not as ambiguously as that, no,' she says, turning away from me on the stool, 'but if someone truly believes they are cursed, in many ways, they are already cursed.' She scrapes her teeth along her bottom lip and says slowly, as though monitoring each word, 'Hatred is the most destructive of emotions. You know that more than anyone. It can make you sad and depressed and physically ill. That is what a curse is, Simon. Nothing more than refined hatred. Now,

174

I think it's time you forgot all this, don't you? For your Mum and Dad's sake, if not for your own.'

'You heard the story when you were younger. Grandpa must have told you.'

'Yes, but that's all it was, a story.'

'What about the ghost at Polders Bridge?'

This time her sigh is impatient. 'I don't remember.'

'Yes, you do. Grandpa told me.'

She runs a finger around her jawline. 'It was just another one of his stories.'

'No, it wasn't,' I say. 'The church came to exorcise it.'

'I don't remember.'

'I do. Grandpa told me. Did he believe in the curse too? He taught archaeology at Cambridge, didn't he? And he had all those books hidden away by his desk.'

Aunty Anne narrows her eyes. Her hands drop into her lap. 'And what does that have to do with anything?'

'I don't know yet,' I tell her, 'but it does. What if a ghost is not trapped in the past at all? What if it lives in the present, only in a place we can't see?'

'Why are you talking like this?'

'She's alive,' I tell her, without turning my head, the patterns on the ceiling moving in the light. 'I know she is. I can feel her.'

Aunty Anne swallows. Tears fill her eyes, which she tries to wipe away without me seeing. 'You should get some sleep,' she says, standing up and moving to the door. 'I think we should all get some sleep.'

Back in my room I get into my pyjamas, put on my Wildlife Explorers' hooded top, swallow two Diazepam, and with dusk being dragged like an old sheet across the fields, the room thick still from the day's heat, I go to the window. The village is dark and two-dimensional. I study it a while, tired yet acutely aware of its presence, as if somehow it has changed over the course of the day, as though a slowly waking demon lies concealed among its shapes and shadows, in the bulbous delineated heads of the holm oaks in the near distance, the straight lines of the Manor House chimneys and, beyond, the sweet chestnut trees and the bell tower. At any moment now, it could unwind itself, stretching its malevolent form across the sky, and consume everything beneath it. Like remoras attached to the thick silhouette of the village, the thatched birds on the roofs of the cottages perch expectantly in the fading light, through which, far out across the fields, long nocturnal smudges of oily grey light are slowly beginning to dissipate.

I go to my desk, take out a piece of paper from the middle drawer and lay it down neatly in front of me. Next, I turn to the back of Woods's book, take a pencil and write down the names and the years of the people who have supposedly gone missing as a result of the curse; then, first looking over my shoulder to the door and the far corner of the room, I start up the laptop.

NINETEEN

The screen opens by default to my Wildlife Explorers' forum, where a thin dark green bar at the top of the window tells me I have one new message and two unread messages. I click on a little green envelope as a car drives out of the village. I don't get up to see who it is. All has turned quiet. The village is as still and dark as the fields it drifts in. They stopped calling for Charlotte some time ago. They've gone inside and left her to the night. Moonlight briefly twitches along the edge of the curtain as I read that yesterday, Rapture informed me of marsh harriers being spotted over Gedney Drove, merlins to the north of Thorney, and that a hen harrier was seen circling above Crowland Abbey, but I doubt that's true, not in June. It was most likely a kestrel. The black tips on their wings are easily mistakable. I don't reply. I rarely do, and besides, I'm not sure how good at identifying Rapture really is. Gull Girl, on the other hand, reports a sighting of a white-tailed eagle over Swaffham, which is backed up by four other names I recognise, and there is a message from The Swan Lands. He, or she, is claiming this afternoon to have seen a black kite over fields near Glennfield.

I sit back on the stool, the shock of seeing the name of the village reigniting the paranoia that has been seething in the corners of my thoughts since all this began. I've never seen a sighting of anything in the village before, never mind a black kite. They are almost extinct, sightings only really coming from Cumbria or Lancashire, and most of those are undetermined, seen from afar. But that's not the point. This is something else. It's a trap. It's not right. There is no way a black kite could have been anywhere near the village. For a start, Mr Skinner would have told me. It could have been mistaken for a juvenile harrier or the sparrowhawk Inspector Sly and I saw hovering above the house earlier, but anyone who knows anything about raptors would know the difference.

Mrs Neal's owls hoot. I go to the window and peer out into the street, but there is no one there. The village is dark, its edges already shaped with moonlight, the chimneys and the thatched birds embossed against the velvety texture of evening. Tentatively I close the curtains and go back to the desk, but almost as soon as I sit down, more letters skitter across the screen.

Your swan is dead.

I sit up and in one swift terrorised movement jolt backwards, fearful for a second that whoever this is can actually see through the screen. I watch the words disappear before me, as does the previous correspondence, and The Swan Lands signs out with a little pinging sound so harmless I question, even, whether it was ever there at all.

I push the laptop away, and with one eye set guardedly on the screen, open Woods's book and flick anxiously through the pages. The paper is coarse against my fingers. I should tell Mum and Dad really, although now is hardly the time, and what would I tell them anyway? I'm being watched by some spotter on a website? No. Even if they believed me, which they wouldn't, it would do no good. My family is in crisis. It's in mourning. It's breaking at the seams. They have more important things to be concerned about. I am being watched, I repeat over in my head, fitfully turning the pages in the light of the desk lamp. Is this a threat or is someone trying to help me? Or is it more sinister than that? I think, trying to picture what I saw today on the plinth of that statue in the old grounds of Glenn Gate House. *And at the Pit of Acheron, meet me i'th' morning: thither he will come to know his destiny.*

Nathaniel Woods never made the connection between the Hecate and Glenn Gate House or Arthur Bradley's involvement in the cult, yet he knew of its existence, claiming it was set up two hundred years before Bradley owned the house, by Richard Cromwell and the new Lord Gibbins. Three years after writing the book, he was at a dig at Coppingford Manor, warning the Montagu family that Charlie was in danger, the very night he went missing, but that isn't the thought easing itself like venom into my skin. There's another connection, a closer one, that ties Charlotte and me directly to the curse. If there is even a semblance of truth to the story, our ancestors would have been here that day. They caused this as much as Lord Montagu and John Morton and the rest of the villagers who committed this terrible act of murder. Grandpa must have known that. He was an archaeologist. He lived for the past, particularly his own. He was obsessed with history and the mysteries of the Fens. I picture the titles of the books I had found in the box by his desk: *Paradise Lost, Fenland Families, Lure of the Sinister*; those ancient coverless spines leaning down on me from the walls of his room in Cambridge. If he knew of the curse, he must also have known of the Hecate, and I'm certain now, my mind guided by some sort of newly acquired prerogative, that he knew Nathaniel Woods, that none of this has fallen on us by chance.

A freight train passes. I turn and listen to the front door opening and closing, shut the laptop, put Woods's book in

179

the bottom drawer of my desk beneath my binoculars, and get into bed. My eyelids fall like shutters. My heartbeat slows. My body sags. Sleep oozes through my veins, warm and viscous like honey. I see Charlotte standing on the roof of the beach hut. She's calling to me, the wind pulling at her hair and filling the glittery light around us with the scents of the sea and the marshes. Overhead, gulls spin through the nebulous glare of the sun.

'Are you going to save me, Simon?' she says and then she laughs, and then she's gone.

Someone nudges my shoulder.

'Simon?' It's Uncle Pete. He's shaking me, his face large and round and suspended just inches from mine. I rub my eyes and scan drowsily the digital clock. Mime artists in little fluorescent green suits tell me it's 23:48. I've only been asleep an hour, but already I'm dehydrated and damp with sweat.

'I was asleep,' I say.

'I know. Sorry. Turn on your light.' He sits on the edge of the bed, those heavy dark eyes of his drawing across the room as though uncertain where they should be. 'Listen,' he says, staring at the wall, not at me, 'finding that blood doesn't mean Charlotte is...' he retains the word in the bay of his mouth. 'You know.'

'I know,' I say.

'I was talking to some of the villagers. Apparently you're under the impression there is some sort of cult here. That they may have done something to Charlotte.'

'Don't you think it's odd someone left a rose on the stone circle at the copse where the blood was found?'

'All this is odd,' he says. 'It doesn't mean the village is against us. They're trying to help. They've been out searching for days.'

180

'What about the curse?' I say, feeling a little foolish sitting here in my pyjamas in the navy glow of night, Uncle Pete sitting on the edge of my bed as he used to do on those early visits to Norfolk, reading us stories. 'Did Grandpa ever talk to you about it? Did he ever mention the word Hecate or someone called Nathaniel Woods?'

At this Uncle Pete closes his eyes and drops his head, the contours of light from the bedside lamp drawing out the colour in his cheeks, magnifying little pockmarks of stubble nesting beneath the skin. 'That has nothing to do with what is going on here. Aunty Anne's told me what you said to her earlier.'

'I'm just asking, Uncle Pete. Did Grandpa ever talk to you about it?'

He sighs. 'He was obsessed with it,' he says eventually, his voice taut with disappointment, and he sniffs like a bull, pats his hands emphatically on his knees and gets up off the bed. 'Gordon Proctor's organising another search for tomorrow morning. They were out until late tonight. They're not giving up, Simon. No one is. They're nice people. They're not involved and they don't like the idea people think they are. There's enough suspicion floating around as it is.'

I shuffle back on the bed, pressing my spine against the headrest. 'Tell me about Grandpa,' I say.

Uncle Pete crooks his neck. 'I don't know a great deal about it,' he says, 'only that towards the end he wouldn't talk about anything else. Sent Anne mad, he did, dug out all his old books, bought new ones, filled every moment looking into it, but he found nothing, of course.'

'Why didn't anyone tell me this before?'

Uncle Pete coats his words with more nervous laughter. 'Because it's ridiculous. That's why. There isn't a curse. There aren't any curses. You know that as well as I do. He was losing it towards the end, talking about all sorts of stuff, ranting mainly. As far as I could make out from his notes, he found no evidence there was even a coach held up here, but that didn't stop him. He wrote pages and pages of the stuff. It was insane.' He locks his fingers together and pulls them over the back of his neck like a brace.

'Where is all this stuff now?'

He shrugs. 'I don't know. I don't have it.'

'There was a box by his desk in Cambridge,' I say. 'Was that it? Because if it was it should have gone to London. I wrote on it specially.'

'I don't know, Simon,' he says.

'And what about Nathaniel Woods? Have you ever heard that name before?'

Once again, he shakes his head. I watch him walk to the bookshelf, then to the window, peering curiously through the curtains, before going over to the desk, where he squints harshly and turns over various notebooks as though looking for something in particular.

The bird clock flickers to 23:51.

'Uncle Pete?' I prompt him.

'I found a letter,' he says and he picks up one of my notebooks and holds it to the light, but I don't think he can see any of the words, and after a few seconds, he drops it back down and starts looking around the desk for a switch, knocking over my pot of pencils as he does. They scatter noisily across the wooden surface. 'Where's the switch?'

'On the base of the lamp. Right in front of you. What was in the letter, Uncle Pete?'

'It was written in the sixties,' he says, clearly dismayed at already having allowed himself to tell me this much. 'It was from this Nathaniel Woods to Grandpa. I found it in one of his books before he died. It was in that box. I don't know where it is now. It doesn't matter.'

182

'What did it say?'

'He accused Grandpa of not supporting him. He'd written a book about the curse and was hoping he could help get it published through the college.'

'But he didn't?'

'No.'

'You've been lying to me. All of you.'

'We haven't been lying to you, Simon,' he says sternly, his shadow distending on the wall behind him. 'We've been trying to find Charlotte,' and as though he had just repri-manded himself, not me, he drops his head in his hand and swears under his breath. 'I'm sorry,' he says. 'I didn't mean it like that. God! I can't believe all this is happening.'

I watch him a while longer, his head moving indiscrimi-nately from side to side, his breaths amplified in the stillness, and when eventually he looks up, he says, his voice distant, as though fearful of his own thoughts, 'That day on the beach, when we found Charlotte. Do you remember?'

I don't answer this. I'm not entirely sure he is expecting me to. I'm not even sure what he's talking about or why he's using that tone, as though he doesn't know who I am anymore. That day on the beach has nothing to do with this. His mind's been tampered with, corrupted by fear, by the house itself. Everyone's breaking. It's beating us, breathing its maligned pneuma into the shadows. Still, I see her standing on the apex of the beach hut, the most extraordi-nary blue sky behind her. It's sparkling with heat, radiant and indeterminable, its edges soft and hazy and melting like ice into the universe beyond. Salt air plays on my tongue. There's a hint of burning tar and marram grass in the breeze. Seagulls flicker through the glossy surface of light.

'You were standing right beside her,' Uncle Pete says. 'You were holding the wire in your hands. Your fingers were cut to shreds.'

The light changes. Charlotte laughs, then waves and leaps into the sky.

'I heard her screaming,' I tell him. 'I went to her.'

'But you didn't call for help, not even when we were shouting for you.'

'No,' I say.

Uncle Pete looks at me for a few seconds. 'Why not?' he says.

'I don't remember,' I say, tears filling my eyes. 'Time disappeared. I didn't hurt her, Uncle Pete. I'd never hurt her. I was trying to untangle the wire. It was all around her neck. She was just lying there, not moving. I thought she was dead, but she wasn't. She wasn't dead. She was breathing. I could feel her heartbeat in my hand.'

'I'm sorry,' he says, the words breaking in his throat. 'I know that. I shouldn't have brought it up. We're all confused. We're not thinking straight. None of us are,' and he lowers his head and pinches tightly the bridge of his nose.

'Uncle Pete?' I say.

'No,' he says firmly, and he turns off the lamp. 'I don't think that at all, and neither do you.'

After that, I don't sleep. I listen to the rhythmic goading of the ash tree, its fingernails scraping with a measured slowness back and forth against the roof tiles as though belonging to some shadowy old witch. Part of me, I guess, must be dreaming for I imagine her peering into the windows of a crudely designed dolls' house. It's this house, the Old Abbey, as it was the day we arrived, cold and guarded, Grandpa's mantelpiece clock our only contribution to its solemn decor, its green walls and broken windows, its foul smell. I stand at the window in the darkness and stare across the moonlit fields and the thousands of stars peeking through the vastness of night and, watched by the witch of my dream, I think about death; not mine or Charlotte's, but of death itself, the waste not of life, but of all those memories gathered, all those millions of moments of colour and sound and smell that our subconscious minds so blithely retain.

Occasionally Mrs Neal's owls hoot or a sudden gasp of wind, steered off course from somewhere far from here, thuds into the wooden board sealing up the fireplace, but other than that we are completely alone. We are adrift and helpless in our leaking vessel. All night the stairs creak. The still breath of the village laps against the hull. The house offers its musty scent as people tiptoe uncertainly on the landing and up and down the long corridor dimly lit by the wall lamps, trying not to wake me. It's best, I guess they're thinking, not to wake me. No one is sleeping tonight, though. Sleeping is giving in. It's admitting Charlotte is dead, that they have failed in the one simple task bestowed on them by life, so they wander aimlessly about these moonlit decks, avoiding each other where possible, or sometimes, I imagine, sitting silently, as one, around the kitchen table, exposed in the harsh electric light as to who they really are. Mum occasionally cries.

Laboriously the mantelpiece clock winches forward another day until, at some indefinable time later, a flat grainy light seeps across my ceiling, and thrushes and blackbirds begin to flute to each other in little repetitive calls that it is safe to come out of their nests, that darkness has passed.

DAY FIVE

188

TWENTY

Just before five o'clock I go to the bathroom. In the mirror I study the cuts and bruises chased into the surface of my skin. Still, I am uncertain of exactly what happened in the grounds of the Home yesterday. My right eye is bloodshot, the brow swollen. My forehead is scratched and the rash on my neck has come out in a scree of blisters that's beginning to look more like a burn. I brush my teeth, floss, brush my teeth again, shower, put on a clean pair of jeans, a long-sleeved beige shirt, buttoning the sleeves at the wrists, and open my curtains. The moon, white and distanceless, its marbled texture as vivid as a stain, hangs in a cerulean blue sky above a single star, both millions of miles away yet seemingly in reach of each other, and me. They look lost, left behind, where others have turned and made their way home, and I wonder if this could be my last day here.

'You're dressed,' Mum says at the door.

Lightheaded from lack of sleep and food and the obscene amounts of medication I seem to have been taking since I returned from hospital, I watch as she walks across the room. She stands directly beside me, closer than we normally allow.

She's in her pyjamas, her red cardigan unbuttoned and fraying still at the sleeve. Her feet are bare, the bones pushing against the skin like beach groynes. 'It's beautiful, really, isn't it?' she says, her reflection meeting her at the window. She waits a moment, allowing time to cushion the air around us. 'There's going to be a church service tomorrow. You can wear the suit I bought you for Grandpa's funeral. It's hanging up in your wardrobe.' Her voice is sedate and absent, and yet there lies in her expression a trace of animosity, as though part of her is challenging me to respond.

I step away. Her hair is matted, the light picking out thin wires of grey. That terse pragmatic shell of hers, the husk that contained the person Grandpa and Aunty Anne and possibly even Dad knew, that Charlotte and I never did, has started to dry and crack, and I can't help think that all that has gone on before, the unbidden detour to her perfectly planned future, has been my fault, that I have marshalled her to this place, to this tragedy. I close my eyes and breathe in her scent: sweat and dead skin and unwashed hair, all things untampered with, all things belonging not to the person standing beside me, and I try to bring to the surface a memory of the two of us before the fits began, but if it's there it doesn't reveal itself.

'She's going to be OK,' I say.

Her smile is forced. 'And have you remembered anything?'

'Like what?'

She straightens and releases a contentious little puff of air. 'About what happened between when she came to see you and when we found you?'

'You know what happened,' I tell her.

She walks away, over to my bedside table, where she opens the drawer and takes out the bottle of pills. She holds them up to the light. 'You've been taking these?' she asks.

'Of course.'

She shakes them and looks me directly in the eye.

'Why would I not do that?'

'I'm not sure,' she says. 'I'm not sure I know why you don't do a lot of things. And did you take them that night?' When I don't answer she shakes them again, a little louder this time, as though to make a point, and puts them back in the drawer, her eyes never once leaving mine. 'Why don't you go back to bed for a few hours? You look terrible. The television people will be here soon anyway. Probably best to keep out of their way.'

'I had a grand mal. I could have died.'

'But you didn't, did you?' she says so quietly it's almost as though she wants me only to hear the reflection of the words, not the words themselves, as though I am supposed to think it was something I'd imagined, made up myself, and as its meaning begins to thread its way pitilessly through my thoughts, she smiles as though nothing has happened. 'And I'd better make myself vaguely presentable too,' she says with a little laugh. 'What do you think?'

I watch her, hardly able to comprehend what I think I just heard, if indeed I did hear it. Of course I took my medication. Why would I not do that? It would literally kill me not to, and she can't possibly be thinking I did anything to Charlotte. It's perverse; and yet the intensity of her glare, as malicious as it is seemingly maternal, tells me that deep down she does, that she will always hold these little sideways glances for longer than required. She will always be watching me.

'I don't know what happened that night,' I say. I'm almost weeping now. 'I don't know where those hours went. The bell wasn't rung at one o'clock, so whatever it was I thought I heard could have been just before the fit, or before she even came to see me. That's all I know. She came to see me. She wanted to tell me something, but Dad came in and sent her to her room, then everything went black.'

Her lips pinch.

'Mum,' I say, 'you have to believe me.' I step towards her, but she doesn't react. She just stands there, waiting for me to come to her. When eventually I do, I press my head against her chest, feeling the coarse fabric of the cardigan against my skin, the sharp dry scent of stale cigarette smoke reaching like tendrils into my lungs. I put my arms around her as I think I used to when I was younger, only those memories are lost now. Maybe they were never there. Maybe I'm inventing them, extracting them from a photograph or a film I may have seen, from something that happened to someone else, and I start to cry, in the hope that she will fold her arms around me and we can mourn together. But she doesn't. She pats the top of my head, takes my hands in hers and releases my grip.

'Why don't you get yourself back to bed?' she says.

Despite Uncle Pete's erratic movements, there is an odd stillness to the kitchen. Everything feels stifled and remote. Everything feels denser than it really is. The kettle clicks. Aunty Anne, her back set to Dad and Uncle Pete and Constable Witt, her fingers shaking, timidly begins to make coffee.

I put my backpack down on the floor by the corner table and go over to help, finding a jug from the overhead cupboard beside her, then going to the fridge to get the milk. 'Why didn't you tell me about Grandpa researching the curse?' I say, my voice flexed, more resentful than I intended.

She doesn't answer. She tightens her jaw against a swell of tears and stares out of the long narrow window, through the swollen branches of the ash tree. Three or four lupin petals, I notice, have fallen from their stem onto the work surface. They glimmer like beach shells.

'What is everyone hiding?'

'No one's hiding anything,' she says. 'Grandpa started looking into it. That's all. It doesn't mean anything. He didn't find anything because there was nothing to find.' She stirs the coffee.

'Why haven't you told the police any of this?'

'What would be the point?' she replies tightly. 'They're out there trying to find her, trying to find out what's happened. We can't burden them with silly things like this.' The spoon clinks against the glass of the cafetière. She closes her eyes and draws in a breath. Still she doesn't look directly at me. No one is looking directly at me anymore, apart from Mum, afraid, perhaps, they may see something they won't recognise.

'So why did you tell me that stuff last night, about curses being the wishing of ill will on to someone or something?'

She bites her lips.

'Is everything OK?' Uncle Pete says.

Aunty Anne carefully lays the spoon down on the work surface. With a little squeaking sound, as though an old door is being forced open inside her, she quietly begins to cry. Uncle Pete pulls her under his arm. He kisses the top of her head as I go to the cupboard, take out five mugs, and place them on the kitchen table.

'Dad, can I speak to you in your office?'

He doesn't reply. He waits in the silence, in his own thoughts. Outside, in the still leaves of the ash tree, a pair of juvenile blackbirds are eagerly whistling to each other.

Eventually Constable Witt speaks. 'Go on, David,' she says in a quiet voice. Her white shirt is so clean it's almost incandescent, the silver numbers on her epaulettes gleaming like medals. Her scent is both faint and obtrusive.

Dad continues to look at the table, legs juddering up and down like pistons, his fingers laid flat on the wooden surface. He's so deep in concentration, I'm not sure he even knows I'm here, never mind if he heard what I said. Part of him is waiting now, I guess, for the news that will eventually break him. His breaths are shaky and erratic. 'If you like,' he says.

Dad sits in the chair by his desk. The office is cold, the morning light pressing through the diamond-shaped panels in the arched window illuminating a venous pattern across the chipped stonework, the marked wooden floor and the oak shelves full of books. It's the smallest room in the house, frowsty and ancient, unwoken by time. Whenever I'm in here, I feel as though I am standing in the core of the abbey, in the very organ that manufactures its silent watchfulness. His face is drawn and ravaged, eyes set so far back in his head they look bruised. Something's changed inside him. Fear is slowly mutating into grief, possibly even vengeance. He looks as he did last summer after his business collapsed. He smells the same too, unwashed and mawkish. To the left of the desk, hanging over long-faded floral wallpaper, is a framed photograph of me and Charlotte. It was taken on a failed walking holiday in Cornwall a couple of years ago. We're huddled stoically against the rain, the wind snapping at our flailing cagoules. We're making faces, although I don't remember why. Mum had stayed at the hotel that day.

A narrow rug, old and bleached from the sun, runs beneath my feet under the desk. The reds are now pink, the blues grey.

Without really seeming to think, Dad picks up some loose papers from the desk, shuffles them noisily into a pile and sets them down again beside a copy of the village magazine. The Three Sheaves Bell Ringers are on the front cover, smiling imperiously in their cream blazers, the bell tower inclining lazily behind them.

I shuffle back on the rug.

He breathes out, composing himself, nodding his head methodically. 'Whatever you want to say to me, you can.'

'Are these Grandpa's books?' I ask, turning my head and examining the shelves. I recognise some of the titles. Their spines are frayed at the edges, their colours faded, the titles embossed in gold and green and yellow: *The Birth of Modern Britain, The Archaeology of Britain, Isles of the Many Gods, British Archaeology*. They are not in any order, as Grandpa had them, but mixed up with encyclopaedias, dictionaries, thesauruses and hundreds of novels both old and new.

'Simon,' Dad says, reeling back my attention.

'Did these come from Cambridge?' I say.

'I guess so. Tell me what you remember.'

'Where's the rest of his stuff?'

'It went to a charity shop, I think.'

'There was a box full of his notes labelled for London.'

'I don't know,' he says irritably. 'They're in the attic possibly. Now tell me what you remember, please.'

'I was awake when she came home,' I say, almost by rote. 'You were arguing about something in the kitchen.'

He picks up a pencil from the desk and swivels it around the top of his fingers. He did this when we were younger, I think to impress us. I wasn't sure it was something he still did. 'And then she came to see you,' he says.

'She wanted to tell me something.'

'What was it?'

195

'I don't know. You came in and told her to go to her room.'

He nods astutely. 'And then what?'

'I don't know,' I tell him. 'That's just it.'

He closes his eyes. 'It's OK,' he says as calmly as he can. 'Take your time. You're not in any trouble.'

My eyes steer back to the books on the bookshelf. They flicker between two times, one here with Dad in this cold stone office with Charlotte missing, one with Grandpa in the mildewed smell of his living room, the last time I ever saw him, his eyes worn and milky, trying to tell me something his mouth wouldn't allow.

'I think I knew something bad was going to happen even then,' I say.

'Something bad?'

Grandpa disappears into the light.

'My seizure,' I tell him.

The pencil pivots back and forth in Dad's fingers. 'But you didn't come and get help?'

'I was frightened.'

'Because she had frightened you?' When I don't answer, his other hand runs over the soil-brown surface of the desk, as though wiping away dust, but I know it's to settle himself. He breathes in, holding the air in his lungs a little longer than he needs to, and says, firmly this time, 'Simon, did she frighten you?'

I shake my head vigorously, almost childlike, fear expunging whatever resolve I thought I had conjured within me. 'No,' I say. 'She would never frighten me.'

'And after that you went straight to sleep. Is that right?'

I look to the floor. 'Yes,' I say.

He exhales and says, carefully, trying to administer a sense of evenness to his words, 'And the next thing you remember is being in hospital?'

196

I nod my head. I'm struggling for breaths now. The air is damp and sticky, the light dark and red from a strip of stained glass bent across the top of the window. 'You didn't find me until two o'clock in the morning,' I say. 'I thought I heard the church bell, but I couldn't have done, which means she could have been taken anytime between you sending her to bed and finding me.'

'Been taken?'

'She's not the first, Dad,' I say. 'Other people have gone missing, all on the same date. Do you remember Holly Thompson from the news? She lived near here. She also went missing on the thirteenth of June, and there was a boy called Charlie Montagu in nineteen seventy-three.'

He screws up his face, I guess as a way of disguising the actual thoughts invading his mind.

With a trembling hand I pass him the folded-up sheet of paper with the names of the missing children.

'What are these?' he says, taking it off me.

'You know what they are,' I say and look away, up into the corner of the room, noticing a fly caught in a web stretched across the top of the window. I squint against the light, imagining the thin grey lines of the web as coronary vessels, that I'm trapped inside some giant eye, looking out. They move gently against the glass, although I can't be sure whether this is caused by the wind coming through a gap in the lead, or if the fly is still alive.

Out in the hallway, a door opens. I look over my shoulder then back up to the fly as Dad opens a page on his computer.

'Are these real people?' he says, and I realise I haven't even checked this. I've only looked up Charlie Montagu. Woods could easily have made them up or simply taken random names of missing children. Something cold and acidic wraps itself around my stomach as a white page

197

appears on Dad's computer screen, the irritation in his face watermarked over the words being vehemently typed into the search engine. When he hits the return key, a scratched black and white photograph of a young girl, ten or eleven years old, forms out of the glaring whiteness. Before I have a chance to read any of the print beneath it, Dad types in another name. A picture of a girl appears, around fifteen years old this time, with blonde hair tied in plaits and huge crystal-blue eyes. She, too, disappears as Dad's fingers blatter down on the keyboard.

I can hear his breathing getting louder. I can see his head, his jaw locked and shaped like the bow of a ship, eyes set forward as another girl materialises on the screen. She's possibly thirteen years old. MISSING appears in bright red text above her dumpy face, then she's gone, replaced by a boy of about nine, but before I get a chance to really gauge him, he is supplanted by another, then another, photofits of children I have never met and will never meet.

Dad sniffs and wipes his eyes, his fingers continuing to hammer into the keyboard as though he's trying to hurt it, as though every face revealed on the screen is another thread of his soul being steadily unwound from his body.

'Dad, please,' I say, stepping forward. 'I didn't check them. I'm sorry. They may not mean anything.' I think about putting my hand on his shoulder, but he shrugs me away before I even get a chance, his wrist flapping behind him and making a wave through the dust.

'These are people's children, Simon,' he says, openly crying now. He taps more faces on to the screen. 'Do you understand? You can't do this shit. This isn't one of your stupid dreams. This is real. She's missing. She's actually missing. My baby girl is missing.' He almost chokes on the words. His eyes flare, red and fierce, and as though to stop himself from saying anything else, he cups his face in his hands and looks at me through the top of his eyes.

My mouth opens but the words don't come. I feel sick. Each mote of dust wafting through the harsh vermilion light seems bright and defined. I step back, half closing one eye as the corners of the room pulse and thicken, swallowing the edges of the web and the fly. 'Of all the species of bird on this planet, the Bewick's Swan *Cygnus columbianus bewickii* must be one of the most appealing. It starts with an unfair advantage over many other species simply by being one of the swans, birds whose grace and pure beauty has been the subject of legends and fairy tales since the dawn of time.'

'Simon,' Dad snaps through his fingers, 'stop that. Please. I need to think.' He exhales and focuses.

'Are you going to show it to the police?'

'I don't know. You should have told me this before.'

'I tried.'

'No, you didn't,' he says. He glares at me, breathing erratically, unable, it appears, to rip his glance away, even if he wanted to, and then he says darkly, 'What else are you not telling me, Simon?'

The words hit me like a club. Time shifts. Everything becomes slow and thick and torpid. I feel cold and childlike, and for a moment I'm standing in the bathroom in our house in London, entombed in bright electric light. I'm staring into the mirror over the bath at a boy of about twelve. He, too, is crying. My pyjamas are soaking wet. My legs sting and my mouth has dropped awkwardly to one side and tastes of sick. Beyond the door, just a few feet away, but what feels to me as distant as another universe, everything is black and silent. It is a place far removed from this floating box of light, a place where, even when eventually lit by the breath of morning, I know I will never really belong, a place that belongs only to Dad and Mum and Charlotte.

Dad folds up the sheet of paper, stands and, concentrating hard, his trembling fingers betraying him, making him fight against his own instincts, places it in the top pocket of his shirt. The gauzy red light reflects on his temple where he has started to sweat. He stares but he doesn't speak, tears streaming freely down his face, and I see him not as Dad, but as a reflection of Dad, the stranger who occupied his space before I was born; as a child, frightened and exposed for the first time to the realities of his previously guarded world, the distending shadow of something inside that, until this moment, has lain dormant within him.

TWENTY-ONE

The heat hits me like a wall. The sun has blanched the air almost to white, giving it the same soapy texture that until now I have only known in the aura, or in dreams. Through the haze I see Mr Scott standing outside Mrs Neal's front gate. Jet is sitting obediently by his feet, as black as oil. I cup my eyes with my left hand and half wave. He doesn't wave back. He just stares at me, curiously, as though he's never seen me before, and so, head down, thumbs hooked behind the straps of my backpack, I walk through the delicate web of shadows cast beneath the cherry and almond trees. The scent of wheat is so robust there's almost no air to breathe. It burns the back of my throat, and yet, weaved within its fabric, as always, lies that faintest lick of sulphur, as though it's waiting there on the other side of the sky, waiting to push its way through.

At the edge of the village, standing in the middle of the road, their clean white shirts already gleaming in the light and the heat, are two police officers. The photographer isn't there. I turn away and, with a furtive glance, see Emma up in her bedroom window. She's speaking on the phone, staring out over the chimneys of the Manor House, her hair a damp tangle of lemony gold. She seems intent. I feel the faintest of tremors in my chest as her head drops, but I don't think she sees me. If she does, she doesn't register it.

Three doors down the violin is still being played.

As I cross the road, I glance up at the pub sign, the red Apothecary's Rose similar, according to Woods, to the rose encrusted with rubies on the chest of gold meant for Naseby that day. I try not to think about the connection too much and look over my shoulder instead, back towards our house, a place I vaguely know. It seems distant, as though on another shore. Mrs Neal is standing beside Mr Scott. They're both looking at me. Through the blaze of the day, a shiny black Range Rover emerges, as though spawned from a mirage. The windscreen glares. I watch it turn into the open driveway of the Manor House, crows and rooks cawing dutifully from the bloated bellies of the holm oaks.

'No news then?' Fred, the landlord, says. He crooks his neck and wipes his forearm, a sodden beer towel drooped like a flap of rotten skin in his fat stubby fingers. 'Terrible business,' he adds, and he stares at me, eyes narrowed expectantly, as though it is customary, whatever circumstances may have fallen on a fellow villager, that they answer.

I try to walk on.

'It's Simon, isn't it?' he says after me, his pitch rising. 'She was in here that night. The police know all this, of course.' His voice is low and steady. There's a long pause. The Trust's heron calls into the empty sky. Its cry is sharp and vexed and seems to ricochet across the surface of the sky as a scream. It sounds almost human. The violin stops. To my left a window opens, pivoting the sun directly into my eyes. I squint.

'Only, we was wondering why she went down to the copse after. And in that storm too.'

I don't answer. He's testing me. I can see it in his eyes, and in the coarse lure of his smile.

'Your uncle was in here last night,' he continues. 'People are saying you think we might all be involved in this somehow, that we're part of some cult. Is that right?'

I let my arm drop to my side.

'They tell me you're a bit funny up here, see,' he says, tapping his head, and then, as if to revoke his comment, or enhance it maybe, I can't tell, so plain is his expression, he releases a little laugh from the corner of his mouth.

I breathe in through my nose.

'We're doing all we can to help,' he says, narrowing his eyes once again, thick sweaty brows collapsing like dunes from his forehead, and he turns slowly away, looks up to the sky and lets out an exasperated breath. 'I wouldn't be out here too long, if I were you.'

I step forward, defiance simmering in my veins. Fred is a mere silhouette against the glare. 'Can I ask you a question?' I say. 'Why were people even looking there? Why would they go to the copse in the first place?' I look back up to the sign, picturing the same rose on the chest of gold from that night, rain hammering violently into its wooden surface amidst the chaos of the storm and the stench of rotten earth. 'It's an odd place to look, don't you think?'

Fred follows my gaze. 'Not out here, it's not,' he says, screwing up his eyes as he, once more, peers skyward. 'Now you look after yourself. Best stay out of this heat, if I were you, boy of your condition.'

I walk on, my pace quickening, my trainers squelching on the hot tarmac, until I get to the corner of Farm Lane, where Mary Murphy lives. The stones of her house have been painted white. Red ivy climbs up the side of one wall. I look up, straining my eyes against the sun. There's a thatched pheasant on the apex of her roof. It's stiff and proud and staring at the church.

In one of the ground floor windows there is an A4 size

poster of Charlotte. MISSING it says beneath her in bright red capital letters. She's in her school uniform, her face turned away from the camera to hide the scar. She would have hated us using it. It should horrify me, really, seeing her picture like this over that incurable word, but it doesn't. The girl in the photograph isn't Charlotte. The girl in the photograph has been stripped of all those provocative little nuances that only I knew. The girl in the photograph is missing. Charlotte is still here. I can feel her.

I cross the lane without looking and stand at the base of the war memorial, craning my neck. It is nothing more, really, than a stone obelisk. Its edges are rough. At its peak is a crude engraving of the village crest, three sheaves of wheat bundled together with twine.

The church bell chimes, sending a faint convulsion through the village that rattles inside me like a memory. I soon found a routine here, out of London. Mum and Dad were right. A change was needed, and each evening, as compliantly April fell into May, Charlotte and I, as well as Mary, Ned and Finn, got off the little green bus that took us to and from school in Spalding and went with a self-appointed unspoken understanding our separate ways, me to the Trust, the others somewhere else. Charlotte never told me where. I had the feeling I wasn't supposed to know. Somewhere in the direction of the church, anyway.

Charlotte sat with me on the bus, though. She made sure of it, her in the aisle, me in the window seat, the faint margins of her dark unremitting mien distending just enough to cover the both of us, and when, a few weeks ago now, the lagging sun blurring the windows of the bus, she nudged me in the ribs with her elbow, I felt for a moment as though we were back where we started, wide-eyed and featureless and staring at each other in the same carmine light that coloured our dawning.

'It's all so fake,' she says. 'Don't you think?'

I don't answer. Instead, I look down to her hands, thin and nearing skeletal, her metacarpals resembling the outstretched claws of a kestrel or hawk.

When she sees me looking, she pulls down her sleeves. 'Everything's so clean, so perfect,' she says. 'It's not real.'

But it is real, I think, turning my head to the glass. It is more real than she can ever imagine. It was the city that was fake. The air has taken on a greyish quality, the clouds, dirty and streaked, appearing low on the horizon and making me think of the early morning gutters of London after they had been washed down with a foamy disinfectant. I can smell them too, from somewhere near the back of the bus. Over our heads, a few miles out of Spalding, step columns of huge metal pylons, tapering south in long straight lines. I think of them, though, not as pylons, but as iron robots returning from some interplanetary battle. Mist stirs about their feet. In the far distance, I see the clouds, soaked by the red sun, as the fire and the smoke of the burning city they have left behind. They make me think of the wreck at Brancaster and I find myself moving even further back in time, a sudden revelation brought to the surface by my subconscious mind and laid out like a strip of film over the present.

Sand is skimming across the surface of the beach, sharp like needles that sting my arms and face. The sea reeks of dead fish. It's wild and glutinous, lashing out with its swollen fingers at the aerial mast poking up from its belly. Gulls wheel above.

'She's the SS Vina,' Grandpa tells me over the roar of the wind. His eyes are screwed up tight, his head down. 'She was a nineteenth century coaster. Spent most of her life shipping trade across the Baltic. Had her day really until, with the threat of invasion, they filled her with explosives and anchored her at Gorleston as a blocking ship.' He lifts his head to admire her in the waves, grunts and laughs. 'In the end she was bought by The Ministry of War, towed out here and used as target practice by the RAF.'

I nod, feeling about in my anorak pocket for the marble I'd put in there earlier, looking to the sky and opening my mouth to the salty air and sulphuric stench of the sea, and I'm struck quite suddenly with its immense sense of scale. So vertiginous is its scope, I nearly stumble. Grandpa supports me by the elbow. He asks if I'm feeling alright. Daubed across the sky's pale blue surface is a vast and motionless tulle of silvery grey clouds, demarcating one world from another. Its underside sparkles and I think, beyond all I've been told by the people around me, none of this can be that simple, none of this can be as rudimentary as a shard of molten rock spinning uncontrollably through space. If it is, I think, the wind howling through me and making my eyes water, if the universe truly is random, why does it visit me so often, why does it consistently feel the need to let me in?

Overwhelmed with sadness, I squash up my raincoat into a pillow and rest my head against the window of the bus. By the side of the road, a magpie picks at the corpse of another magpie.

'Are you OK?' Charlotte asks. 'Do you need me to stop the bus?'

'I'm alright,' I say. 'I was just thinking.'

She sniffs fondly. 'What were you thinking?'

'About Grandpa.'

She pats my knee and says plainly, 'If I ever left here, would you be alright, do you think?'

I don't answer. A sickness as dense as grief slinks into my belly.

She doesn't say anything else until we have got off the bus. When the others ask if she is going with them, she is silent briefly, then tells them she doesn't want to, she wants to go home with me and it's as we are walking beneath the gently moving branches of the cherry and almond trees, petals lying scattered on the pavement like broken glass, that she stops and looks at me. She seems frightened all of a sudden. The village is deserted, as are the fields beyond. There isn't a sound to be heard beyond the distant breaking of thunder.

'I can't stay here much longer, Simon,' she says, those mournful eyes of hers lifting to the low mottled sky. It flashes. A crude untreated silence falls between us. 'It's this place, it isn't right.'

Daylight surges into me. Charlotte's image splinters into bright red blurs that sink back into the darkness like drying puddles of blood. What did Fred mean by that? That the copse is the only place to hide out in the open fields, or that he knows it's connected to the story of the curse? My vision is muzzy, its edges soft and curved as though being observed through a fish-eye lens. I blink and try to focus on the memorial. A single rose, snow white, its delicate petals sagging like cloth, lies on the bottom step of the memorial. The grass surrounding it is yellow and dry. There are a dozen names engraved on each side, some of which I recognise from the back of the book, but not enough to offer anything more than coincidence.

I turn, fearful I am being watched, but there is no one there. There is only the indomitable glare of the sun, and the heat, and the stark disdainful sound of crows and rooks calling from the roof of the church before me.

TWENTY-TWO

A small overgrown footpath leads from Farm Lane to the back of the churchyard. Brimming with swollen clumps of ivy, bramble and elder, it's hard to get through in places without side stepping. Nettles pick at my ankles, thistles scratch my arms. Filling the narrow space is an overriding smell of hawthorn. It's so thick I can almost sense it closing in. I feel oddly safe here, though, disconnected from the village, and as I walk, part of me expects to be stepping out not into a graveyard, but the wide-open stretches of beach at Brancaster, binoculars clenched in my palms, gulls quivering high in the grey light, Scolt Head a blurred strip in the distance.

On my left, the Burtons' farmhouse and yard are hidden behind a high matted screen of yew and birch trees through which I can hear Charlotte's name being called. There's an almost relaxed note to their voices now, as though they are searching for nothing more than a lost dog. On the other side of the path, the Cowleys' garden releases into the tart bite of hawthorn the scents of honeysuckle and white viburnum. Clumps of campanula cling to the top of the wall. Insects scrawl through the haze. Splayed like a firework, a single almond tree drips over the corner of the graveyard near the Green as though having fallen there by mistake. Everything else is a dark mossy brine beneath the towering yew tree at its centre.

A stack of maybe twenty gravestones has been piled against a drystone wall. Nettles and long chaffs of uncut grass fringe the dark ground beside them. Of those I can see, most have been defaced with time. Bending beneath the stiff branches of a holly bush, its sharp needles scratching the back of my neck, I make my way along the graves on the southern edge of the churchyard, the sun and the heat once again smothering me like a vapour, until after twenty minutes or so I recognise one of the names from the book. The surname was also on the memorial. Matthew Spencer, 13 June 1922. The only other words are *In memory of* carved in italics above his name.

A tractor starts in the yard beside me, a low and drowsy grumble that soon disappears west, out towards the fields. Other than that, I hear no evidence of life until, at some indefinable time later, the sound of shoes pitter urgently down Chestnut Grove and I find myself ducking down onto my knees and hiding behind one of the graves. The foot- steps belong to Norman, the church organist. Tall and gaunt and clutching a pile of papers in both hands, as though some eternally lost schoolmaster on his first day of lessons, he turns swiftly beneath the lychgate, ever looking about him, before heading into the church itself. Sunlight glares off the roof tiles as an indistinct glow, soaking the leaves of the sweet chestnut trees lining the edge of the graveyard.

Accompanied by the dull lament of organ pipes, I continue to look over the graves on this side of the church. Other than a small area by the gate dedicated to the recently departed, their stones black and polished, garnished with wilting roses and lilies and purple lilac, the

graves and tombs of the churchyard, those long established, are each in their way elegant, forgotten as they are
and carved with cherubs and wreaths and poetic inscrip-
tions. I'm not entirely sure what I'm trying to establish
here, but I'm doing something, I tell myself. I'm being
active. I'm trying to find her. Wherever she is, she is not
lying dead out in those fields. That much I know. None of
the graves, however, takes me further back than 1829, and
the only other names I recognise from the book are Howe
and Richardson, both also, I notice, with the words *In
memory of* carved in italics, but these, too, are pretty
common names and don't really prove anything beyond
them having died on the same day of the year. There's even
a Mary Murphy from 1902. I get much the same results by
the path, where straighter more Victorian-looking stones
have been lined up in close proximity around the yew tree,
and I start to think maybe Woods really had just taken
random names of missing people from newspapers.
Perhaps he even borrowed some from here and the
memorial.

There is still no one around, only Mr Baldock standing
by his gate, watching me working my way along the rows
of stones to the muffled drone of the organ. Along the top
of the roof, each panel seemingly a different tint of grey in
the hot sun, perch two or three dozen crows. They watch
inquisitively, heads tilted, as I make my way through the
scorched smells of cut grass and lavender until finding
myself standing in the porch amidst a complex pattern of
geometric shapes falling through the open wooden structure. An oddly nostalgic scent of old stone drifts from
inside. It's both refreshingly cool and stagnant.

Norman has left the door open, and as I stand here a
moment, listening to the notes bellowing inside, the little
squeaks and laboured breaths of the pumps, I can hear also

the muffled drone of rain on the roof. The sounds compete with each other, jostling for space in my head. The light in the porch quivers and I notice a small table by the entrance. It's stacked with frayed green hymn books and piles of service sheets. By the door to the bell tower, spotlighted by a single beam of reddish light angled through a stained-glass window on the far side of the church, is another longer table full of brass-rubbing paper. A porcelain vase stands in its centre, cradling a wilting bunch of white roses, and beside that an old wooden wine box with a number of opened cartons of wax crayons nestled in its hull, along with a small brush and a pair of silver scissors.

The stone floor beneath is speckled with rose petals, and as though time has unexpectedly short-circuited itself, my vision flickers between two different moments, both stereoscopic and ghostly, neither one more consequential than the other. The organ murmurs, and yet at the same time all I hear is the sound of rain, wind forcing its way through the straining branches of the yew tree in the graveyard and across the roof of the church itself.

Charlotte glances at me as Mum steps ahead, her shoes sharp and immodest against the hard stone floor. She faces the altar, bowing her head so tightly it's as though she doesn't want us to see. Charlotte grins and goes to stand before the bell tower door. It's been left ajar, and a thin disjointed slice of grey light has carved itself across the table. It moves to the sound of rain. I follow. The door is dark and panelled, designed for someone far shorter than either me or Charlotte. Its square frame, made of elm I think, has been intricately carved. It looks like one of Grandpa's books, as though something greater than we lies within it. In the centre is the village crest pressed within the carved sides of a shield. The border, which also runs along the top and bottom edges, is adorned with hundreds of tiny birds.

Charlotte picks up the top piece of paper and shows it to me, her bottom lip curling with disdain, the way it does. It's a brass rubbing, also of the village crest, about a foot in length with an inscription beneath so smudged it is almost illegible. 'And behold,' she says, adopting a priestly note, 'into this land of wheat and rape you each shall die of eternal boredom.'

'Don't be silly,' Mum says quietly, widening her eyes and glancing around the empty church. The left side of her face creases disobediently as she catches our eyes, and for the briefest of moments the space between us contracts and the noises of the world fade and the light turns from grey to red and we are each together as we once were, sharing the same air, the same smells, the same deafening heartbeat. 'You might even enjoy it,' she adds, which is when I realise there is someone standing behind me.

In the arch of the porch, Mr Scott is holding a fresh bunch of roses across his chest. Despite the heat, he is wearing a coat, a cream-coloured waterproof jacket that stops half way down his thighs. He smiles, diffidently, as though he wasn't expecting to see anyone, especially me, and looks down at Jet, who in turn looks up and opens his mouth expectantly, his tongue steaming and lolling to one side like a piece of meat. I stutter, part of me desperately trying to bring back to the surface the veneer of the memory of that day in the rain.

He frowns beneath whiskery grey eyebrows and looks down at Jet again, shrugs indifferently and walks past me into the church. I watch as he goes to the long table by the bell tower door, puts down the flowers, pulls out a news-paper from his coat pocket, unfolds it and carefully, as if they had once been dear to him, lifts the old roses from the vase and lays them in their paper cerement. He doesn't once turn around, but still I feel him watching me so I don't move. I just stand here in the entrance, in the chaos of shapes pouring through the wooden frame, until he takes the vase in two hands and walks slowly to the unhurried dirge of the organ to a small columned area at the back of the church. It is only when he moves out of sight that I go inside, into the cool reflective light.

The scents of dried incense and stone and old books, damp from somewhere beneath, fill the small church. On the floor by my feet, the inscription carved into a huge flagstone has been almost eroded away. All that remain are the starts of sentiments, swept into one corner like jigsaw puzzle pieces: *In Memory... Edward... June... Who.*

The church is no more than fifty metres in length, predominately made up of a wide nave and the aisle where I am standing. The high wall before me, set between the roof beams and three stone arches, is bright white and windowless, adorned in part with paintings faded almost to nothing, the myrtle green and blue ghosts of past priests and abbots, what appears to be an offering to the sun, and a painting that is unquestionably the slaying of a horse by a knight. Muted red blood, now pink in colour, lies in a pool beneath it. I turn my head away, trying not to see too much in it, trying not to pattern everything into the story of the curse, but it's almost impossible. It's everywhere I look. It's seared into my every thought.

Arched like a banner over the stained-glass window behind the altar are the words THE EARTH IS THE LORD'S AND THE FULLNESS THEROF, through which splays the most extraordinary rush of coloured light. Norman turns his head as he plays, watching furtively as I walk over to the table, pick up a roll of paper in one hand and pull from

213

the wooden box a crayon. Something clinks at the back of the church. I look up as Mr Scott returns with the vase, balancing it carefully in both hands. He nods, expression-less, and stands beside me at the table. His face is unshaven, pale and leathery, like an old rag, dark eyes hidden in the deepest of its folds. His breathing is nasal. His breath smells of stale milk. Not once does he look at me as he concentrates on arranging the fresh flowers until, with some hesitation, feeling nauseously exposed just standing beside him like this, I take a short and wary step to my right and reach for the iron handle of the bell tower door.

Before I can even touch it, he produces from his throat a sudden and hostile rasp that stops me instantly. When I turn, he smiles gingerly, the dead roses wrapped in news-paper across his chest. He glances over his shoulder to Norman, I think to make sure he is not being observed, although I can't tell, and motions resolutely with the side of his head to the south wall. Then he turns and leaves.

Either side of the square window where he pointed are maybe twenty stone plaques. I walk along one of the rows of pews and, with the organ slowing, the crayon and the paper clenched in my fingers, I read each one. They are mostly the eulogies of past priests. Lord Gibbins and his ill-fated troop of volunteers even have a stone, dated 14 June 1645, but that is the only connection to the story of the curse. At my feet is a series of brass panels, which I guess is what Mr Scott was pointing to. There are six in total, more priests by the look of it, and there at the top of the aisle, engraved on a brass plate beneath the village crest, is the memorial tablet for Arthur Bradley, his wife, Mary, and their daughter, Elizabeth, killed on 13 June 1879. Beneath it, most of its letters dissolved now into the footings of the church itself, is the quote from Hecate.

'And at the Pit of Acheron,' I tell myself, the low notes of the organ juddering through me, 'Meet me i' th' morning: thither he will come to know his destiny.'

With the church falling quiet, I almost kneel down before the words and rub them, but I don't bother. I shove the crayon into my pocket and head for the bell tower door, gripping firmly onto the iron handle and yanking it to the side with a reverberating clatter. It's locked. When I turn, part of me expects to see someone standing directly behind as they have before, but there is no one there. There is only Norman, fingers submerged into the keys of the organ, regarding me suspiciously over his shoulder. Frustrated, I drop the paper down onto the table and head out of the church, along the path and around the back of the bell tower.

The organ slips, spilling a flat incongruous note that peals around the church like a factory alarm, before finding its rhythm once again. With an unwarranted sense of danger coiling itself about me, I swallow two more Diazepam without really thinking about it, drink some water and make my way to the old rose garden, looking up to the open bell tower behind me as the highest and most exposed bell, peeling and russet with age, begins to chime midday. It stirs the crows, who make lazy unenthusiastic shapes in the sky before settling once again on the slate roof.

I look away, noticing as I do, through the crumbled remains of a series of ivy-clad pillars set back in the furthest corner of the churchyard, two ancient-looking rose bushes, each one swollen with bright white roses. On the grass in front of them, petals lie scattered over two large rectangular areas which I guess must have once been graves. There are no stones, only an archaic looking tomb set some way behind, partly hidden in shadow and sitting

215

horizontally beneath long sprigs of bramble. In loose piles beside it are crushed cans of cider and lager, bleached from the rain and the sun, most of which have been drawn into the brier by ground ivy.

There's no inscription, not on the front facing me or on the sides, or the rough grey surface of the lid. And so, uncertain of my own convictions, my faculties even, that familiar sense of detachment passing through me as a quiver, too afraid perhaps to connect all these things together, to commit Charlotte to the same unearthly ending as Holly Thompson and Charlie Montagu, I lift myself up and sit where I guess she would have sat that night in the rain with Mary, Ned and Finn. I stare down at the white roses and the shape of the ground around them, the stone trimmings exposed as though the bones of some primitive beast, and I tell myself, without hesitation, that beneath lie the bodies of Frances and Elizabeth Johnson; that four hundred years ago, people constructed from the same blood that runs through me once stood here in the dark and the rain and the foul stench of the deeper earth, the bodies of those they'd killed laid out beside them.

TWENTY-THREE

As Mary appears, two juvenile blackbirds scramble about in the trees behind me, spilling dust into the motionless air, before darting like sunspots out into the polished light. She pauses when she sees me, although I suspect she already knew I was here, and without saying anything, she sits beside me on the lid of the tomb. She smells strongly of body spray, cheap and unimaginative. Tiny droplets of sweat stipple her forehead like dew. After a long while, and starting to look bored more with herself than me, she takes out a can of cider from a black canvas bag, clicks it open, takes a small sip and offers me some.

I decline.

'I saw you in the graveyard,' she says. 'I heard about the copse, about them finding the blood.'

'She's not there,' I say. 'They can dig all they like, but they won't find her.'

The sun folds around her puffy white cheeks, catching the deep ruby-red of her lips and that small slightly upturned nose of hers, and for a brief moment I think she may be smiling, but she's not. She's frightened of something, possibly even of me.

'So where will they find her, Simon?' she says.

I don't rise to this. I look away, out in the direction of the village.

She takes another sip of cider. Its acidic tang fills the air between us.

'Why did she go to the church?' I say.

Mary shrugs. 'I told you. I don't know.'

'You're lying. You all are.'

She faces me, frowning with a grim pride that contorts her face like dough. 'We went to the pub then we came round here, but the storm was coming, and...' She shuffles back on the lid of the tomb, pulling her knees up and folding her long black dress around her legs. The movement dislodges a bramble by her head, which she hooks back onto the ivy before wrapping her arms around her knees as though she's freezing cold. I notice the ring attached to the lace bangle on her wrist with a small black chain, my mind hurriedly trying to fit all the jagged little pieces together. It's gaudy and brash, a glimmering six-leaf flower in its centre that part of me now thinks I recognise from somewhere.

'What is that exactly?' I say, not bothering to hide the derision in my voice. 'You said it was some sort of charm.'

She doesn't answer, not at first anyway. She sniffs indulgently, contemptuously even. Bees hum around the rose bushes. I watch them a while, the hypnotic rotation of their glistening bodies and the tiny drone of their wings reminding me that I haven't really slept now for three nights.

'Mary,' I say sharply, as though trying to wake her, 'you have to tell me. Why did you give her that bangle?'

Her lip quivers. Her eyes begin to well. 'I was trying to help her,' she says eventually.

'Help her with what?' I say. A single tear works its way down her left cheek, slowly moving over a thick layer of foundation. I should pity her, but I don't. I feel only anger.

She takes another sip of cider, dangling the can from the tips of her fingers as though it were the weight on a pendulum. Pushing sluggishly through the trees behind us, the sound of a freight train judders through the graveyard. 'It's an apotropaic symbol,' she says quietly, looking at the rose petals left scattered like confetti over the graves before us. 'It was supposed to protect her.'

'Protect her from what?'

'You know from what,' she says, and she looks up to the church, not at me. A door shuts on the other side. She closes her eyes and releases a number of slow breaths, as though preparing herself for meditation. Footsteps, light and arrhythmic, shuffle away towards the Green. I look back down to her boots and the pale white skin beneath her dress. She bites her bottom lip and glares back at the church then up to the sky. Her chest and shoulders rise and fall as she breathes. 'You don't get it, do you?' she says, her voice trembling now, holding back tears. 'No one ever comes back,' and looking straight ahead, she sucks in air, wipes her eyes and takes a long meaningful gulp of cider. I watch her, fear tightening my jaw, narrowing my eyes to mere slits, as though trying to hurt her with my mind. She doesn't turn. She continues to look ahead.

'Did you know Holly Thompson?' I say.

She takes another sip of cider.

'Emma Proctor told me she used to live near here.'

She doesn't reply.

'You believe the Horses have taken them, don't you?'

She glances up impatiently, a slight billowing in her cheeks. 'I was trying to protect her,' she says, looking down into the can and swirling it gently.

'What about the rose?' I say. 'The one they left at the copse? What does that mean?'

'We were trying to protect her,' she says bitterly. 'Can't you see that? We were trying to protect her.'

With the sun splattering a complex mosaic across the Green, I step out through the lychgate and walk across the grass, a ruthless strain of terror previously unknown to me coursing through my veins. I'm not really sure anymore what Mary meant, or what I'm supposed to take from it; whether it was a warning or a release of her own insecurities, her own fears. Maybe she was simply preparing me for the inevitable, as an act of kindness. I don't know. *No one ever comes back.* Only a few seconds ago, her words had slipped inside me like a frost, but now, disentangled from the verdant shadows of the churchyard, they appear in my head simply as words. Groundless. Most likely she meant no one ever comes back after five days missing, as Mum and Dad and the rest of the village, despite their relentless searching, are all thinking. Not that the victims of the curse never return. These sentiments, I'm pretty certain now, belong only to me.

Terry Baldock is in his garden on the far corner of Chestnut Close. He nods his head as I pass. I vaguely return the gesture, crossing the road at the junction of the Bukehorn. A high-pitched beeping sound fills the air to the east, where flickering in the watery glare of the sun I can just make out the flashing red lights of the crossing. I see myself walking back from the tracks the day I found the swan. My fingers are bleeding. My head is pounding. Birds circle overhead. I spoke to her, I think. We spoke to each other as we did before, when we were younger, silently, in the room with the animal wallpaper and the alphabet poster. Why, I ask myself, has this returned to us now, here, in this desolate place where everyone is watching our every move, where our house belongs still to someone else, where birds gather in great congregations as though the souls of the dead, and I think maybe the village itself has been acting as a connection between us, a portal, in the same way the aura links me to the black world beyond it.

As I think this, the ground trembles and a sudden rush of sound and heat pours through the light before me. A horn blasts. I step back and steady myself as the fast train rushes north. I stare at it, wide-eyed and frightened, as if my own life were accelerating before me, reflected in the blurs of coloured light in the windows, thousands of memories spiralling through the air, going from one place to another. And then they're gone and the barriers lift and the flashing lights cease.

I stick close to the Old Hermitage wall, pausing only briefly at the main gate, where I try to picture a view of Glenn Gate House as it was before the fire that killed Arthur Bradley and his family, the lawn falling away behind it and the statue over the quote from Hecate uncovered by ivy and bramble and bathed in glistening sunshine. One of the top floor windows of the Home closes. A jackdaw spits its discontent from the slanted roof of the hermitage.

The old Mini is parked still by the picnic benches in the Trust's car park before a measureless pool of blue, the hazy spires of the Deepings as distant as another continent. I shrug off as well as I can this insistent notion of isolation, and with my trainers crunching decisively on the ruptured tarmac, push my way through the double doors, where I'm met with the staccato sound of the photocopier clunking away in the office.

'That you, Simon?' Mr Skinner calls out.

'Whose car is that?'

The photocopier whines to a stop.

I know there's something wrong as soon as he steps out.

His eyes are both trying to look away from me and trying to look at me at the same time. He's wearing an old brown polo shirt that's too big for him, and he's unshaven, the bristles grey and stained. 'I was going to call you,' he says, 'but, you know, what with everything.' He scratches the back of his head. 'She was fine when you were here yesterday. Then when I went in to see her in the afternoon, after you'd gone...' He stops himself and purses his lips. 'As peaceful as anything, she was.'

The words float about my head. Charlotte, my twin sister, the very anode of my soul, has been missing for five days now. Yet in some shadowy part of my mind, this feels even more catastrophic, as though the swan's death is in some way more tragic than Charlotte's. I try not to think about her, try not to picture her as Mr Skinner described, or see her lying at the side of the tracks that day, brambles entangled around her neck.

'Whose car is that?' I say again, and for some reason, as though the answer had simply dropped like a leaf from a branch in my head, I know exactly whose car it is, and I know also who the man who has been sitting on the village bench watching our house for the past few days really is. 'Where is he?' I ask.

'Outside,' Mr Skinner replies. 'You sure you want to hear this?'

We bury her beneath a young ash tree on the eastern edge of the grounds, overlooking the wheat field, the animate scents of meadow grass and thistle rising up from the dried-up ditch that separates us from the land beyond. Buttercups, orchids and huge dandelions turn their necks to the light as we each take a few steps back and bow our heads, an odd directionless breeze shaking the leaves above and sprinkling us with dust and pollen.

'Do you want to say anything?' Mr Skinner asks.

I shrug and turn to the photographer. He, too, shakes his head.

Mr Skinner clears his throat, screws up his face as he thinks, and says quietly, 'From the sky to the soil.' Reverently he nods his head, and together the three of us walk out on to the path. The crane calls. Its voice is untamed, almost tropical in this stifling heat. In the water to our side, behind a line of silver birch trees, savaged in places with ivy and elder, something makes a hollow plopping sound as it drops into the water. Mr Skinner wipes his forehead with his handkerchief, pushes it back in his pocket, and sits down on the bench beside the copper beech tree. The photographer and I sit either side of him.

'Nathaniel was my father,' the photographer says, as if I had asked him the question. He leans forward on the bench so he can look directly at me, his back hunching awkwardly. His skin is rough, his jaw grey with uneven hanks of stubble. Sweat permeates through his black shirt in odd shaped patches, the scent of which, in this thick stirless air, floats about me like the smell of something dead.

I look down to his long dirty fingers. They are scratched and pockmarked with little sores, the bones almost visible beneath the skin. He looks older than I suspect he is, his eyes the colour of the sea in the morning in summer. 'Why the secrecy?' I say. 'Why the pretence? Why not just knock on the front door?'

'It doesn't work like that.' His voice is strained and bronchial. 'These are hard times for parents and families, as you know. They don't want people like me preaching the impossible.' He looks over his shoulder towards the Home. 'Besides, I have to be careful.'

'Sly knows who you are?'

'Not exactly,' he says, 'but he knows what I want.'

'And what's that?'

He looks at Mr Skinner, as though for clearance. 'I'm looking for evidence, Simon.'

I, too, lean forward, resting my head in my hands and staring down at the ground beneath me, at the dandelions and the speedwell slumped thirstily across the stones. The sun beats down on my neck. Across the water thousands of tiny fragments of light appear to be rising up into the air. Coots and moorhens drift impassively through them, gathering expectantly by the wooden pier, where silently they tread water over their own reflections. At my side, Mr Skinner pats both his pockets. He shrugs apologetically. 'No more secrets,' he says.

The photographer nods his head. His movements, I notice, are few but erratic, as though with each one he is finding himself waking from a dream. Far in the distance, they are calling Charlotte's name.

'Your grandfather taught my father at Cambridge. He admired him greatly. He told him never to accept the impossible until all other routes had been explored. My father, before he died, encouraged me to do the same.' He frowns heavily, as though in pain, scrunching his eyes into folds of grey skin and vigorously scratching the top of his head. 'And yet when that time came for him, no one listened, not even your grandfather.'

I know this already, I think. Or at least, I suspected it. I just wouldn't accept the connection before. It was better off hidden beneath the nostalgic dust of those memories. But Grandpa did believe it, in the end.

'My father was sent down from Cambridge,' the photographer continues, still hunched forward on the bench. 'You've read his book. You know the rest. Every attempt he made at making this public was rebuked, right up to his death.' He runs his arm across his forehead, legs shuddering beneath him and shaking the bench. 'The same thing's happening to me. I've been continuing his work since I was a teenager. I've dedicated my entire life to it, but nothing I ever try to publish gets through.' Nervously he sucks in air through his teeth. He looks over his shoulder, and with eyes stretched sternly open, as if clamped, he turns and stares deliriously at the Home. 'That's why the need for secrecy.'

I let out a dismissive puff of air. 'The Swan Lands?'

Mr Skinner catches my eye. 'They're watching us, Simon. They always have been. We've been trying to tell the world for years, Nathaniel, the two of us, Ethel and a handful of others, but nothing gets through. There's no way through.'

'Why didn't you tell me this before?'

Mr Skinner turns to the flat motionless water idling before him. 'I'm sorry,' he says. 'I wanted to.'

'I went into the grounds of the Home,' I tell them both in a languid voice, 'directly behind us. It was part of Glenn Gate House. There's a statue there above a quote from Hecate. Arthur Bradley was part of the cult. He painted the horse's head in the sky that's in our living room. He could see things other people couldn't, things that I can. They worshipped the curse. That's all. They protected it. I think people still do now. They are the ones conspiring against you. Detective Sergeant Daniels is a member. He wears the symbol of Hecate on his signet ring. A pentagram encircled in a wheel.'

'Why don't you help us?' the photographer says.

I look out across the pond. A pair of ducks turn themselves upside down in the water. They bob there a while, inverted as they are to the world above them, concerned only with what they can see beneath, before reappearing, a little startled, and heading back to where they came from.

225

'What are these things you see, Simon?' Mr Skinner says.

'I don't know yet,' I tell him, staring still at the patch of water where the ducks had been, its creases slowly diffusing into the smooth metallic surface of the pond. I face the photographer. 'I'm sorry my grandfather didn't listen,' I tell him. 'I'm sorry for everything that's happened, but you have to leave me alone now. I don't care about evidence or proving to the world what is happening here because I don't really know what is happening here. I only know what is going on in my head. I have to save Charlotte. That's all that matters. That's all I'm required to do. I'm sorry, Mr Skinner.'

'And how are you going to do that, Simon?' the photographer says, but I don't respond. I listen to the crane and the heron and the gentle lapping of the water against the wooden pier and, far off, the voices in the fields calling Charlotte's name.

TWENTY-FOUR

We are all alone. We are born alone. We die alone. Only Charlotte and I know any different. This is how we became who we are. We lived once in a world unseen by others, encased in an embryonic darkness so bright we could see each other's thoughts, touch our slippery webbed fingers and toes together and stare at each other through swollen eyes not yet developed. We knew no other love. No other love existed. Our world belonged only to us. We felt each other's heartbeats and lived each other's dreams.

If she was dead, I would know she was dead. But she is not. She is alive as I am alive, detained perhaps in some ineffable dimension the boundaries of which I'm starting to believe are not too far from here, within me even. Or maybe she is simply in another place, in another town or village, and all this has been some appallingly misjudged cry for help. Maybe she really is in London with Tom. I don't know, but she is alive, of that I'm certain, and she is alive in the same moment of time that I am alive, a steady abiding time that is different to the time that tows with it my physical self; a slower more indistinct time that beats only in the space between the past and the present. We are in harmony. Our pulses throb, still, to the resonant vibrations of each other. I can feel hers as prominently as I feel my own, sense the lingering residue of her presence, and in some weightless part of my mind, I can hear her too, her voice low and distant as though passing through a great mass of water, being carried resolutely on a current from her to me. She's talking directly to me, as she did before in that sonorous vermilion realm of our beginning, as she did that day by the railway lines, and she's crying. She's telling me she loves me, that she's sorry, that I have to work this out on my own, and then, stretched thinly across the texture of her voice, I picture her standing in my bedroom the night she disappeared, her scarred porcelain face blazing in thin slashes of metallic light.

'There's something I have to tell you,' she says, and then she's gone.

Sly is standing at the gate, watching the television people load up the last of the boxes into a large black van, although, really, I suspect, he has been waiting for me. He looks old and tired, colourless in the sharp glow of the day.

'Your mum and dad are inside,' he says in a tone suggesting I should not go inside, that I should stay outside with him.

We sit on the wall to the left of the gate. A faint breath of hot air brushes over my face as I look out across the rape field. It's frayed and grey compared to the lush flaxen glare of the wheat beside it and the fields falling steadily west beyond.

'Simon,' he says, letting slip for the first time a note of sadness, submission even, as though this place and its mournful essence have at last got inside him, 'we've established nothing from the CCTV in Peterborough or any other town near here. Nor has she been seen at any of the London stations.' He takes a wheezy breath and turns his head remorsefully, and beyond Holly Thompson and Charlotte, I wonder just how many people he has never found whose soundless two-dimensional faces appear in his dreams. 'We're pretty certain she hasn't travelled anywhere publicly and we know she hasn't used her bank card.' He shakes his head again. 'There hasn't been a single sighting of her anywhere, in five days.'

'And there's no body at the copse,' I say.

Sly waits for the men to shunt a bulky silver case into the back of the van. The sun glares off its mottled surface, making us both wince as, shirts sticking to their bodies, their faces glistening, they close the doors with two firm repetitive thuds. Turning and puffing air into their top lips, they each briefly but purposely catch my eye, I guess as some mark of respect or even to put a face to any muted rumours before, eyes averted, sheepishly heading back to the house. 'No,' he says. 'We've found nothing else at the copse. We've searched every property, and the church and the Home and the Trust. I don't understand it. It's as though she never even left the house.'

'What about the blood?'

He makes a noise at the back of his mouth. 'It's not Charlotte's,' he says without turning his head.

Over by the bench I hear the chatter of finches. Something flashes in the far distance, and for a moment I find myself simply staring through the wispy afternoon heat, thinking not of Charlotte and the curse, but of how calm everything is, how soothing, the flat endless swathes of farmland, the distant shimmering of the horizon, the sky, rich and unsullied and as vivid as it is impalpable. Nothing seems real. The world has taken on the appearance of a painting or a model, something designed without flaws, wildly disparate in every way imaginable from the one three months ago we left behind.

'What is it, then?' Charlotte says, sitting down beside me on the same wall I am sitting on now. I regard her suspiciously. 'The bird,' she says with a wry grin. 'What else?' and she points with a straight arm towards the village sign.

With Sly watermarked in the light beside me somewhere in the future, I look back to the fields and the female merlin that's been hovering some twenty metres or so above the bench. 'It shouldn't really be here,' I tell her matter-of-factly, my fingers tapping on the worn leathery surface of the binoculars hanging from my neck. 'Do you want to have a look?'

She declines with a little laugh.

A tractor is ploughing the edges of the rape field, terns and crows circling endlessly behind, while closer to hand a pair of wrens busy themselves on the grass verge by the village sign. Daffodils crane their necks.

'There's something strange about this place,' she says, 'don't you think?'

'No,' I tell her. 'I think it's wonderful.' I look up to the thatched owl on the roof of Mrs Neal's house, then back out to the open fields. The merlin has gone.

We both turn our heads as Rupert Gibbins strides across the road from the entrance of the Manor House, his shiny brown brogues eagerly tapping out a little dance on the tarmac. A mop of floppy black hair, becomingly speckled with grey, falls over a face so eminent it almost appears ugly. He's carrying a box of wine. There's some sort of ornament resting on the top.

He smiles broadly, more at Charlotte than me. 'Charlotte and Simon, I assume,' he says in a low sardonic voice, holding on as long as he can to Charlotte's gaze. 'I'm Rupert. We're neighbours. Welcome to Glennfield.' When neither of us responds, he says, 'Nice to meet you too. Are your parents in?'

Charlotte shrugs.

I tell him they are, that they're in the house and that we're pleased to meet him, noticing the figurine on top of the box of wine appears to be a bronze bird of prey, a bit like the one Grandpa had. 'Is that a hawk?' I ask.

Rupert stops and smiles, at Charlotte, not at me. 'Buggered if I know,' he says through a laugh, and he capers off up the path to the house where we both hear Mum inviting him inside as though he was an old friend.

'Welcome to Hell,' Charlotte tells me evenly.

I look up with a start.

'OK?' Sly says. The lean shadow of the lamp post stretches behind him like a scythe. Across the road Mrs Neal opens her front door. Her wicker basket is nestled in her arms. She smiles seriously, red lipped and pale skinned, and heads off at a pace into the village.

'Why did Daniels ask me if I believed in God?'

Sly faces me. 'He shouldn't have,' he says. 'If he has offended you, I apologise. He has no right to ask you questions of that nature.'

'It didn't offend me,' I tell him, sensing the hackles on the back of my neck. My voice is calm, but inside something is snapping, something brittle and intractable. I can almost hear it, like a whip. It rages through my thoughts at a different pace to the world outside them. 'I just wonder,' I say, 'why no one has listened to what fifty years ago Nathaniel Woods tried to show the world yet your detective feels it's acceptable to ask me if I believe in something that possesses, in evidential terms, as much credence as the curse. That the reverend is permitted to offer God's hope to my parents and arrange a service of prayers in his church,

231

and yet no one will offer a single thread of feasibility to any alternative form of what is still fundamentally the supernatural. Who decides that one story is more valid than another? Isn't that your job, to decipher which narrative is true and which is make-believe?'

Sly pinches his lips, I think as a subtle form of recognition, although I guess it could easily be nothing more than patience earned from years of experience. It's hard to tell. The smoky scent of his jacket doesn't seem so potent today and the air about us is stuffed with the smells of lavender and grass.

'My grandfather was also researching it,' I tell him before he can respond. 'I don't know what's going on here and I'm not saying for a moment that Charlotte and Holly Thompson have somehow been taken by a curse, but something's not right. There was also a boy taken in the seventies from Coppingford Manor, the home of Lord Montagu.'

He looks over to the empty village bench. 'You've met our friend, then?'

I follow his gaze. Chaffinches flutter in the waxy air beside it, hovering at the edge of the village as though unable – unwilling, maybe – to pass over its threshold.

'People have been looking into this for decades,' Sly says calmly. 'I have been looking into it for decades. There is no evidence of anything supernatural.'

'There is no evidence of God either,' I say curtly, 'yet we're allowed to talk about Him as though he was a neighbour. Our courts are even sworn in by His name. Thieves and murderers are sentenced in His word.'

'That's not for me to discuss. What I'm saying is, there is no evidence that could possibly offer a sense of plausibility that the curse has any foundation, tangibly, metaphysically or historically. I am a policeman, Simon. I have to think logically and laterally. That is my job. Other people are entitled to do as they please, as are you, as clearly so were Nathaniel Woods, his son and our friend Mr Skinner, Ethel Roberts even.' He looks skyward a moment. 'I understand your frustrations. In many ways it's the easiest answer, but it simply isn't the truth. After Holly went missing I spent almost every minute I had trying to find a connection between the disappearances, but there isn't one. There's nothing.' He exhales, his eyes steering to my backpack. 'And I've read that book many times. I've spoken to the families. I've investigated those names, believe me. I even tried to track down Woods on the off chance he was still alive, as some people seemed to think, but he wasn't. His body was found four months after his disappearance, washed up in Norway.' He sighs. 'There will always be ghost hunters, Simon, as there will always be priests, as there will always be police inspectors.' He looks into the village. 'And there will always be those whose beliefs will never be altered. I don't know why Daniels asked you such a question, but I do know what I know, and the answers are always far more removed and far more prosaic than any perceptions of the supernatural. I will never stop looking for Charlotte, believe me, as I'll never stop looking for Holly Thompson.'

A quiet mournfulness falls across his face, and I'm just about to tell him about Daniels wearing the symbol of Hecate on his ring, that he, among others, more than likely those close to him, have been impeding his attempts at finding the truth all these years, but I don't. I stop myself, realising it wouldn't do any good. All it would do is depreciate his work, make his unfeigned efforts, his unbridled commitment, appear to the world and the parents of those children he has been searching for all these years less essential, less consoling than they actually are.

'You be careful now,' he says, picking a cat hair from his jacket and letting it float gently to the ground.

Aunty Anne is waiting for me by the door. She shakes her head when she sees me, the fear and uncertainty, the childish bewilderment reflected in her swollen red eyes releasing into the air the freakish abhorrence of what it is that's happened to our family. It lies in every corner of the house: in the shadows trapped between long stretching batons of sunlight sifting through the porch window, in the fireplace beneath the mantelpiece clock, already laid for a winter that may never come. Things are settling now into our new environment, our new domain, into this pristine unexplored version of reality that will forever be our lives.

The clock ticks behind us. Aunty Anne leads me processionally into the kitchen, where Dad is sitting opposite Constable Witt at the table, going through a pile of police photographs. He turns his head only slightly, as though thinking about acknowledging me but unable physically to go through the mechanics of doing so.

'Pete's with the search party,' Aunty Anne informs me in a whisper, 'and your mum's upstairs. We've given her something to help her sleep. Shall I make you a sandwich?'

I shake my head, filled with an enormous sense of grief, not for me or for Charlotte, but for Dad. In London, after he lost his job, in those slow misshapen days when the house constantly smelt of coffee and toast, he constructed a model railway set in the basement. Mum had plans for it to become a cinema room. It took him over a month to build, in which time a matted gingery beard had slowly germinated on his face like a fungus. It didn't suit him in any way.

A few weeks after the completion of the railway set, he shaved off the beard and set up his new business. The

234

layout was based on Wiveliscombe station in Somerset, where he grew up. His parents had died before we were born and we have never been there. I'm not sure Mum has either. There were three lines with changeable connections, each with their own signs and signals: a Class 22 Diesel working a milk service from Torrington; a Bachmann 2-6-2 Prairie Tank which would carry a three-coach local service for Taunton or Barnstaple; and a Pannier Tank shifting freight to and from Taunton.

Dad hardly ever went down after he started working again, but I sometimes used to sit there at night with all the display lights switched on, in the heat and the glare, accompanied only by the metronomic clicking of the washing machine in the room next door. I never started the trains. I just used to observe this perfectly assembled world and its silent population encased, only in part, by a large sheet of MDF that he had sanded down and painted bright blue to look like the sky. He never got around to painting the clouds.

I felt like God down there – maybe Dad did, too – bathed in that white artificial light which sometimes caught the air and gleamed like the corona of some distant world, while everyone else slept, with the power to simply switch everything off in an instant if I so desired.

TWENTY-FIVE

The attic is baking hot. It smells of decaying wood and mothballs, dried out rat pellets. Sunlight pushing against the roof tiles has given them a rusty almost transparent glow that makes me think I'm walking through the hull of a capsized ship. The boards creak beneath me. Dust covers everything: boxes, old trunks, pictures, a broken chair. It makes creases on the wooden floor and sparkles in the light coming up from the ladder behind me. It clusters around the lightbulb. A cracked mirror, its edges blackened, has been partly covered by a grey blanket at the far end of the makeshift walkway. The mirror blinks as it catches the light, as I see myself walking towards it, towards the empty space over the laundry room, the air abundant with an overwhelming sense of beauty that after a while I realise is that familiar scent of lavender: the quiet stolen breath of the house when darkness appears.

I've only been up here once before, with Charlotte a few weeks after we arrived.

'You remember that film in Balham?' she had said with her back to me, rummaging through some of the boxes. There had been an odd burning smell in here that day. The air was thick and sharp, frantic with millions of flecks of fibreglass from the recently laid insulation that clung to my moist skin and scratched the back of my throat. The bulb was buzzing, the dull yellow light flickering across the side of her face, where her scar, a dark brownish colour, appeared to be crawling out of her eye like a centipede. I stood by the hatch and watched her.

'There was silence in Heaven about the space of half an hour,' she'd said. 'Do you remember? You recited it to me and Tom when we met you outside.'

She looks around, gazing anxiously at the sloping walls as though trapped in a cave beneath the ground. 'What do you think it means?'

'It's from Revelation,' I tell her, an odd sort of lucidity to my voice. 'The Seven Seals were given to Jesus when he ascended into Heaven, as a reward for cheating Death.'

'For cheating Death,' she says quietly, almost to herself.

'And there was silence in Heaven about the space of half an hour, where God, before the end of times, allowed his chosen few to live.'

'And then what?' she says with a faltering nervous sort of laugh. 'Everyone else just died?'

I don't respond. We never talk about religion. It's a family tradition as old as religion itself.

'Can I be one of them?' she asks, I think playfully, although I can't be certain, so staid is her manner. 'Can I be one of the chosen few? Can I also cheat Death?' She smiles, and after a long while says, 'You walked me back in the snow. Do you remember?'

I nod measuredly, not really sure why she's talking like this.

'I love him, Simon,' she says without warning, her voice as exposed as it is stern. 'We want to be with each other.'

The words congeal inside me as a paste. 'So that's what

it was all about then was it, leaving me in the cinema so you could be alone with Tom in that flat?' There's a sharpness to my voice I hardly recognise as my own.

She shivers and allows her gaze to drift briefly to the open hatch beside me, her eyes glistening a little in the tawny light. 'It's not just that,' she says timidly, 'it's this place. It isn't right. We shouldn't be here,' and she pulls out some old books from one of the boxes. She holds one up in her hands. The wooden cover is frayed at the edges, a worn mahogany brown embossed with a floral pattern. The only print is on the spine. It's one of Grandpa's. 'A New Theological Dictionary,' she says, half laughing and opening it at a marked page. 'The society that embraced this new discipline ran in multitudes, composed of persons of both sexes, and all ranks and all ages, through the public streets with whips in their hands, lashing their naked bodies with the most astonishing severity, with a view to obtain the divine mercy for themselves and others by their voluntary mortification and penance.' She looks up. 'Why would Grandpa have this?'

I stare intently, eyes fixed, an immutable vehemence carving its way across the length of the attic. 'He was an archaeologist,' I tell her evenly.

'He was an atheist. He didn't believe in anything superstitious.'

'No,' I say, walking to where she had sat that afternoon, the ghost of the memory sinking back into the wavering shadows, 'I think he believed in everything superstitious.'

I can vaguely see the folds in the dust where she had been sitting. The box is still open, just as she left it, the flaps closed but unsealed. A dried-out twisted strip of masking tape hangs down one side, where I had that day in Cambridge written LONDON while Mum was in the kitchen. I sit exactly where Charlotte sat, the mirror slanted at my side and throwing a contorted square of pale light on the wooden boards. The crack in the glass flexes on the rough surface.

Soothed by the distant hum of a train making its way south, its mechanical scream muted through the slate tiles and sounding monotonous and trance-like, I scrape the box towards me, wedging it between my feet. Resting on top of half a dozen or so other tatty looking history books and Ordnance Survey maps, a number of cardboard folders, each crammed hastily with pages of either typed or hand-written notes, is the same book that Charlotte had read from that day. I rest it in my lap, running my fingers over the waxy surface of the page, the smell of the stained greyish paper lifting into the dry air. I am feeling the same material she felt. I am inhaling the same scents, the same molecules, and as though part of me is trying to get into her mind from that day, become part of her once again, I, too, read the preface out loud, imagining myself standing by the hatch, watching as I had done then.

Swaddled now in some sort of hypnagogic state of shock, anaesthetised at seeing all these titles again, a foggy grey texture having suffused the air about me, I slowly pull out the folders and skim through his endless notes, turning each page over as though it belonged not only to Grandpa but the past itself, delivering into the air amidst the fuggy scents of dust and old books and pipe smoke such a profound sense of sadness I start to cry. Pressed disorderly among them are a number of pages torn haphazardly from other books, and numerous Polaroids. Some I recognise as having been taken in the village, their colours bleached by time, Grandpa's fraught and discomposed thoughts enmeshed eternally within them, his almost illegible ideas scratched briskly in the space beneath in blue biro. There are images of this house and the painting and someone standing beside it, who I assume is Ethel Roberts. Her expression is as blanched and distant as the image itself. There are also photographs of the Home, Mr and Mrs Skinner, a young Nathaniel Woods, hair down to his waist, and the church, both inside and out, and among all of this, a single sheet of tracing paper, its edges sharp, on which he has made a brass rubbing of the eulogy for Arthur Bradley and his wife and daughter.

Wiping my eyes with the back of my hand, I put the folders down and go back to the box, lifting free a large and heavy leather-bound book. Embossed in faded gold lettering, the title reads *The Origins of English Villages*. At first, I simply stare at it, just as Grandpa used to do, inhaling its musty scent as though it was something to be revered, something animate that first needed permission to be opened and explored. It was published, according to the inner leaf, in 1832. The pages are fragile, frayed along the spine. I go straight to the index at the back and read the letters aloud, quickly scanning the minute print until, at last, I see it: *Glennfield*. It's been underlined in pencil. The word fires out at me, augmented and surreal, and for a second or two I see Grandpa, his eyes vivid with both fear and excitement, in his mangy green cardigan, turning fervently through the pages just as I am now, a current simultaneously running through the pair of us, as if it were some sort of cure, some sort of magical denouement.

A moth hisses against the lightbulb, its blurred dilated shadow dancing wildly about the roof of this tight inverted space as the page opens almost of its own accord, the hinge wedged with a small paper-thin envelope. It's become grey with age, one edge dotted with little specs of mould. I turn it over. Written in neat flowing handwriting I recognise as Nathaniel Woods's is Grandpa's name.

Dr Hendry

As you will have heard I have been sent down. I leave immediately. You will be my last correspondence with an establishment I once held in great admiration. For one last time, I implore you, do not, simply by way of rigid expediency, repudiate what is not known. You have my notes. You have my manuscript. We have discussed this at length. I am not, therefore, pleading with you to reconsider my proposal. I am asking you to listen for the sake of your own family. They are at risk. Understand this wholeheartedly. Your family are at risk.

Perhaps, Dr Hendry, our duty is not simply to uncover the truth but to attest it.

My sincerest regards
Nathaniel

I put the letter to one side and skim over the text in the book, barely registering the words, before turning the page to a copy of an ink drawing. It's of a large but unpretentious two-storey residence. In italics beneath it are the words *Glenn Gate House c. 1861*. At the bottom of the same page is another sketch, possibly drawn by the same hand. It's of a formal garden. Set between a square of apple trees is a statue of six rearing horses. I pause and look up and take a shuddering breath as darkness passes over me before, with an almost imperceptible buzzing sound, as though time had temporarily fused, the moth settles on the wooden beam above the lightbulb and the shadow disappears.

I gather the book and the envelope and head for the attic door. The television is on in the living room beneath me. I can hear Constable Witt with that eternally professional voice of hers talking to Aunty Anne, something about needing to give us space as a family. I ignore its connotations and go straight to my room, closing the door behind me and starting up the laptop. My head is thick with ideas and already my mouth tastes of copper, but I ignore the signs. I don't have time for that. I don't even go to my bedside table drawer for the Diazepam, if indeed I should even take any more. I've lost track of how many I've had over the last few days. Maybe that's why everything's moving, why the light is stinging my eyes, why I feel weightless, suspended like a ghost between two moments of time. They're keeping the seizures away, though. That's all that matters for now. They're blocking their paths.

Gathered outside Mrs Neal's gate are a dozen or so villagers, some of whom I'd seen earlier on the Green, their shadows inkish and taut, stretched like guidelines across the tarmac. The air moves around them, the sun mercilessly regurgitating heat, glaring in every window. Mr Scott looks up, as though he heard a sound. He stares at me, eyes narrowed beneath thick grey brows. He seems threatening, despite the indistinct creasing of his mouth, despite me having known his diffident politeness for three months now, having been entrusted, even, to walk his dog all those afternoons under the open skies. So, too, does the village. It's conscious and watchful, obedient only to itself. My gaze draws to the thatched owl on the roof of Mrs Neal's house and quickly, as though alerted to some terrible threat, across to Mr Scott's hawk and the neighbouring pheasant and the kestrel and the stone raven perched on one of the chimneys of the Manor House. Each of them is facing the church and, standing here, detached as I am not only from the village and all its secrets, but from my own family's private grief, I begin to think that they, too, are in some way connected with all of this, as though they are nothing more than the perfectly placed, perfectly crafted figures of a model village.

Mr Hinton, I notice, is holding his straw boater against his chest. He's wearing his cream blazer with the crest of The Three Sheaves Bell Ringers. The top of his head, chalky-white skin stretched almost to breaking point across his skull, gleams like a beacon. Both Mr and Mrs Cowley are there too. A child of about eight or nine, heavy brown hair and tiny eyes that seem almost to be touching each other, is hiding behind the legs of Mr Cowley, playing some sort of game with himself, or me, the child's stern hypnotic leer never once retracting from my window. Even Mrs Yearsly is there, standing but a foot away from Mr Chaplin, a few stems of bright white roses cradled in her arms. I don't know the names of the others, not even the kids kicking a tennis ball about in the middle of the road beneath the holm oaks, their bikes left twisted like the bones of animals. They all know I am here though, up in the window, staring back at them as they stare at me.

I wash my face in the bathroom, go back to the desk and pick up Grandpa's letter. The screen in front of me, bright and fuzzy, tells me I have two new messages. My head sinks as I wait for the letters to focus, to find themselves in the light. The first is from Rapture informing me of a sighting of a Cetti's warbler over Whittlesey Fen just an hour ago. She's included a photograph, which seems genuine enough, although I've not heard of them drifting this far inland before. It's more than likely a nightingale. The second is from The Swan Lands. I glare a while at the letters, smirking at its crass simplicity, picturing the photographer on the bench beside Mr Skinner this afternoon, scratching the back of his head like some stray mutt. I delete the message without reading it and, with the black weight of sleep sinking through me like a tide, lie flat on the bed, the letter cradled loosely in my fingers, and stare at the door and the Montagu's harriers and the empty space in the corner, and all the while I feel the darkness inside, distending as a gloom, pure and endless and teeming with voices and memories not yet woken. Charlotte, too, is in there somewhere, as she always has been, courageous and unorthodox, all things I am not. She is calling me.

From my bedside table drawer, I clumsily take the bottle of Diazepam and swallow two more pills with the few drops of water left in the glass, relinquishing myself deferentially to something I know is without question stronger than me. I dream of Brancaster beach, of the sound of the waves in the far distance, the thin fabric of the earth stretched to its limit, glittering under the sun and broken only where the wreck has split through its surface like an abandoned toy. Stints and dunlins prod at the wet sand by the channel, curlews among the long glittery frieze of broken shells that appear to move in the light like melting snow. Avocets speckle the air over Scolt Head. I smell the marshes and the sea in the distance. I see Charlotte on the roof of the beach hut, the sky behind her so blue it doesn't seem real. The wind blows her hair. She smiles.

'So are you going to save me or not?' she says, and then she's gone.

DAY SIX

THE LAST DAY

TWENTY-SIX

I wake early. The sedate morning light is vague and hesitant, a developing fluid gradually soaking through a negative, slowly transposing the components of darkness to objects more recognisable: the finer edges of the furniture, the corner of my chest of drawers, the shelf with my bird books.

On the desk, the laptop gently murmurs. I see the letter laid out neatly beside it. I don't get out of bed though. I let the half-light assemble my thoughts, my head weighed down into the pillow, anchored not only with exhaustion, but an indomitable sense of foreboding. I stare at the numbers on the clock, waiting for them to move on their little black stage. On the far wall the Montagu's harriers are hidden still in their dark frame as though passing a window at night. Thrushes and blackbirds, wrens and finches call to each other at the edge of the village. Every minute the numbers shift, spilling a faint fluorescent glow across the sheets where in some part of my mind I hear a police car or ambulance caterwauling its way along Tooting High Street, blue lights blinking across the animal wallpaper and extending the shadows of the books on the shelf by the window.

247

Is it so wrong, I think, that Charlotte and I have an ability to protect each other, and, if so, why are we governed by the necessity to keep this a secret? I know, deep down, this makes her feel guilty. She wishes things were different. But they aren't. It was a decision made for us, not by us. For Charlotte, it is already a curse, an unbidden incursion that over time she will have to come to accept, if not embrace, that we are interminably tied, we coalesce as one shadow. The course of her life is dependent on me honouring that wish. It is up to us, surely, to sculpt this any way we want. Such a gift, if that's what it is, doesn't have to be warped or evil. Ötzi could have forgiven those who killed him. Elizabeth Johnson could have absorbed the last few cognitive moments of her life for reflection, not revenge. We are not possessed, Charlotte and I. We are tied. We always have been.

Back in the flimsy remembrance of South London, a taxi passes. It's being driven in the wrong gear, an eerie middle-eastern chanting leaking from the radio out into the stillness of the evening. Laughter crackles from the pub at the bottom of the road, through which drips a timid shuffling of feet, a voice shouting into a mobile phone. As Charlotte turns in her bed, the dressing covering the entire right-hand side of her face, stained and patchy in the muted glow, catches the edge of a red light as it slips diagonally across the ceiling. In the far distance a siren wails.

She was given her own room at the end of that week, the spare room. She took all her clothes, the large mirror and the alphabet poster, even though I know she didn't like it.

Mum and Dad are sitting at the kitchen table in their pyjamas. There's a strange smell of early morning sunlight and old wood and the distant fusty stench of the house itself, that insistent air of age and neglect, decay and inhospitality that has never once left the perimeter of my senses. Part of it will always be deserted and abandoned, I think, stinking of dead rats and coated in the warm spring light of that first afternoon. Charlotte will always be there in that doorway among the bones of dead birds, hands pressed sternly against her chest. Henry Roberts will be walking back and forth along the corridor upstairs, peering tenuously out of my window into the past, and so too Ethel, staring at the painting in the cold and the dark.

'What is it?' Mum says.

Dad gets up and guides me into a chair. 'You alright? Take your time,' he says, rubbing my shoulder affectionately. 'Have you taken your pills?'

I don't answer this. The smell of fresh coffee floats beneath me. I glance around the room. The work surface is clean, taps glimmering, the fence and the branches of the ash tree clear against another radiant untarnished synthetic sky.

'Simon,' Dad says seriously, speaking to me at eye level. There are red marks around his eye sockets. 'They showed the appeal on TV last night. If she saw it, I'm sure she'll get in touch.'

'Right,' I say.

Mum looks up from her mug. Her hair is matted, coiled in unkempt barbs. Her eyes, too, are red and inflamed. Nervously, her mouth quivering, she motions for me to look down at the table, where there are three or four newspapers spread out in a large fan, as though prepared purely for my benefit.

'And the nationals have run it too,' Dad says, muting a desolate note of excitement in his voice. 'Someone must recognise her. Someone will be in touch. I just know they will.'

I reach over and, straightening my posture, start nonchalantly flicking through them.

'I've left another message with Sly,' he tells me. 'He's going to call as soon as he hears anything.'

I turn over another page, eyeing Uncle Pete at the far end of the table.

He shakes his head.

Constable Witt stands and asks me if I'd like a cup of coffee.

'The service is at ten o'clock, remember,' Mum says, pinching her lips and heading up the stairs.

Heat pours from the sky, hotter than I think I can ever remember it. It feels as though we're each standing directly before the reverent might of the sun. It swaddles us as we walk down the path, our clean black shoes clicking on the tarmac, the last remaining souls on earth. It sticks the cotton of my shirt to the skin on my back. It feeds into the rash on my neck where my tie has been done up over my top button. It draws out like a ventilator the stiff fragrances of lavender and dried grass, roses, magnolia and rhododendron. The light, too, seems exaggerated. It's blurred yet crystalline, throbbing with a chemical energy far too bright for this earth, and beyond, on a shoreline I can almost see, as though coming into port from a long journey, I smell the aura, its thick swirling vapour waiting in the edges for the exact moment of contact.

A huge carrion crow swoops low over my head, resting on the corner of our wall. It turns to me and squawks.

'Wretched things,' Mum says, looking fearfully around the village.

I half close my eyes and follow her gaze. There are hundreds of them, I notice, perched ceremoniously on the roofs of the houses, beside the thatched birds or on the tops of walls: crows and rooks, blackbirds and jackdaws, hunched together, the dour solemnity lacquered across their sharp silvery eyes almost respectful, a show of deference. They're each looking at us, adorned in black silk, minding our every step. Occasionally one calls out, breaking rank and stirring the others, who look about each other skittishly, as though not sure of the reason they have been gathered here today.

The sun gilds the long misshapen branches of the holm oaks. The birds screech atop the chimneys behind them, as slowly the church bell starts to chime. It's faint and distant, but everything's faint and distant, turned into a gas. Everything is strange and beautiful at the same time, and as I think this, despite the brittle currents of fear flowing through my blood, I allow a wry grin to cast itself into my mouth because it makes perfect sense. Of course dimensions are different, perspectives disparate and inconsistent. Of course the light is hazy and stereoscopic, the air so full of scents it can't quite contain them. Of course the heat is incongruous, colours garish and faux. There are no boundaries in here. There never have been. Within the arms of the aura I am God, with the power to switch everything off in an instant if I so desire.

Waiting for us at their gate are Gordon and Annie Proctor. Rupert Gibbins is standing beside them, dressed in a thick yellow sports jacket, despite the heat. Gordon is wearing his cream blazer with The Three Sheaves crest stitched into the chest pocket. Emma is at the door behind them, a silver sheaf of wheat pinned to the lapel of a thin cotton jacket, the same design as on her mother's pastel green cardigan. Their faces glare at me, broad and indistinct.

'You OK, Simon?'

251

I don't answer. I'm not even sure who said it. All their voices sound the same. When Gordon bows his head, I notice tufts of grey hair protruding from his ears. He offers Mum and Dad some words of support, as does Rupert.

'Your ancestors,' I say, my words noticeably thick and accusatory. 'I know all about them.'

Dad puts a hand on my shoulder. He peers into my eyes. 'You sure you're up for this?'

I tell him I am.

Rupert smiles thickly. 'Well,' he says, holding my stare with dark speckly eyes set so cavernously deep into his face I can almost see their shadows, 'when this is all over, you can come and tell me about them, hey?'

Bile swirls around the inside of my mouth.

I straighten, pull at my collar and let them walk ahead, the dried petals of the cherry and almond trees stirring on the ground at their feet as though caught in a breeze, but there is no breeze. There is only light, a fog as oblique as it is incandescent. It's swelling. The light is swelling. It bleeds through my skin. Through its haze, I notice the back of Mum and Dad's hands touching briefly, as though by mistake. I study them with interest as, in the glare, their fingers twitch uncertainly beside each other before eventually, like two magnets being pulled across a vacuum, they link.

As a distraction I glance at each door, each brightly coloured slab of wood slotted neatly into its frame. Faces, plain and emotionless, occasionally move in the windows. I look, too, at their perfect gardens and their neat white fences and the smooth rounded edges of Mr Chaplin's hedge. I listen to their low voices. I smell the idyllic meddling of fragrances. I look at the wisteria and clematis, the purple ivy that climbs adoringly over the stonework of their model houses. I hear the freight train, thudding and

252

distanceless, and I think of the swan lying dead beneath the ash tree at the Trust and of Charlotte in the smoky light of the afternoon I found her, the train tracks steadily falling away to the south, the smells of cut grass and hogweed and nettle. I look, again, at the thatched birds on the roofs of the houses, each facing the church, and the villagers waiting for us by their gates, dressed in their smartest clothes, jackets and ties, their collars creased, long skirts, children looking bored in checked shirts and shorts, their elder sisters, necks stiff, standing there like porcelain versions of their mothers. They walk behind us, each in step, as though the whole thing has been rehearsed. Sound bellows in my head. Into the stagnant heat, their gardens spatter the scents of hostas, anemones, lupins and lavender. Colours bleed and congeal. Columbines and white daisies, hollyhock and hydrangea are each humming with insects, the sheen of their petals as glossy and as synthetic as enamel. The rich pinks of Mrs Yearsly's dame's rockets glare against the darkness of purple iris and blue delphiniums. Everything moves. Everything's moving. Everything ripples as though nothing more than the reflections of what they actually are.

'You alright?' Emma whispers, dropping back to my side, and at once I see her not as Emma, but as Charlotte the morning she disappeared. We had walked to the bus stop together, the hypnotic summer light spearing through the trees, the birds circling the hot air as it moved and shimmered about us, giving them the appearance not of birds, but of fish oscillating just beneath the surface of water.

The church bell chimes.

'Why don't you come into Peterborough with us today?'

There's a quiet leaping in my chest. 'Really?' I say. 'Why?'

'I just thought you might want to, that's all.'

'I thought you were going with Mary.'

'I am.' She half laughs at the idea and arches her brows. 'She's got a present for me, apparently.'

'So why do you want me to come?'

She looks at me sternly, almost pityingly, and glances first to the bus stop, then to the roofs of the houses. Her expression softens. 'I just thought you might like to. That's all.'

'Why?'

There's a jackdaw on the grass by the corner of the bus stop. It's watching us.

'Everything's going to be OK,' she says after a while and she smiles again and touches my arm just below the elbow. 'Whatever it is you think is happening, everything's going to be OK. You have to trust me.'

Lavender, aged and scraggly, swollen purple flowers grey in the glare, fringes the side of the church path, where even more villagers are gathered. Until now I didn't think this many people lived here. I'm not even sure they do. Perhaps they've travelled in from the Deepings, consumed in pity for a family they've never met, their mere proximity to such a tragedy enough to warrant a show of unification; or perhaps they belong somewhere else entirely. The steady hum of their undisclosed sentiments is low and respectful. They look, but are careful not to catch our eyes, to reveal themselves as voyeurs, as witch hunters. Cordially, a contented pleat in his thin mouth, Spragg, adorned in long white robes, slowly nods to each one of them as they make their way into the hallowed shadows of his church, hands clasped tightly together, holding on to something metaphysical they will never understand. He spots us through the crowd. Dad nods. I look away. Over the gravestone at

254

my side a dragonfly is hovering in the air as though trying to read the inscription.

'You'll be OK,' Uncle Pete says at my side, taking hold of my arm and pressing a hand against my back as though I were a blind person, guiding me through the shattered lines of light encaged inside the porch. His face is glistening, his eyes flared and nervous. Aunty Anne, clinging to his other arm and dressed in one of Mum's old blouses, attempts to offer me a look of conciliation, but it does no good, not now.

All the while the bell tolls.

Most of the pews are already full. Some of the congregation turn and look over their shoulders. They seem furtive yet quietly gratified, content at God smiling down on them from the enormous arched window over the altar, His universe splintered into stretched batons of coloured light, cobalt blue, yellow and selenium red, and for a moment I, too, feel His strength pouring into me. Among such wild seraphic colours and smells, I sense time separating; there is the invariable time of my thoughts, my memories, the seemingly endless passages of my dreams, the languid all-conquering time of the aura, and there is this, a time within time. Each exists alongside the other. I understand that now.

Mary Murphy smiles from the end of the pew nearest me, her gaze curiously unsettled, frightened, I think, not of the curse and the power it holds over her and the village, but that I am a threat to it, that I may still expose them. With his back to the nave, Norman, long arms bent like a spider's legs, waits expectantly over the organ. When I see Mr Skinner, he reluctantly raises a nervous finger and nods his head. I don't respond. I wait and I breathe. My skin is numb, and as Mum and Dad make their way to the front of the church, guided silently by Annie and Emma Proctor, I grit my teeth, turn and, aware of everyone looking at me, walk towards the bell tower door.

Charlotte is standing beside me from that day with Mum in the rain, a grin cut into the delicate fibres of her lean white cheeks.

Wind scrapes across the slate roof.

The bell stops.

The organ starts.

Everything's out of sync now.

Time has ruptured itself.

The stench of sulphur pours from every particle of light. I can physically see it, stained and watery and engulfing me as fog.

I stand beside the long table, anaesthetised and floating. Nothing seems real. Everything is beautiful yet frightening.

The door opens with a thin grating sound.

Finn Cowley steps out from the bell tower and offers me a grin so permissive and clownish part of me wants to laugh. He's wearing the cream blazer of The Three Sheaves Bell Ringers. He lowers his head and compliantly steps aside.

'Hello, Gordon,' Mum says brightly beneath the drone of rain.

Gordon smiles. 'Sorry,' he says, 'but they're not supposed to be in here. This door is always kept locked.'

'Why?' Charlotte asks, and in another moment altogether, a moment suspended within itself, the murmuring behind me simmers and the scent of roses and dust surges through me as a wave, a subjugate black mass rolling in from the horizon, gulls and terns fleeing inland.

Birds scamper on the tiles.

Gordon Proctor is still here, sketched in keen slashes of silvery light. He asks me if I'm feeling OK.

'What's happening?' I say meekly. 'Where's Charlotte? What have you done to her?'

He looks at me uncertainly, his expression strained with wonder as he lowers his voice to a stealthy whisper. I grip the edge of the table. 'You still don't get it, do you?' he says.

At the altar, Spragg bows his head.

The church settles.

'In death there is life,' he begins.

Someone coughs, and it is only then, when I turn around, that I see her, I see Charlotte, half running, half walking through the splintered maze of lights in the porch. She flickers as though the emergence of a memory, but this is not a memory. This is real. I feel her presence as much as I do my own, sense the gaps in the air between us contracting. A police siren whirls in the distance. Someone gasps. Mum screams. Charlotte glances at her, then looks back to me. She's moving towards me, time slowed almost to nothing, the stench of sulphur flooding into the church behind her, the light, bulging and white-hot, struggling now to hold back the darkness behind it.

The ground shifts. Heat disperses. I look up, half closing both eyes to focus. Tears are streaming down her face. Tom is beside her, Daniels holding firmly on to his arm, trying to pull him away. Beside me, Finn swears. The organ stops. Everything flashes and goes silent. My muscles betray me. My arm jolts. My legs fail. I fall forward. Charlotte reaches out. She's crying. She's telling me she's sorry, that she loves me, that she'd never leave me, not really, that she was stupid, that she thought I'd understand, that she thought I'd heard her in the darkness. Her hair is neatly brushed to the left, as smooth and as burnished as granite in this intense light, revealing the scar that runs down the side of her face, and for a second or two, I can't be sure, time

257

disentangling itself from the now, I see her not as Charlotte, but as a swan, snow white and elegant, wings stretched back into a silver sky, her neck supple and lithe and twisting free, at last, of the shackles of thorns that had held her to the ground.

She looks at me. She looks into my eyes and, without speaking, she tells me we'll never be apart again, which is when my head connects with the hard stone and all I see are sharp glittery lines of golden light.

Already I feel myself going, my mind with all its timeless memories detaching itself one last time from my physical self, but I have no regrets. I am not frightened anymore. This darkness is no longer dark. Charlotte is safe. I found her. I brought her home in the snow.

Through the shapes of light, I see her kneeling over me. Tears fill her eyes. Her ring catches the skin below my ear. 'Hold on!' she screams, although I can hardly hear the words or see her face anymore, but it doesn't matter. I have saved her, as I was destined always to do, from that very first glimpse in our own glassy world. She is safe, she is alive, the shadow of my heartbeat rippling in hers, and so I allow my soul, if that's what it is, to rise from my wild convulsing body that I'm not sure ever really belonged to me. I stretch my arms way up high, the delicate fibrous bones of my wings crackling slightly as achingly they begin to form a new life, intricate and aqua blue.

Soon we'll be together, as we once were in that red embryonic glow, as we were in that room in London with the animal wallpaper, in the darkness and the silence, in a place where time exists not as it exists here on earth, for the space of half an hour, and as I look back to the blurry light, each particle glimmering like a star, forming the shape of an enormous chart stretching into the furthest corners of the sky, the light flickers and I am high in the radiance of the sun, the salt air in my lungs. I hear seagulls above, avocets and dunnocks gathered in their hundreds across the waxy swathe of Scolt Head, and Charlotte, arms stretched on the roof of that half-buried beach hut in the sand, telling me to follow her, which, of course, I do.

ACKNOWLEDGEMENTS

Untold thanks to Louise Walters, Jennie Rawlings, Leigh Forbes, Alison Jack, Susan Davis, and Nicholas Russell-Pavier, without whom I wouldn't have been able to write their names just here, in the back of our book.

ALSO FROM
LOUISE WALTERS BOOKS

Louise Walters Books is the home of intelligent, provocative, beautifully written works of fiction. We are proud of our impressive list of authors and titles. We publish in most genres, but all our titles have one aspect in common: the high quality of the writing.

Further information about all LWB books and authors can be found on our website:

louisewaltersbooks.co.uk

THE LAST WORDS OF MADELEINE ANDERSON
Helen Kitson

"Writing is like a love affair, or should be.
You get to know your story, it intrigues you,
if you're lucky it enthrals you, and ultimately
it ends, leaving you wretched and abandoned."

ONCE UPON A TIME Gabrielle Price wrote and published an extraordinary novel.

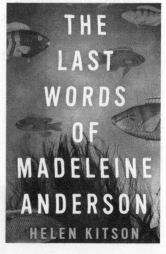

But twenty years on her literary star has dimmed, her "work of genius" is all but forgotten, and no further novels have materialized. She now lives an unremarkable life: middle-aged, living alone in the sleepy village she grew up in, and working as a housekeeper for the local vicar. Her lonely existence is dominated by memories of her best friend Madeleine, who died young, in tragic and mysterious circumstances.

Gabrielle's quiet world is turned upside down when she meets and befriends Simon – young, attractive, a would-be writer, and enthusiastic fan of the astonishing novel that Gabrielle published all those years ago. Charmed and flattered, she recklessly invites him into her home and her heart. But Simon is mysterious and manipulative, and it's not long before he forces Gabrielle to confront the demons in her past. Gabrielle's obsession begins to destroy her carefully cultivated life, and she comes to feel increasingly threatened by Simon's presence. Who is he? Why did he seek her out? And what does he really want?

The debut novel from acclaimed poet Helen Kitson is a joy to read: mysterious, reflective, and darkly humorous. Diana Cambridge describes it as "Barbara Pym noir".

Available in paperback, ebook and audio.

DON'T THINK A SINGLE THOUGHT
Diana Cambridge

"Hello? Hello? Emma, is that you? Emma!
It's only me... Hello? Are you there, Emma?"

1960s NEW YORK, and Emma Bowden seems to have it all - a glamorous Manhattan apartment, a loving husband, and a successful writing career. But while Emma and her husband Jonathan are on vacation at the Hamptons, a child drowns in the sea, and suspicion falls on Emma. As her picture-perfect life spirals out of control, and old wounds resurface, a persistent and monotonous voice in Emma's head threatens to destroy all that she has worked for...

Taut, elegant and mesmerising, *Don't Think a Single Thought* lays bare a marriage, and a woman, and examines the decisions – and mistakes – which shape all of our lives.

An elegant, fascinating novella that grips the reader from the first sentence, and with the added bonus of being a slim book that will fit easily into handbags and busy lives...

Available in paperback, ebook and audio.

Louise Walters Books extends its gratitude to our Supporters. Supporter subscriptions are invaluable to a small publisher like us.

Please visit louisewaltersbooks/lwb-supporters if you would like to receive a year's worth of books, invitations to launch parties, exclusive newsletters, early glimpses of forthcoming covers, and many other nice bookish things.

Heartfelt thanks to:

Karen Ankers

Francesca Bailey-Karel

Tricia Beckett

Liz Carr

Pippa Chappell

Eric Clarke

Karen Cocking

Jill Doyle

Diane Gardner

Andrea Harman

Cath Humphris

Seamus Keaveny

Moon Kestrel

Karen Mace

Cheryl Mayo

Rosemary Morgan

Jackie Morrison

Gillian Stern

John Taylor

Sarah Thomas

Penny Tofiluk

Ian Walters

Steve Walters

Elizabeth Waugh

Alexis Wolfe

Louise Wykes